Judgement and Wrath

ALSO BY MATT HILTON FROM CLIPPER LARGE PRINT

Dead Men's Dust

Judgement and Wrath

Matt Hilton

W F HOWES LTD

39210763

This large print edition published in 2009 by
W F Howes Ltd
Unit 4, Rearsby Business Park, Gaddesby Lane,
Rearsby, Leicester LE7 4YH

1 3 5 7 9 10 8 6 4 2

First published in the United Kingdom in 2006
by Hodder & Stoughton

A CIP catalogue record for this book is available
from the British Library

ISBN 978 1 40743 856 6

Typeset by Palimpsest Book Production Limited,
Grangemouth, Stirlingshire
Printed and bound in Great Britain
by MPG Books Ltd, Bodmin, Cornwall

FSC
Mixed Sources
Product group from well-managed
forests, controlled sources and
recycled wood or fiber
SA-COC-1565
www.fsc.org
© 1996 Forest Stewardship Council

To my wife, and best friend, Denise

The seventy-first spirit is Dantalion.
He is a great and mighty duke, who governs
thirty-six legions of spirits. He appears in
the form of a man with many countenances,
all men's and all women's faces. Dantalion
knows the thoughts of all men and women,
and can change them at will.

The Goetia: The Lesser Key of
Solomon the King
A Crowley

Hell is empty and all the devils are here

The Tempest 1.2
William Shakespeare

PROLOGUE

Caitlin Moore opened the door to her living room and stepped into Hell.

Or that's how it seemed to her for the remaining three minutes and twenty-seven seconds of her life.

The clock began ticking when she pushed the door to with a nudge of her hip and reached for the light switch with an expertly aimed elbow. It was the usual Friday evening routine. Coming home from Collinwood High School with her arms filled with books and test papers for marking, she could hit the switch every time.

Except this time blackness prevailed.

'Goddamnit,' she muttered under her breath, swinging round to place the papers down on the sideboard next to the door.

It was the creaking of the easy chair by the TV that made her pause.

'Are you awake, Nate? How about giving me a hand here? The power's down.'

Nathaniel Moore was also a teacher at Miami's Collinwood High. But Caitlin's husband was a track coach and didn't have to attend the Friday evening tedium of the faculty meeting. He always got away three hours earlier, picked up Cassie from the sitter and went home. Once Cassie was tucked up in bed, and a couple of Jack Daniels were residing in his belly, Nate would doze in front of the wide screen with the Discovery Channel doing its best to cover his snores.

Routine.

'Nate?'

But tonight's routine was blasted into smithereens.

There'd be no supper. No cuddling on the couch while watching a late movie. No fondling their way to bed where a rejuvenated Nate would prove he was still a jock when it came to stamina-based sports.

'Hello, Caitlin.'

The voice was soft, but still enough to shock her to the core. She jerked, her spine knocking on the sideboard, papers spilling from the pile. That wasn't the voice of her husband.

It wasn't the voice of anyone she knew.

The easy chair creaked again, and there was a shifting of the darkness around her. The mystery voice was on the move.

She almost turned for the door.

Then she remembered Cassie.

Eight-year-old Cassie would be asleep in her room. If she ran, what would happen to Cassie? What *had* happened to Nate?

A flashlight was thumbed on, the beam stark in

Caitlin's eyes. She croaked, throwing an arm across her face.

That rush of movement again and a hand clamped on her throat. The fingers were long and slim, but they felt like steel where they dug into her flesh. Caitlin's lungs bucked in her chest.

She had no way of resisting. Air gone, she didn't have the strength or the will to fight. She was turned in a lazy circle then ushered to the centre of the room. Sparks popped and fizzed behind her eyelids. Without air she'd be unconscious within seconds. Then the fingers were gone from her throat and she was retching: gag reflex on overdrive.

'Hello, Caitlin,' the voice said again.

'Who are you?' Caitlin gasped. 'What do you want?'

The light was still in her eyes. She couldn't make out the figure behind its beam. Did she know the voice after all?

'I want to give you a choice.'

The torch went off and darkness slapped its hood over Caitlin's head. Around her a breeze eddied. The stranger was on the move again. Caitlin swung with the breeze, trying to determine where the stranger was now.

'Do you love your family, Caitlin?' The voice was barely more than a whisper.

'More than anything. Please! Don't hurt them. I'll do anything you say.'

'Anything?' the voice sounded strangely disturbed. 'You'd debase yourself for them? You'd lie down and give yourself to a stranger?'

'Anything,' Caitlin sobbed. 'Money! You want money? I'll get you money.'

'I don't want money, nor do I want your body.'

'Then, what?'

'I told you. I want to give you a choice.'

There was a metallic click above her: a bulb being turned in its socket. Pearlescent light bathed the room.

And Caitlin saw the figure and knew that her life could be counted in seconds.

He was tall. Slim almost to the point of emaciation. His face was too pale, a wax mask that made Caitlin think of a reflection in a steamed-over mirror. His hair was silk-fine, as pale as his skin, and hung to his shoulders beneath the wide, circular brim of a hat. His coat was shabby: a long, ankle-brushing raincoat that was missing all but the topmost button. A thin silver chain looped from one side to the other, where something bulged in the pocket. On his feet were grimy deck shoes that were threadbare where his toenails pushed against the fabric.

The stranger had a look about him that spoke of sleeping under cardboard, drinking from bottles concealed within brown paper bags, and ranting at alcohol-induced phantoms.

But Caitlin knew: this was no street person who'd found access to her home. This man was the type that even the hardiest of the streetwise shunned.

Two things told her.

The silenced pistol he held loosely in his hand.

And the stone killer intensity of his eyes.

'I'm going to give you a choice,' the man offered again. 'Who will you save, Caitlin? Nate or Cassandra?'

Caitlin followed his gaze. On the opposite side of the room, two wooden chairs had been dragged from the kitchen. In each of them sat the people she loved most in the entire world.

Nate was bound and gagged. He strained at his bonds, his eyes huge. In contrast Cassandra was very still, her features lax.

A wail swelled in Caitlin's throat.

'Make your choice, Caitlin,' whispered the man.

How could she? How could she? How . . .

'Cassandra has been anaesthetised,' the stranger said. 'If you choose Nathaniel she will never know. Do I kill her, Caitlin?'

Nate's veins were standing out on his temples like blue ropes. He was shaking his head in denial. Caitlin met his eyes and he sank back in the chair.

'Please,' Caitlin said, 'don't harm our daughter.'

The stranger nodded. Then shot Nate in the forehead.

'You made the best choice. Your child will be safe now, Caitlin. You can rest easy.'

Then he lifted the gun to Caitlin's face.

CHAPTER 1

Sometimes you make rash decisions that you instantly regret. Other times you just have to go with the flow.

Like when I walked into Shuggie's Shack – a roadhouse north of Tampa, Florida – and parked myself on a stool at the corner of the warped and stained bar.

Shuggie's is the kind of place that self-respecting souls avoid unless they're dragged inside by the hair. The tables are planks nailed to barrels, seats 1970s retro-vinyl from the first time around. The atmosphere is redolent with beer fumes and cigarette smoke, and the stench of unwashed bodies. Tattoos seem to be the order of the day. Muscles and hair, too. And that's just the women.

You finish your meal of grease over-easy, and the kind of gratuity you offer the staff is thanks that you get out with your face still intact.

I was made as a cop by every man, woman and beast in the place within the time it took me to catch the bartender's eye. Every last one of them was wrong, but I wasn't averse to letting them wonder.

7

'Beer,' I said. There didn't seem to be any choice. It was that, or chance the brown liquid masquerading as liquor in the dusty bottles arranged on the shelf behind the cash register.

The bartender moved towards me reluctantly. He glanced around his clientele, as if by serving me he was betraying their creed. Not that he looked the type to worry about people's feelings. He was a massive man in one of those cut-off leather vests designed to show the size of his biceps. He had a black star inked into the rough skin beneath his right eye, and a scar that parted his bottom lip and ended somewhere in the braided beard on his chin.

'Don't want any trouble in here, mister,' he said as he set down a beer in front of me. 'I suggest you drink up and get on your way.'

Holding his gaze, I asked, 'Is that what you call Southern hospitality round here?'

'No,' he sneered, 'in these parts we'd call that good advice.'

Besides the long hours I'd already put in at the wheel since leaving Tampa, I could foresee a long night. A relaxing drink would have helped my mood. Maybe a little pleasant conversation would have helped, too. Didn't look like I was going to find either in here.

'Thanks for the heads up,' I said.

Flicking dollars on the bar top, I stood up and walked away, carrying my drink. It felt warm in the glass. By contrast, the barkeep's gaze on the back of my head was like ice.

Passing a group of men sitting at a table, I inclined my chin at them. They looked back with the dead eyes of men wary of the law. One of them shivered his overdeveloped pectoral muscles at me and they all sniggered.

In the back corner of the bar sat a man as incongruous to this setting as I was. A small bird-like man with nervous eyes and a way of oozing sweat through his hair without it moisturising the dry skin on his forehead. His right hand was in continuous motion, as though fiddling with something small in his palm. I may have caught a flash of metal, but his hand dipped to his coat pocket and it was gone.

Without asking his permission, I placed my beer on the table and took the chair alongside him. The barrel made it awkward to sprawl, so I leaned forward and placed my elbows on the planks. I turned and studied the man but he continued to watch the barroom as though fearful of who might walk in next.

'When you said I'd know you when I got here, I see what you meant,' I said. 'You don't strike me as the type who hangs out in biker clubhouses.'

'We agreed on this place for that very reason,' the man said. 'It isn't as if anyone I know is going to be here.'

'It wasn't a good idea,' I told him. 'If you wanted anonymity, you should have chosen somewhere where you'd blend in. Where *we'd* blend in. Check it out; we're on everyone's radar.'

Maybe the bartender's advice wasn't so bad after all.

'We should go,' I told him.

The men gathered at the table further along had turned their attention to the spectacle we presented sitting in their midst. They didn't seem pleased, as if we spoiled the ambient testosterone.

The man wasn't listening. He dropped a hand from the table and dug beneath a folded newspaper. I saw the corner of an envelope.

'Everything you need is in there.' He quickly grabbed at his own drink, taking a nervous gulp. 'The balance will be paid as soon as I get the proof that Bradley Jorgenson is no longer a threat to me or any of my family.'

Sighing at his amateurish game of subterfuge, I left my arms resting on the table. It gave me cover for when I dipped my right hand under my coat and caressed the butt of my SIG Sauer P228.

'I'm not sure I want the job,' I said to him.

The man stiffened.

'I'm not who you were expecting,' I said.

He finally glanced at me and I knew what he was thinking. Is this a set-up? Was I a cop like everyone in the damn bar thought?

'You can relax, Mr Dean. I am Joe Hunter.' I folded my fingers round the butt of my gun, placing my index finger alongside the trigger guard. 'What I mean is I'm not a hit man.'

'Jared Rington told me that you would help,' Richard Dean whispered harshly.

'I will help,' I reassured him. 'I'll get your daughter away from Jorgenson. But I'm not going to kill the man without any proof that he's a danger to her.'

Dean nodded down at the envelope. 'Take it. You'll see what I mean. All the proof is there.'

There was movement among the men at the next table. One man with jailhouse tats stood up. He picked up his beer, held it loosely in his hand. He gave me a look that said we'd outstayed our welcome. He sniffed loudly, then jerked his head at the two men nearest him.

Oblivious, Dean said, 'Please, Mr Hunter, I need you to get my daughter away from that monster. If it means killing him to do that . . . well . . . I'll pay you any price you want.'

'Pass me the envelope,' I told him. 'Under the table. I've got your phone number. I'll be in touch with you, let you know my decision.'

Dean had panic in his eyes. Whether it was about relinquishing the cash already in the envelope without a firm agreement, or because there was a *real possibility* I was going to do as he asked, the nerves got a grip of him. He wavered, his fingers plucking at moisture on his glass.

'Two seconds and the deal is off,' I warned him.

He quickly slipped the envelope into my outstretched left hand.

'OK. Now go.'

He opened his mouth and I gave a slight shake of my head. Suddenly he was aware of the Aryan Brotherhood approaching us. Coughing his excuses, he started from his seat, dodging round the tattooed man and his two compadres. They heckled him but allowed the little man to go.

Pushing the envelope into my waistband, I stood up.

'I'm going, guys. You can relax.'

The man with the jailhouse tats barred my way. He lifted a grimy nicotine-stained finger to my chest.

'You're not welcome here.'

'Didn't you just hear what I said?'

'Can't say I did. What is that funny accent?'

I get remarks like that occasionally. Comes with being English. And northern to boot.

'Look, guys, you've caught me in an awkward predicament,' I said to Tats. 'You don't want me here; I don't want to be here. Truth is, normally I wouldn't sully myself by entering a shit hole like this. But here I am.'

My words had the desired effect.

I got a laugh.

Stepping forwards, I found they parted for me.

That should have been it. Playing on the paradox of self-deprecating humour, I should have got myself out of Shuggie's Shack without any injuries. The problem was two things got in the way.

First, Tats' question: 'What did that little freak hand you under the table?'

Second was the surly mood I'd been in when I arrived. Which wasn't helped by the bullshit Richard Dean had subsequently laid on me.

'None of your fucking business,' I told him pleasantly.

The jukebox was spitting out heavy rock music. Earjarring stuff, but expected in a place like this. It played on. If there'd been a pianist in the bar he'd have stopped at that moment.

'You're in *my* place,' Tats pointed out. 'That makes it *my* business.'

'Oh, so you must be Shuggie, then?' I swept my gaze around the barroom. Shook my head at what I saw. 'You know, place like this dump, you should be ashamed of yourself.'

'I ain't Shuggie, asshole. And that's not what I meant.'

'Yeah, I know what you meant.'

'I own this place. I own what goes on under this roof.' He stuck out his grimy hand a second time. 'Hand it over.'

I shrugged.

'OK.'

The SIG was between his eyes before the smirk had fully formed on his lips.

Chairs scraped and there was a chorus of shouts as just about everyone leapt to their feet, pulling out guns of their own. A couple of the more delicate customers headed for shelter.

It was like DefCon Five had just been announced and anarchy was the new world order.

It kind of matched my mood.

'This is how it's going to be,' I said. My words were for everyone in the room. 'Everyone relaxes, puts away their weapons and gets the hell out of my way. The alternative is that Biker Boy will be throwing his very own wake in the near future.'

'He's only one fucking pussy,' an anonymous voice shouted from out of the crowd. 'We can take him out.'

'One pussy with a gun at your stinking boss's head,' I reminded the shouter. Turning my attention to Tats, I asked him, 'How would you like things to go? Bit of a party animal, I guess. Should be a good turnout for your wake.'

'Put down your goddamn guns,' Tats yelled. 'Any of you muthas with itchy fingers, you're gonna answer to me!'

Smiling at him, I grabbed a handful of his denim cut-off.

'Me and you are going to walk out of here together,' I told him.

He was shorter than I was, but bulkier in the chest. Slightly awkward for getting a hold round his neck. Making do with bunching his cute little ponytail in my left hand, I stuck the SIG under his ear. That way we moved towards the door.

A man to my right maybe still had it in his mind that I was a cop. Cops will always warn before they shoot. He lurched at me, trying to grab the gun away from Tats' throat.

But I'm not a cop.

My sidekick found his knee. There was a tendon-popping twang and his leg now had a two-way joint. His face screwed around the agony, a good

14

target for my elbow. He went down, but at least in his unconscious state he wasn't in pain any longer.

In the fraction of a second that it took to take the idiot out, the SIG had never wavered from its target.

'Any more of you assholes want to test me?' I growled.

They hung back like a pack of hyenas, wary of the lion in their midst, starving but too afraid to try to snatch away its kill.

Taking that as my cue, I dragged Tats backwards and out of the door. Arrayed along the road outside was a row of chopped and converted Harley Davidsons and other bikes I didn't recognise. I shot at a few of them, putting 9 mm ammo through their gas tanks. One of them went up in the air like the space shuttle, trailing fire and burning fuel that splashed most of the others. Rapidly I dragged Tats away from the conflagration, even as others began to spill out of Shuggie's. Suspended between their desire to get Tats free and saving their beloved bikes, there could only be one winner. I was able to bundle Tats into my Ford Explorer without anyone else trying to play the hero.

Screeching out of the parking lot, I pushed the SUV into the eastern lane approaching eighty miles an hour and gaining.

'Fuck, man!' Tats said from the passenger seat. 'You didn't have to go as far as blowing the bikes to hell.'

15

I smiled. The action had done my bad mood the world of good.

'Had to make it look real, Ron, otherwise they might've guessed you were a willing hostage.'

CHAPTER 2

I'm not a cop. I'm not a bounty hunter. But I didn't mind the cash kicked back my way for taking Ron Maynard in.

He was grateful for the service, even thanked me for my help as I passed him over to his bail bondsmen on the outskirts of Tampa. I nodded at him, but didn't accept his hand. After all, he was a punk criminal who'd hurt too many people in the past. His only endearing quality – and the reason I'd agreed to the job of getting him out – was his desire to get away from the lifestyle and go whistle-blower on his gang's activities. His testimony would put a shitload of his friends behind bars. Not as satisfying as if they'd been sitting astride their bikes when I blew them to pieces, but there you go. Still a good result.

It was the small hours of the morning but the sub-tropical heat was like a wet hood thrown over my head. An air-conditioned room and comfy bed seemed like a nice idea, but I'd arranged to meet with my friend Jared Rington first. Didn't matter what time it was. Rink would be waiting up for me.

17

Rink has a condominium up in the wooded lands northeast of Temple Terrace, but he keeps an office for his private investigations business in downtown Tampa. It was outside his office that I parked the Ford. Few people were out on the street, and what traffic there was in the area was reduced to the occasional police cruiser or taxicab. The blinds had been drawn on the window to his office and a 'Closed' sign was hanging in the door, but when I twisted the handle the door swung open.

Rink was sitting behind his computer tapping keys as I walked in and shed my coat. He just didn't look right at the desk. He should have been in a wrestling ring or octagonal cage. If he was a foot shorter and one hundred pounds lighter he'd have looked like the hero from a 1970s Kung Fu movie. He owed the blue-black hair and hooded eyes to his Japanese mother, while his size and muscular build had to have been passed down from his Scottish-Canadian father.

'Got a call thanking us for a job well done,' he said. He gave me a grin, his teeth flashing white against his tawny skin. 'Course, we might have to do a little damage control over the shit storm you left at Shuggie's Shack. Did you have to burn down the entire building?'

'It burned down?' I couldn't help the chuckle. 'Never mind, it was a pigsty. Shuggie will likely thank us.'

If things worked out with Maynard, Shuggie's

wouldn't be getting as many customers in the future. The owner would get more from the insurance payout than the place was worth.

Pulling out the envelope that Richard Dean had passed me, I put it down on the desk next to Rink's computer. 'What do you know about this client, Rink? Impression I got was he's on paranoia overdrive.'

'Just your run-of-the-mill white-collar worker with a mortgage to support,' Rink said. His Arkansas drawl always made me think of Wild West heroes; which was apt considering Rink was as quick on the draw with a gun. All that was missing was the white Stetson.

'So how does he come up with that kind of cash?'

On the drive over, I'd pulled into a rest stop. The way in which Dean had conducted the meeting had set off a worm of unease inside me. The envelope contained a number of photographs and a wad of cash. Twenty thousand dollars to be precise.

'Maybe he's done a little digging into his daughter's college fund. It ain't like she's gonna be needin' it.'

Moving the cash to one side, I laid out the series of five photographs. The first showed a pleasant – if homely – looking young woman smiling into the camera. She was slim, her slightly prominent ears emphasised by her tight ponytail. She wore only a dab of make-up and her jewellery didn't extend beyond silver studs in her ears and a delicate

19

crucifix on a chain at her throat. Her clothes were a conservative blue cardigan over a white blouse. Richard Dean's seventeen-year-old daughter, Marianne, looking shy and uncomfortable in front of the lens.

In contrast, the young woman in photos two and three could have been lifted directly from a celebrity gossip magazine. This woman was the type you usually see hanging on to a movie star's arm. If it weren't for the crucifix I wouldn't have immediately made the connection to the insecure child in the first photograph. Marianne had definitely blossomed from drab duckling to radiant swan.

The final two images gave me most concern. The first showed Marianne in the back of a limousine. She was drunk, her hair disarrayed, clothing twisted askew. The man sitting beside her was mugging for the camera as he slipped his hand up the hem of her dress. His face was cruel, mindless of the token effort that Marianne made to push his hand away. Then there was photo number five. A flat portrait shot lifted from a Miami P.D. file.

Marianne had been crying. Her hair was dark with sweat and clung to her forehead. Mascara was smeared down her cheeks, but failed to hide the bruises round both eyes. Her top lip was split in two places, and an earring had been torn from her left lobe, leaving dry blood streaking her neck.

The most poignant thing that was instantly noticeable to me was the lack of her crucifix.

There was a note pinned to the final shot. Handwritten by Richard Dean, it said, 'Will the next photograph be taken from the M.E.'s post-mortem report?'

Maybe he had a point.

Recalling his final words to me, I thought about what he expected. '*Please, Mr Hunter, I need you to get my daughter away from that monster. If it means killing him to do that . . . well . . . I'll pay you any price you want.*'

When Rink and I were in the Special Forces together we'd both killed men. Government-sanctioned killings of terrorists and gang lords. I never saw myself as an assassin; still don't. I saw the death we doled out as a necessary evil. The scum we put down deserved what they got, and it usually made life so much better for the innocents who had suffered under their reign. Maybe I'd been a little too quick to deny Dean's assumption that I was a hit man. There were some men in this world that needed killing: Marianne's battered face was all the proof I required.

'The asshole in the limo,' I asked, 'I take it he's Jorgenson?'

Rink swung the computer monitor so that I could see it. The same face smiled out at me from the screen. He was a clean-cut-looking kid, early twenties, reddish hair. Bradley Jorgenson was one of the playboy elite who were gaining media attention on the Miami scene.

'He do that to her?' I tapped the police photograph.

'Marianne wouldn't go through with any official charges. She denied Jorgenson was responsible. So did more than two dozen partygoers at his mansion that night. Course, when they were out of earshot of the police, talk was different. They said Jorgenson must have beaten her for the hell of it. He was pissed off about some deal or another going ass-up: Marianne was the nearest punching bag he could find.'

'But she went back to him?'

'Don't think she had a choice in the matter.'

'We'll see about that.'

Three months ago, moving out here had been a big decision. It had taken me all of about one minute to consider whether I could build a new life in the sunshine of Florida. It meant leaving behind my old life in England, an ex-wife who I still cared for, and my two dogs, Hector and Paris. Diane took the German Shepherds and I took the first flight out. Rink's offer of work had clinched the deal. When we were in the forces together we'd worked as equals. Although – according to the sign on his door – Rink was at the helm of this P.I. outfit, we were still equals now. So there was no need for an executive meeting to decide what we were going to do about the Marianne Dean situation. I pressed buttons on my mobile phone.

'Mr Dean. You're still awake. Good.' I looked

down at the portrait of his daughter. The fear behind the flash-washed image couldn't hide. 'You still want me, I'm going to take the job.'

I'd have taken it whatever his answer.

CHAPTER 3

Mention New Orleans and certain images come to mind. The world famous Mardi Gras carnival. Jazz musicians. River boats plying the wide Mississippi. Then there are those pictures that people wish to cleanse from their minds. Hurricane Katrina. Floods and devastation. The dead and the displaced. Thousands of families still living in transit, suffering for all they had lost when nature unleashed its pent-up fury upon them.

New Orleans is a potent mix of extravaganza and destruction, magic and mayhem, wonder and desolation.

It would be hard to imagine a human equivalent, a poster boy for the city. No one would instantly bring to mind the face of Dantalion. But, in his own estimation, he was the very essence of this contradictory place of enchantment and woe.

Outwardly, he accepted, he was no great shakes to look upon. Some might even say that his un-healthy pallor and emaciated frame spoke of disease and decay. Initially people would avoid him, but in the end they'd come when he wished. They would bend to his will and give him what he desired. He had that power. It was his gift.

It was what had made him a master of his craft.

Why he was much sought after when certain people required other persons dead.

He was meeting *certain people* today.

Not in New Orleans, the place of his birth, but far to the east in Miami. The whisper had gone out among those certain people that he was in town and available. A coded message had come through on his BlackBerry, requesting a meeting. This was why he found himself sitting on a bench in Bayside Park overlooking Biscayne Bay. Nearby the Macarthur and Venetian Causeways carried traffic over the holiday-brochure water towards the island where the world famous Miami Beach could be found. The Mildred and Claude Pepper Fountain was just visible through the trees, and to his left he could make out the Miami *Queen* at its permanent berth, allegedly Miami's most unforgettable attraction. Dodge Island was a low-slung beast hunkering in the water. Pale against the turquoise sea, it was like a great white whale aground in the shallow bay. Industrial units and storage containers made up the barnacles on this creature's back.

He wasn't there to appreciate the sights, not a tourist. But that was how he would appear to anyone walking by. His pale skin was at risk from the sun, so he'd be forgiven the wide-brimmed hat and dark glasses. His billowing white coat, like

25

the cassock of a medieval monk, was a little strange when taken at face value, but not compared to the garb of some visitors.

Behind his sunglasses his pale blue eyes were watchful. The stark light pained him, but it was necessary that he be vigilant. Sometimes certain people wished *he* was dead, too.

Three men were walking towards him from the mall area next to La Marina de Miami. One, dark-haired and permatanned in a cream linen suit, headed directly towards Dantalion. The other two, men with guns concealed under their jackets, stood kicking their heels as though admiring the bronze statue commemorating Christopher Columbus. But their eyes never left the man on the bench.

Scanning right, Dantalion saw a further two men on the parking lot of the Bayside Park amphitheatre. Not interested in the band stand, they too were watching him. There could be yet more, but it was enough to be getting on with. Discreetly Dantalion slipped a hand beneath the tail of his voluminous coat, as though scratching an itch on his thigh. He unsnapped the holster holding his 90-two Beretta semi-automatic. It had the capacity to fire off seventeen 9 mm rounds as rapidly as he could caress the trigger. Enough for the five men and then some.

The tanned man sat down on the bench next to him. There was no preamble. No checking of identities; each man knew who he was there to see.

'I'll take care of your instructions personally. The information you need is already where you asked,' said the client. He brushed a speck of lint off his suit. 'In return I need something from you.'

'I know what you want from me.' Dantalion's voice came out in a whisper. It wasn't practised, merely an effect of his feeble genes. His words were lilting; not effete, but androgynous, as though spoken by a pre-pubescent child. There was no trace of his Cajun heritage in its inflection. 'Confirmation of death. One target has been eliminated. The others will soon follow.'

'Sooner rather than later would be appreciated.'

'You have a choice,' Dantalion pointed out. 'If you simply wish these people dead, you could send your dogs around—' he nodded at the two nearest the amphitheatre, just to let his client know that he was aware of them – 'or you can be patient and allow me to do *what I do best*.'

'The killings can't be traced back to me,' said the man.

'So you choose me?' Dantalion nodded slowly. He placed a hand on the man's wrist. He saw the cringe worm its way up the man's arm and into his face. Dantalion smiled faintly and slowly drew back his fingers. His touch caused that reaction in most; they were repulsed by the scaly look of his skin, the thick yellowing nails.

'You know my terms?' Dantalion asked.

'You will be paid half the sum up front. The remainder on confirmation that the targets are dead. You are trusted to do the job . . . I have no problem with that.'

Dantalion's chuckle was like the whisper of bats' wings through the night. 'Those are not the terms I'm referring to.'

A pale flush crept over the man's features. He looked across at the two men keeping Columbus company. 'Along with the targets you have the right to choose how many others die. Yes, I understand. That's up to you.'

'Yes,' Dantalion agreed. 'It's up to me. But, worry not, I don't charge extra for a high body count. I'm just happy with the job satisfaction.'

'Just make sure nothing can be connected to me. You do realise what's at stake here, don't you? *How much* is at stake?'

'I thought you trusted me to do the job?'

'I do. Your record is impeccable. Only . . .' he coughed. 'You can't blame me for being nervous.'

'No need to be nervous.' Dantalion smiled, showing his caramel-coloured teeth. He shifted his sunglasses so that he could lock gazes with the man. 'It's not as if I'm coming after *you.*'

The man stood up fast. He swayed, looking down at the killer on the bench. His face said it all.

'Please,' Dantalion laughed. 'Sit down. I'm only funning with you.'

'You don't look like the type to make jokes.' The client didn't sit down again. His gaze sought Dantalion's hand where it disappeared below his coat.

With a flourish the killer swept his hand out. The man flinched, but then saw what Dantalion was holding. A book, attached to his body by a silver chain. With a thumb, he flicked open the book. He rifled through the pages, displaying rows of numbers.

'They're all listed,' Dantalion said. 'The names numbered. Each correspond to a different person I have killed. Do you know how many there are in this book?'

The man shook his head.

Dantalion neglected to enlighten him. The plethora of handwritten pages should be evidence enough.

'I am still walking free,' Dantalion said. 'None of my clients has ever been tied to my work. Does that make *you* happy?'

'I'm happy.' The man stuffed his hands into the pockets of his linen jacket, scrunching the cloth between his sweating palms. He took a discreet step away. He glanced around at the men near the statue.

'The alternative is I walk away,' offered Dantalion. 'The downside of that is, well, you've seen me. You can identify me. If you aren't happy, you'd best set your dogs on me now.'

Out on Biscayne Bay a speed boat swept by, throwing out a phosphorescent spray in its wake. Music drifted on the air from the nearby Hard Rock Café. Strolling couples talked in low murmurs. The fountain danced to life amidst a chorus of wonder from the gathered tourists. It was a strange setting for the stand-off that Dantalion had just offered.

Finally the man turned and walked away. Over his shoulder, he said, 'I understand your terms, and I trust you. I'm happy, OK?'

Deal done, Dantalion stood up. He straightened his long coat over his lean frame, adjusted his hat. The two men over by the amphitheatre were watching him with their jaws set. Dantalion flicked the brim of his hat at them – just to let them know.

CHAPTER 4

It was hot in Miami. But that was OK. I was enjoying the sun on my face and making the most of the sightseeing opportunity. Other times I'd been in Miami, I'd got off a plane, then hightailed it elsewhere. Breezing along the causeway in my Ford Explorer, I had the AC on high, and a John Lee Hooker CD belting out of the surround speakers. My idea of cool.

Interstate I-95 connects Miami Beach with the mainland. Straddling Biscayne Bay, it's the main route on to the island, and at this time of the day it was relatively free of traffic in both directions. Sometimes people refer to Miami and Miami Beach in the same breath, but Miami Beach is a city in its own right, a distinct municipality of Dade County. I was heading for the South Beach area – again not just a beach, but an urban sprawl – which was regarded as an affluent area these days. Considered one of the richest commercial areas now, it had suffered from urban blight prior to the fame lavished on it by the TV show *Miami Vice*. I knew it was just a veneer: in SoBe, as it was known, poverty and crime were still rife, just a kick in the ass away.

31

Cutting across the city, I picked up Washington Avenue and followed it south until I saw the Portofino Tower, a huge terracotta-coloured edifice that Rink had told me about. Here I swung west, back towards the marina overlooking Baker Island. There's no road across to Baker Island; the rich and famous demand privacy. The only way across was by boat or helicopter.

Once the Vanderbilts owned exclusive rights to the island, but after it was sold for development in the 1960s more than two hundred homes had been erected on the man-made land. It still remained exclusive to the super-rich set, and once had equalled nearby Fisher Island as one of the richest per-capita locations in the USA. Maybe it still did. The northern portion of the island was barely settled, but in the south-west it was well developed with mega-homes. That was where I hoped to locate Marianne Dean.

Jumping a ride over on a water taxi, I arrived at the island among a group of giggling teenagers. It was handy, because there were a couple of body-guards within the group, and I blended in with the stern-faced men who watched me as though I was a challenge to their employment. Once I was back on dry land, I hired what looked like a beach buggy and drove the short way over to yet another marina on the south-west shore. There, Tiffany, my real estate agent, passed over the keys to the condominium I'd leased. The week-long rental had already snatched a significant portion of the twenty K Richard Dean had supplied, but I wasn't there because of the money.

My prime concern was getting Marianne Dean to a safe place. Richard Dean had painted a pretty ugly picture of Bradley Jorgenson and the way he treated the girl, but there was something about the man's motivation that was giving me cause to question how I'd complete my task. Dean wanted Bradley stopped – no longer a threat to him or any of his family – and I knew exactly what he meant by that. He didn't strike me as the overly affectionate type of father and he seemed more concerned with punishing Bradley than with getting Marianne home.

From the balcony of the condo, I looked over a circular swimming pool, which in turn looked over a palm-fringed garden and down on to the marina. Yachts and motor cruisers seemed to be the preferred mode of transport here.

To my left was the house that Jorgenson had leased for the summer. He had his permanent place of residence up the coast at Neptune Island and a boat moored at Puerto Banus, in Spain, but this was my best chance for getting Marianne away from him.

I was there on a scouting mission. Rink would join me later after he'd finished a little business of his own in Tampa. Dressed in shades, a short-sleeved cotton shirt and Bermuda shorts, I set myself up on the private balcony. A glance over the rail and I could see beautiful bikini-clad women frolicking in next door's pool. The deckchair was comfortable and the beer cold; it was mind-numbingly boring on stakeout, but someone had to do it.

By the time the sun started to set, the bathers had disappeared inside and my beer had grown warm. Even the executive-class sun lounger was beginning to feel like a torture device. The sunset made up for some of my chagrin, though. It was spectacular, setting Miami city and Biscayne Bay aflame with bronze and gold highlights.

Also, as if he was a vampire out of lore, Jorgenson made his first appearance.

In a cream linen suit, his reddish hair slicked back, and a mobile phone to his ear, he wandered out on the tiled area next to his pool. The water was like a mirror, reflecting his downcast face. Bradley didn't seem very happy.

'I've told you,' he grunted into his phone. 'Over and over again. No! When is that going to sink into your stupid fucking head?'

Whoever he was speaking to must have pleaded their case. As he listened, Jorgenson chewed his lips, and even from my high vantage above him I could hear the rasp of his breath.

'You know what I should do to you?' Jorgenson suddenly shouted. 'I should have you . . .' His voice faltered, and his gaze nervously searched for unseen watchers. His dark eyes flicked my way, but I'd already moved back out of sight. His next words were whispered and I couldn't hear what

34

was said. But I heard the snap of his phone as he closed it. Then followed the clop of leather heels as he hurried inside. More shouting ensued but it was muffled, then there was a crash, and – I'm pretty sure – a woman's voice crying out.

I'd made up my mind already, but the man's words and actions only served to confirm that. Jorgenson was a bully. And anyone who knows Joe Hunter knows I can't abide bullies.

My plan didn't extend to walking up to his front door and ringing the bell, but at that moment I felt the urge to get on the move. It was the stirring of anger that always drove me to violent conclusions. Rink has accused me of getting a kick out of the violence. But I don't. I only want peace. The problem is, I want that peace to extend to everyone, so if it means cracking the skulls of those causing the rot in the world, then so be it. As a counterterrorism soldier my career was dictated and channelled towards specific targets. Now, free to roam, I could pick and choose who needed sorting. And I'd decided: Bradley Jorgenson required setting right on a point or two.

Despite the glitz and riches, Marianne Dean had to be very unhappy. I'd seen it many, many times before: a woman giving up everything for the man she loves. She will take the beatings and humiliation, won't reach out for help, because, underneath it all, *he loves her*. It must be her own fault.

Domestic violence is a curse on society. Most times it stays hidden, but even when a woman is brave enough to come forward and report what is happening behind closed doors, the finger of blame can be pointed back at her. What was she doing to push her man to hurting her? Likely she got exactly what she deserved!

But I wasn't from that school of thought.

The way I look at it, men who hurt women are only a step lower on the ladder of shame than those who hurt children. Sometimes there is no distinction between the two. Marianne had blossomed into a beautiful young woman, but she still remained the shy child captured in that school portrait less than a year ago. Likely she wouldn't thank me for saying so, but to me, Marianne was still a baby. Suddenly I could understand her father's vitriol, his desire to see Jorgenson dead.

In the past I've been accused of many things. Some have called me a vigilante. Fair enough, I can live with that. But I don't see things the same way. I prefer to be seen as someone who can help. When the full weight of the law can't do anything, well then, that's where I step up. I don't take the law into my own hands. Not as such, not when the law doesn't extend to what is occasionally required.

The thing that stopped me approaching Jorgenson right that instant was one undeniable truth. I still hadn't seen Marianne. I'd no way of knowing if she was even inside the house. Introducing myself to her violent beau at this stage could mean that I never saw her again.

Better to wait, then.

There would be a time for entering that house, but it would be later, under the cover of darkness and with Rink watching my back.

Jorgenson – notwithstanding his sudden rise to prominence as one of Florida's social elite – was third-generation money. His grandfather had come over from Europe in the late 1950s. He brought with him a pharmaceutical supply company that rocketed along with the post-World War II financial boom. The Korean and Vietnamese conflicts didn't do any harm either, and set Jorgenson's father, Valentin, at the helm of an industry driven by military contracts that were fed by Desert Storm and the more recent campaigns in Iraq and Afghanistan. With his father ailing, Bradley was now poised to step up and take the reins. He was the face of twenty-first century consumerism.

My worry, and this was possibly due to my doubts regarding the man's character, was that he was living a lifestyle usually associated with another kind of pharmaceutical. Those that don't come with a prescription.

Two could play to those rules. Whatever he was peddling, I had a painkiller of my own.

I reached for my SIG Sauer.

CHAPTER 5

As a child of the Mississippi Delta lands, Dantalion had been raised on the myths and legends surrounding haunted groves and magical ceremonies performed by High Priestesses of Voodoo. Louisiana Voodoo, Haitian Vodou or West African Vodun in its generic form, had all appealed to the fertile mind of a child with too much time on his hands. From an early age he had eagerly grasped at tales of spells and enchantment, of living dead men, and ritual sacrifice. But in his early teens, he left all that nonsense behind. He turned his attention to other legends, in particular a story everyone knows, though their take on the Fall from Grace was normally mired in the dogma preached by the Church.

How could this impressionable youth not seize on the notion of angels, when his alabaster skin and ice-blue eyes had singled him out and set him above all the other human cattle? His earliest recollection had been of his momma cooing that he was her little angel. They were fond memories. Next came the bullies at school stripping him to see if his wings had been cut down to stumps, then beating the shit out of him when their suspicions had proved wrong. They were fond memories too, which confirmed in his mind that he was better than them. Encouraged him to embrace the reality. The Fallen did not have wings. They were seared from their backs when God cast them into the flames of Hell.

In the subdued darkness of his hotel room in the SoBe district of Miami Beach, Dantalion was not concerned about the stares he received in day-to-day life. In this enlightened age, people were more sensitive to the feelings of others. Still, people passing him in the street couldn't help the involuntary flicker of their eyes as they tried to probe beneath his coverings, seeking out *what the hell he was.*

They were ignorant of his condition. Most assumed that he was an albino, but that was not the case. Vitiligo is an acquired disorder distinguished by patches of depigmented skin. Ordinarily people with vitiligo lack melanin in the epidermis, and form patches of milky- or chalky-white skin. In extreme cases – as in Dantalion's – the hair and retina of the eye are also affected. Various treatments are available, but in cases where depigmentation affects more than half of the body, a bleaching agent named monobenzone is applied to the normal skin to match it with the paler areas. It is not usually debilitating, but the skin can become more sensitive to the sun. Occasionally, dermatitis can be a side effect of the treatment. As long as he remained covered he was in no danger, and thankfully it was only patches on his hands and face that required hydrocortisone creams. Ingestion of immuno-modulating drugs also formed a necessary precaution, though the risk to his bone density was a potential and serious side effect he could do without.

In this room, though, with the dimmer switch turned to its lowest setting, he felt at peace. He was stripped to the waist, his body faintly luminous against the darkness. He had disdained his dark glasses in order to see what he was writing in his book.

He had people to kill.

He was confident in his abilities.

When he chose to kill, there was only one outcome.

He was so confident that he'd already assigned the numbers. Two new figures he jotted down. They were for starters; there were always others he could add if he so wished.

CHAPTER 6

Watching the boats sailing into the marina, I was acutely aware that nothing was getting done. The buzz of adrenalin I'd experienced earlier was wearing off, and I was beginning to get a slightly nauseous feeling in my gut. The beer I'd drunk on an empty stomach wasn't the best idea I'd ever had. There was no public restaurant on the island that I was aware of and I was starving.

Rink was due soon, though, so I sent him a text requesting a detour to the nearest fast food joint for something substantial. He replied, 'YUR GONNA GET FAT!' So I told him: 'I'D PREFER A CHEESEBURGER.'

Told you stakeouts were boring.

With nothing for it, I returned to my recliner and sat watching the adjoining property. Things were silent in the household now, but I knew that Jorgenson hadn't left. His personal boat was moored to the peninsula jutting out into the seaward end of the marina directly at the foot of his garden. Assuming that Marianne was with him, my best course of action was to sit and wait. To kill time, I again took out my SIG and for about the fourth time that evening I stripped it down and cleaned it.

That done, I went inside and shucked out of my shorts, pulling on a pair of black jeans and sweater. Carrying my boots on to the balcony, I laced them up while glancing down into the pool area of Jorgenson's property. I'd only been gone seconds, but already the tableau had changed. A woman was moving through the garden, her arms folded beneath her breasts. Her light brown hair was pulled up in a knot and was pinned in place to the back of her head. In pale blue cardigan and blue jeans she looked more like the girl in the school photograph. Even without a good look at her face, I was pretty sure that it was Marianne Dean.

She seemed lost in thought. Singing softly to herself. Was it a sad song?

Quickly I let myself back into my condominium and took the steps to the lower level two at a time. I exited into the garden nonchalantly, whistling loudly to myself as though I was unaware of the woman on the other side of the palm-fringed border which was all that separated us. Armed with a net, I approached the swimming pool and began scooping bugs and non-existent windblown dross from the surface. The woman must have heard me come outside, and I sensed that she was watching me from between the palm fronds.

I kept up the charade just long enough to make it look natural, then swung round to place the results of my labour on the garden. Widening my eyes, stepping back, I said, 'Oh! Sorry. Didn't see you there. I hope my whistling didn't disturb you?'

Marianne seemed amused. She shook her head. 'I didn't know we had neighbours,' she said. 'Maybe it's us who should apologise about the noise.'

Approaching so that I was leaning through the fronds, I offered her my most disarming face. Studying her features, I couldn't make out any signs that Bradley had been up to his old tricks. 'Just arrived. I haven't heard anything.'

Her lips pinched momentarily and I wondered what had flitted through her mind. 'I had some girlfriends over earlier. They behaved like kids. We had to send them home before they had us run off the island.'

Nodding at her wisdom, I said, 'Beautiful island, isn't it? Wish I could live here all the time.'

'Yeah,' she said, her features smoothing out.

'I'm only here for a few days,' I told her. 'Couldn't afford this lifestyle all year round. As much as I'd like to. What about you? That your parents' place?'

'No.' She didn't expand. There was an uncomfortable second or two. To fill it, I stuck out my hand. 'Sorry, I'm being rude. Name's Joe.'

Her arms were still tucked tight beneath her breasts and it didn't look like she was going to accept my proffered hand of friendship. Her glance skipped towards the house. But then she leaned forwards and shook my hand gently.

'Mari,' she said.

'Nice to meet you, Mari,' I said. Mari, not Marianne. The little girl all grown up and demanding her place in the world. Demanding individuality.

'Were you thinking of taking a dip?' She nodded over at the pool, then looked pointedly at the net I still grasped in my hand.

'No, not just now. Look,' I offered, 'I didn't mean to disturb you. I've kept you long enough.'

'It's OK. It wasn't as if I was doing anything. Just thinking about . . . stuff.'

'Still, stopped you doing that.'

She waved down my concern.

'It's not important,' she said. But her arms went back under her breasts. Defensive body language.

'Anything I can help with?'

She looked at me strangely. 'No.'

Nodding once, I told her, 'If there is anything, well, you know where I am. You just have to say. I *can* help you, Marianne.'

There was confusion on her face now. I'd called her by her given name on purpose, and she'd picked up on that fact. In the past she'd made some bad decisions, yeah, but she wasn't stupid.

'Who are you, *Joe*?'

Staring into her face, exuding honesty, I made her a promise, 'I'm someone who can help you.'

Marianne wavered. Fear flashed across her features, but was replaced instantly by something that looked too much like anger to be ignored. She opened her mouth but the words didn't come. Before things went any further, I stepped back, hefting my net again. 'Well,' I said, 'I'd better get back to work and let you get on with thinking.'

There was a noise from up near Jorgenson's house. A heavy tread on the poolside tiles. 'Mari? You out there?'

I could see a heavy-built guy in a dark suit. His stomach was large and extended over his belt line. Thick rolls of flesh hung on his jowls and made a hump at the base of his shaved skull. He was like a heavyweight boxer who'd gone to seed. He glanced my way once. Then back to Marianne. 'Something wrong, Mari?'

Mari glanced my way, then said, 'No, of course not. I'm just saying hello to our new neighbour.'

The big man – undoubtedly hired muscle – squinted my way. I nodded a greeting which he mirrored with no enthusiasm. Back to Marianne he said, 'Best you come in now, Mari. Mr Jorgenson's looking for you.'

Marianne gave me the tight-lipped smile again, then turned in the direction of the house. I couldn't swear but there seemed less melancholy to her humming now. I watched her until she was back inside the house. The muscle eyed me for a long beat, then he too went inside.

After that, I dropped the net by the pool and took up my place back on the balcony.

I'd come to take Marianne Dean away from Jorgenson. But the opportunity I'd just been given had passed. Obviously I wanted the girl to trust me when I did snatch her out of his hands, and I knew that she didn't yet. But another opportunity would present itself.

To kill time I cleaned my gun again, and watched the boats coming and going from the marina.

I was watching for Rink, but I saw something else instead.

Good job I'd got the gun ready.

CHAPTER 7

As a killer for hire, Dantalion had certain limitations. His looks – the paleness of his skin and hair, the limpidness of his eyes – made him stand out in a crowd. It was never good for one who prized anonymity to be seen and to be remembered. It was one reason why he rarely left anyone alive in his wake. There couldn't be so many angels wandering around in the flesh that he could get away with his trade if anyone should witness his comings and goings.

But because of his individuality he had schooled himself in the art of concealment. He knew how to get in and out of places without alerting even the most vigilant of watchers. He was adept at disguises, could administer theatrical makeup as though born to the movie industry. But sometimes, he knew, boldness and confidence could win the day where all that sneaking around would achieve was raised eyebrows and pointed fingers.

Arriving at the Baker Island marina, he did so in style. He made sure that to any observer he was yet another man of the über-rich set. The boat – a $2.5 million cabin cruiser – might not be the most expensive in the marina, but it certainly didn't look out of place. He was dressed in the finest silk suit and his face and hands were a light tan, his hair concealed under a sleek black wig. Even his eyes, his greatest giveaway, were disguised by tinted contact lenses. To all intents and purposes, he looked at home on the island. The real boat owner wouldn't mind that Dantalion had stolen his identity; he was currently bleeding out through the hole in his head back at Miami Beach.

He purposely didn't moor the boat anywhere near the target's home; that could alert any minders prowling in the area. Better that he stroll in, a man arrived from the sea catching his balance now that he was back on dry land. As he walked he lit a cigar. He didn't regularly smoke, but it was all part of the look. He walked with his free hand tucked into his jacket pocket, where a slit had been cut in the seam so he could reach the sound-suppressed 90-two Beretta strapped to his thigh.

Lights positioned along the dockside attracted swarms of gnats: even mega-money couldn't eradicate the presence of pests. Dantalion ignored them. He was too intent on the row of luxury houses ahead. The buildings looked pink in the yellow haze of the lights, almost semi-circular in construction as they hugged the curve of the land where the marina spilled back into Biscayne Bay. Off to his right was the sprawling length of Dodge Island and beyond it the blazing nightscape that was Miami itself.

The house he was looking for was the one to the extreme right of the three comprising the half-moon shape. The houses, making the most of the view and the afternoon sun, were built so that the gardens and pools faced towards the sea. Entrance to the buildings could be gained from the gardens, but the main doors were at the far side of the buildings.

Taking in the nightscape of the metropolis across Biscayne Bay, he stood leaning his elbows on a low wall overlooking the promontory that gave private mooring to these three properties. A $10-million plus craft bobbed on the swells there, making Dantalion consider the fee he'd set to get this job done; maybe he should have doubled it. Perhaps he still would.

Putting the cigar to his lips, he took smoke into his mouth but no further. Then, exhaling slowly, he turned and leaned his elbows on the wall so that he was looking back towards the houses. It was nonchalant enough that to any observer he would appear simply as a man at peace with the world and enjoying the privileges afforded him. In that brief moment he scanned all three upper balconies of the properties he could see. The building furthest to the left appeared deserted. There was a man, apparently asleep on a reclining chair on building two. Lights blazed throughout the target house but he could not immediately detect any movement from within.

His eyes strayed back to the central balcony.

He couldn't see much of the man, but he appeared relaxed enough to be genuinely asleep. He watched for long seconds but got no reaction. He dismissed the presence of the man: he was probably drunk or sleeping off a long flight. He could always pay him a visit after he was done, make sure that a potential witness was no longer around. Jamming the cigar between his teeth, he pushed off from the wall and walked along the pathway overlooking the sea. Tiny waves made crystalline splashes on the rocks below. He flicked the cigar away, watching it spiral end-over-end like a tiny meteor before it fizzed out in the ocean.

He then moved inland towards the high wall bordering the garden. To look at him, he wouldn't have the strength to catch the top of the wall and swing up as nimbly as a cat, but that was what he did. There he crouched, peering over the top of shrubbery towards the house. He held the pose, gargoyle-like, as though he was an evil sprite fleeing a European cathedral. Pretty apt, considering.

When he was sure he'd gone undetected, he hopped down into the garden, landing surefooted amid a stand of palm. Crouching again, he felt for the necessary tools of his trade. Beretta. Check. Book. Check. That was all he needed. He moved forward, staying within the shadows of the trees. Nothing stirred around him; even the endemic bugs had fallen silent.

The bushes ended at a paved terrace, then came an open space he had to traverse to get to the door. From this vantage point he could see through the doorway to a well-appointed lobby area. An overweight man in a dark suit was sitting on a couch, using a telephone on an adjacent stand. He was giving someone quite express orders judging by the snapping motion of his free hand. Dantalion followed the man's gesture. Another big man, the shoulder holster immediately obvious against his shirt. Two minders at the very least. Could be more on the upper floors.

Calculating figures, Dantalion moved forwards. He lifted the silenced Beretta, took aim. There was a noise like someone slapping a catcher's mitt. The light above the entrance went out. Within the house neither of the bodyguards noticed the sudden darkness outside. Dantalion was immediately on the move.

He was across the terrace in seconds. He didn't pause, pulling open the door in one swift motion. The fat man on the couch was the nearest target, but he was sitting down and had his gun hand full of telephone. Dantalion shot the standing man. The 9 mm bullet hit him centre mass, going through-and-through, putting a hole in the mirror behind him. Blood spray misted the crazy-paved glass.

It was a heart shot, but experience told Dantalion that sometimes that wasn't enough. Even as the target crumpled, he shot the same man a second time, taking off a sizeable portion of his skull.

Barely two seconds had passed, but it was the

length of mortality for at least one of the men. The heavy man had hardly registered what was happening. He swung his gaze from his dead companion to the mystery man in the lobby, his mouth hanging open. The Beretta was now aimed his way. The second victim was more show than substance, his real weapons his size and his fists. Not much good against an expert with a semi-automatic handgun. His response was to sink back on the couch, bringing up his hands. Dantalion shot him twice. Once in the throat to stop his shout of alarm, once in his tremulous gut, just for good measure.

Both men out of the picture in less time than it took to stalk the length of the lobby. The suppressor – though not as effective as Hollywood would have it – deadened the sounds of the gunshots, but there'd still been the sequence of thuds. Most noise had come from the smashing of the mirror. Still, Dantalion wasn't concerned that the people upstairs had been alerted; they weren't familiar with the sounds of death.

Moving to the foot of a staircase, Dantalion swept the remainder of the lobby with his gun. A closed door on his right, possibly an entrance to a kitchen area. He twisted the handle. Didn't want to be going up the stairs only for the door to swing open and disgorge more minders. But the kitchen was in darkness, empty of armed guards. He quickly pulled the door shut.

The door out into the parking area was closed.

No movement beyond it. He returned his attention to the stairs.

There was a young woman coming down, a step at a time, as she hefted a heavy suitcase. She saw the dead man on the couch, jerked her stupefied gaze towards Dantalion. Her eyes widened. A scream began to swell. Dantalion shot her in the mouth. No need of a second shot this time, not with half her skull decorating the stairway. She slipped to the stairs, boneless, making hardly a sound. Not the suitcase, though; it rattled and thumped and banged its way over the steps before Dantalion could reach it and halt its fall.

Quizzical voices were raised from above him. One female, two male. He glanced at the dead woman on the stairs. Slim and petite with a Hispanic look. She was wearing a white blouse, black skirt and sensible black shoes. Housemaid, he determined. That would mean the three upstairs were his targets, plus one more probable guard.

Taking their confusion as cover for his own upward charge, he gained the upper floor before any of them had the notion to come and investigate the commotion.

Walking along the landing, he saw another young woman step out of a bedroom. Anglo-Saxon this one. Light brown hair, blue-green eyes, nice figure. Dantalion smiled at her.

'Hello, Marianne,' he said.

Then he showed her the gun. The woman

immediately yelped and jerked back into the room. Dantalion followed her. He was only a beat in her wake, and he was planning on using her fear against the others.

He blinked, taking in the tableau.

The woman was still running across the room. A young man, reddish hair marking him out, was in mid-pose pulling on a suit jacket. The second man was older, grey hair, slim, distinguished-looking. Sitting at a desk, he had been bending over a laptop computer. More accountant than bodyguard, perhaps, but still a viable threat. Dantalion lifted the Beretta and blew him out of contention.

To the younger man, Dantalion said, 'Bradley, how are you, sir?'

Jorgenson gaped at him. Then he looked down at the dead man slumped over the computer, his fingers arched over the keys as though writing his own eulogy.

'Dad?' Jorgenson croaked. His face collapsed in on itself and he sobbed.

'That was your father? The great Valentin Jorgenson? If it's any consolation, your father would probably thank me for killing him. What was it? Cancer? He was in great pain, was he not?' Dantalion went closer. He lifted the gun so it was aimed at Bradley's heart. 'Do you want a quick and painless death, Bradley? I'm prepared to give you the choice.'

Jorgenson stepped back, bringing up placating

hands. 'Look, whoever you are, whoever put you up to this, I will double the price. Don't kill me.'

Dantalion let out a long sigh like an escape of steam. 'I'm not averse to being handed heaps of cash, Bradley. However, a deal is a deal and you must die.' He turned and sought out the woman. Marianne had pressed herself to the far wall as if she could melt through the brick and escape the horror. 'You too, Marianne.'

Marianne whimpered, slipping down the wall and covering her head with both arms.

Dantalion waved Jorgenson over to the woman with the barrel of his gun. 'Go and comfort her, Bradley. She deserves a hug, don't you think?'

Jorgenson pleaded. 'She hasn't done anything wrong. Please don't kill her.'

'The deal has been made, Bradley. I must.'

Jorgenson was fit and strong. Approaching his prime, before the hedonistic ways the affluence afforded him would make him fat and slow. Dantalion saw him clench his fists.

'Don't be silly, Bradley. The hype is just that. They've dubbed you *Superman*, but, believe me; you're not faster than a speeding bullet.'

'Who sent you?' Jorgenson demanded.

Dantalion tapped the Beretta alongside his nose. 'That would be telling.'

Jorgenson snapped his gaze on Marianne. There was a flash of anger, but then the hardness melted.

'Let her go.'

Dantalion shook his head.

'I will let you choose, Bradley. The woman first?'

'No!'

'Then you first?'

'No!'

Dantalion shook his head. 'You just don't seem to get this, do you?'

'I'm not going to choose who you kill. How can you expect me to do that?'

'Flip a coin if you wish,' Dantalion said. 'But if I kill her first, then we go back to my first offer. Quick and painless or slow and in untold agony.'

Shuddering, Jorgenson looked down at the woman. Her eyes were huge ovals as she looked back at him. 'Mari,' he said, 'I'm sorry I dragged you into this, babe.'

'Not. . . . your . . . fault,' she whispered back.

'Now that's very touching,' Dantalion said. Unconsciously he wiped his arm over his chin. A pale patch of skin drew Jorgenson's gaze. Realising his error, Dantalion shook his head slowly. 'Bang goes the neighbourhood! Now there's definitely no choice.'

With a lifestyle built on giving commands, Jorgenson wasn't one to give in so easily. The shock of seeing his father gunned down, the weirdness of the man threatening him with death, were beginning to dissipate. He squared his shoulders.

'You touch either of us, you'll be hunted down. They won't stop. You'll be hounded constantly and when they get you they will make you *hurt*!'

Dantalion raised an eyebrow. 'They? Who are

these *they* you have so much faith in? *They* will have to find me first. If I don't want *them* to find me, *they* never will.'

'*They* already have,' said a voice from behind him.

CHAPTER 8

Not normally one for moving in the kind of circles the people of Baker Island enjoyed, I could be forgiven for missing *just another rich man* as he took an evening stroll along the dockside. But as one who had spent fourteen years hunting terrorists, and the last four dealing with criminals ranging from moneylenders to a bone-collecting maniac, I recognised a stone killer when I saw him.

An island this wealthy, it was probable that a large portion of the populace was ex-cops, ex-military – and everything in between – employed as executive protectors to those who called Baker Island their home. But something about the sinuous way this man moved told me he wasn't the type who celebrated the sanctity of life. For one, he was too watchful of his surroundings. Even switched-on security men don't act that way when they aren't covering their mark.

The cigar was a prop. Too exaggerated, the way he put it to his mouth, then immediately removed it with a sweeping gesture of his arm. And all the while the other hand didn't move from his pocket.

It fiddled with something that extended much lower than the confines of his pocket. He was packing.

He flicked the cigar away, watching it as it pinwheeled away into the ocean. Leaning back on a wall, the man turned and stared directly at me. I'd been expecting that, so I'd already sunk down against the recliner, tilting my head as though dozing. I watched him through the merest slitting of my eyes. The man ghosted a smile. I'd have missed it in the subdued lighting if I hadn't got a flash of saliva on teeth.

Out of his line of sight I was already mid-text to Rink.

'GET HERE FAST. TROUBLE'

I hit the send button just as the man turned away and walked along the coast path. His very black hair picked up highlights from the lamps along the path, so I could make out his progress beyond the wall to Jorgenson's garden. I blinked and the man was suddenly crouching on the wall like some unearthly bat. Next instant he was down in the garden and he paused to check his pockets. When next he moved it was as if a snake had sprung out of a coil, fast but sinuous at the same time. Then I couldn't see him because of the angle and the obscuring foliage.

Keeping low, I moved to the edge of my balcony. The lights above the entrance spilled across Jorgenson's terrace, making for faux-daytime. Then came a noise like a sharp cough and the garden went dark.

As soon as it did, I was on the move.

But not without hearing four rapid shots from a silenced handgun, and the smashing of glass.

Going back through my apartment would take too long. I swung over the edge of the balcony and jumped to the terrace below. Harking back to my parachute days, I tucked and rolled, absorbing the impact, and came up with my SIG levelled towards Jorgenson's house. Then I moved forward. Further down the garden, only the shrubbery marked the boundary, but here close to the entrances a small wall had been erected to offer privacy to occupants sitting on the terrace. I had to shift a terracotta pot containing some fern-type plant. Then I vaulted the wall and landed in Jorgenson's property.

Another dull thud sounded, then the bang and rattle of something clattering down a staircase. I stepped into the foyer just as the man I'd watched outside raced up the stairs. The big man who'd called Marianne inside earlier was dead. A telephone was still in his hand, but he'd ripped the cord loose as he'd died. Another man sprawled on the floor and his blood decorated the walls and made a crazy pattern on the shattered mirror.

What the hell had I got myself into this time? I couldn't take time to ponder the bad luck that had cast its hand my way. Marianne was up those stairs. Who this killer was I had no idea, but whether or not Marianne was the target she wouldn't get out of this situation alive if I stood there trying to figure out the age-old question.

The killer was already out of sight. Another gunshot, then muffled talking. I swung on to the stairs and saw another corpse. A young woman with half her head gone. This angered me more than any number of slaughtered bodyguards. It also told me the killer wouldn't hesitate to put a bullet through Marianne as well.

Silent as possible, I made my way up the stairs. The killer and someone I took to be Jorgenson were conversing in low tones. I wasn't concerned about what was said – the threat in the killer's voice was enough to keep me moving.

On the landing now, I moved along the hall. A thick carpet beneath my rubber soles ensured silence and I was able to move directly to the bedroom door without raising the alarm.

There I readied my gun. Listened.

'They?' the killer was asking. 'Who are these they you have so much faith in? They will have to find me first. If I don't want them to find me, they never will.'

Conceited, overconfident bastard, I thought. I entered the room behind him. 'They already have.'

Should have kept my mouth shut. Conceit and overconfidence can get anyone killed.

The killer spun and fired even before I'd done gloating.

His bullet missed me. Only just. But it made me flinch and my return fire missed him as well.

Sometimes sudden violence can have a strange effect on the senses. As adrenalin spurts through the system, you can experience a startling slowing of reality so that everything around you seems like a slow-motion, hyper-clear shot on a 3D screen. Really it's your mind racing as it seeks the options for flight or fight, overtaking the responses of the machine that the engine of the brain powers.

There was an overriding sense of déjá vu even as I pulled the trigger again and saw the material of the man's suit jacket trail on the wake of the bullet's passing. Unfortunately there was no blood. Missed the fucker a second time. Then he was lunging to one side and shooting across his body at me. Throwing myself into the room, I fired off a volley of five rounds. Unlike his silenced pistol, my SIG roared like Thor's battle cry.

I was here on the knight errant's quest to save a damsel in distress. I wouldn't be much good to her if I ended up dead.

Swinging round into a sitting position, I levelled my SIG on the killer.

He must have had an equally important reason to live, because he fired back. Burning cold creased my right shoulder. It wasn't a debilitating hit, in fact the bullet had barely grazed me. It was enough to draw my aim though, and my return fire went over his head and struck the door frame as he vaulted back into the landing. The clatter of his feet down the stairs resounded through the house.

Pretty certain he wasn't going to return in the next second or two, I searched for Marianne. She was unhurt, but still in a state of near collapse. Jorgenson was in a duck's crouch of his own, ass almost touching his heels.

'You OK?' I asked the two of them.

Receiving nods from both, I rolled over on my front, swinging to cover the door. 'Jorgenson,' I said. 'Get over here.'

Jorgenson blinked at me, half rose, then sunk down again. Not sure why, but not wanting to approach me either.

I snapped, 'If you want to get out of here alive, you're gonna have to do what I say. Now get the fuck over here!'

I had started this job with the understanding that I might have to kill Bradley Jorgenson. It's funny how fate plays out sometimes. The arrival of this would-be killer had changed the dynamics of my mission. In my mind, Bradley had been someone to be loathed, someone to be put down with all the regret of shooting a rabid dog. And yet here I was, offering to be his protector.

'Are you armed?'

He shook his head.

'What about him?' I jerked my head towards a man folded over a desk.

Jorgenson's eyes teared up. He shook his head sadly.

'Make sure,' I ordered him. 'He could be carrying.'

'He isn't,' Jorgenson said. 'My father. He abhorred violence. He was a man who only wanted to stop pain.'

Noble, I thought, but misguided. Someone who makes their billions from military contracts can't play the moral card when challenged over their source of income. He could say what he wanted, but Daddy Jorgenson was as much to do with causing pain as curing it.

'Check,' I said.

I crept over to the door. Keeping low, I bobbed my head round the frame, then back inside again. I didn't see the killer, but he was likely still in the house. When I glanced in his direction, Jorgenson was gently patting around inside his father's jacket. He was looking at me, his eyes full of disgust.

'Nothing,' he spat, moving away quickly.

'Get Marianne,' I told him. 'Take her over there.'

Jorgenson helped Marianne up. She looked shaky, but unhurt. On rubber legs, she allowed Jorgenson to lead her past the dead man to the far end of the room. Her eyes swooped, like birds chasing insects at dusk, never still, never in one place.

'Do you know that man?' I demanded. I snuck a look round the door frame, noticing a play of shadows from below.

'No,' Jorgenson said. 'And I don't know you. Who the hell are you?'

It was Marianne who offered an explanation. 'He's Joe. He's here to help.'

'You've no idea why he wants you dead?' I asked.

No reply. When I looked, Jorgenson was holding Marianne to him, his hands cupping her head against his chest. Marianne was sobbing into his shirt. The picture of young love. It didn't look much like Marianne had ever suffered at his hands. Maybe she'd only traded one lesser terror for another.

There'd be time for resolving the Jorgenson problem later. Right now there was a far greater danger to Marianne's welfare. The killer was downstairs and he was up to no good.

'Is there another way out of here?' Studying the windows, I decided that we could smash one of them and climb out. It would be a fair drop to the ground but we were all capable of it. What I didn't like the idea of was the killer waiting for us, picking us off from below as we clambered from the window.

RINK HOW FAR AWAY

My text was hurried. Thankfully I received his reply in seconds, but it wasn't what I wanted to see.

FIFTEEN MINS

Not soon enough. The killer wasn't going to wait that long.

I heard a clatter and dull thump from below us.

'What's he doing?' Marianne asked.

I'd been thinking the same thing. Sounded like he was in the kitchen.

MEET US SOBE, I sent to Rink.

In her schoolgirl guise, Marianne might not have been much help in these circumstances. But as the sleek trophy Jorgenson had made of her, perhaps there was something she could bring into play.

'Marianne, you have perfume in here?'

Marianne stared at me as if I was mad. In all honesty she wasn't so far removed from the truth. 'Perfume?'

'Good stuff. Concentrated.'

She nodded, pulling free from Jorgenson's embrace. She took a wide berth round the dead man and went to a credenza where she pulled open a compartment and grabbed at bottles of scent. Judging by the brands and designs of the bottles, she handed me the makings of a bomb that would cost thousands of dollars.

Checking that the killer wasn't sneaking back along the landing, I snatched a look. The sounds from below reassured me he was still being industrious in the kitchen. For a second I considered leading Marianne and Jorgenson out of the bedroom, taking our chances on getting out while he was busy with whatever the hell he was doing. He'd hear us, though, and would pick us off as we came down the stairs.

When I turned back to the bedroom, Jorgenson had joined Marianne beside me.

'This better not be what I'm thinking,' Jorgenson said. His head shake was pure denial.

'We have to make a diversion; otherwise we

aren't going to get out of here alive.' I began unscrewing tops off the perfume bottles. 'Find me something larger than these. That wine bottle over there will do.'

'But my father . . .' Jorgenson croaked.

'Your father is already dead,' I pointed out. 'But I'm pretty sure he'd want *you* to live. Now go and fetch me the fucking bottle.'

I stepped out on to the landing and peered over the railing. The killer immediately shot at me, and I ducked back. I unloaded five bullets directly through the floor. Not really an attempt to hit him – the wooden joists would probably sap much of the velocity of the rounds – but it was enough to force him back into the kitchen.

Two could play at the same game. The killer's bullets drilled upwards, lifting tatters of carpet in front of my eyes. I jumped back into the room. Good enough, I thought, I'd got his attention. Plus he was using the kitchen for cover.

'Empty the perfume into the wine bottle, and get me some sort of rag for a fuse,' I whispered to Marianne. She understood my train of thought and nodded. She turned to the bottles I'd set on the floor.

Jorgenson brought the wine bottle. He walked slowly, and his eyes never left the still form of his father. His father was a sick man, dying from cancer as I recalled, but I don't think that Jorgenson expected to be cremating him so soon.

'If there was any other way,' I said, by way of

apology. His face was set in stone. There'd be no consoling him. It'd be pointless trying, so I turned away, concentrating on keeping the killer at bay.

Behind my back Jorgenson sobbed for his murdered father. It was enough to make him step over a precipice.

The stupid son of a bitch swung the bottle and smashed it over my skull.

CHAPTER 9

The appearance of the mystery gunman was an unfortunate – and unforeseen – complication. Dantalion recognised the man who'd been dozing on the balcony next door, but couldn't at first understand his reasons for intervening. Dantalion didn't think the man was in the employ of Jorgenson. The targets had been as surprised by his appearance as Dantalion had been. Plus, however much cash you could throw around, you didn't hire a condominium adjacent to the one you're living in and set the guard up as sole occupant. This man had another reason for being here.

Recalling the meeting with his client back in Bayside Park, Dantalion thought of the subtle threat he'd levelled at the man. Bad idea in hindsight. Maybe his employer had set this man up to kill him after the hit had been completed on his targets. Insurance that Dantalion wouldn't come after he'd been paid for his services. Or that Dantalion didn't become a liability: someone who could lead back to the client, implicating him in the murders.

Fucker! Well, if that was the case, the client better watch his ass. He was numbered now.

But first he had to finish what he'd started here.

Bradley Jorgenson and Marianne Dean must die. So must the gunman. In fact, the gunman took priority because he was stopping Dantalion getting the primary job done.

Time was against him.

He'd come with a silenced gun but the other man hadn't been so discerning a killer. He'd been shooting off a barrage of loud volleys. Place like this where the populace of the island lived on tightly wound nerves for fear of robbery or kidnap, dozens of people would be demanding the immediate arrival of Miami P.D. The cops didn't have a station house on the island, but there'd be plenty of rent-a-cops en route. The police wouldn't be far behind.

There were two possible ways for this to play out. He could get the hell away now and take a second shot at his targets later, or he could try and kill them now and take his chances with the swarm of uniforms bearing down on him.

He wasn't worried about security guards or cops. They'd never been capable of stopping him before.

He made his choice.

He exited the kitchen and looked up. He saw a head glance over the balcony. Quickly, Dantalion lifted his Beretta and fired. The man had seen him, though, and ducked back out of sight. Then Dantalion had to dance to avoid the bullets blasting holes through the balcony above his head. Splinters of wood rained down on him, but miraculously none of the bullets hit their mark.

Dantalion fired back.

Then he was back in the kitchen. His mind made up. Choice made.

The island wasn't supplied with a gas main. Electricity was the overriding source of power to these houses. However there were secondary sources, too. Oil tanks. Propane gas. Jorgenson's house was equipped with a full cooking range.

Reaching down alongside the range he found a rubber pipe attached to a valve on the wall. Dantalion grabbed a knife from a nearby cutting block and swiped it through the rubber pipe. He heard the hiss of escaping gas. Then he moved back across the room to the door. Listened. A mutter of voices from above. Good, they were still in the room.

Dantalion looked back at the range. He imagined that there was a haze over the cooker now, but knew that was only fancy. The gas was invisible. But it was there, the cloud growing exponentially by the second.

The scorching flames of hell would scour this house, do his work for him. How appropriate for one who fancied himself as one of the Fallen. It would be just like home.

Above him he heard smashing glass. Not a window, more a dull thud followed by tinkling. A second more solid thump and he almost believed that he saw the balcony above him shift under the weight.

He went into the foyer, training his gun on the bedroom door. Two forms raced out, bent low as they charged along the balcony towards the rear of the house. Startled by the direction they'd taken, he was a split second behind them as he fired. His bullets found only plaster, then the two were out of sight behind a turn in the hall above.

A gun poked over the balcony. Firing blind. One of the bullets snicked a bleeding chunk from Dantalion's right thigh and he was forced to swerve away. Back towards the kitchen. In the doorway he searched for the front door. Should have opened it first. But never mind. He'd take his chances. He took out the lighter he'd used to ignite his cigar earlier. Back out under the balcony, using the wall as a shield, he flipped the lid open and spun the wheel of the lighter. A flame guttered, went out. He hissed, spun the wheel again and this time the flame stood an inch tall.

As he slid the lighter across the floor towards the cooking range, he was already running.

The gas caught with an imploding cough, then expanded as the flames raced through the kitchen.

Two feet from the front door, Dantalion held his breath in anticipation. He grabbed at the handle, tugged open the door, was through it. That was when the flames backed fully down the exposed rubber pipe, found the reserve tank and exploded like Hiroshima.

The impact knocked Dantalion sprawling. His ability to hear deserted him. His vision was full of raining debris and flames and smoke. His body was pummelled by flying dust and fragments of wood.

But he was happy.

No way the people inside could survive that explosion.

Back on his feet, his first concern was for his book. He felt in his pockets while his ears whooshed and squealed as they sought to regain normal function. His book was there, attached to his belt by the ever-present chain.

Numbers needed adding to the list.

CHAPTER 10

Bradley Jorgenson was a man capable of beating the woman he supposedly loved, so I should have expected something like this from him. He didn't want me to burn down the house where his father's body lay. Fair enough. But my plan to lob a jerry-built fire bomb at the killer was only intended to keep him at bay in the kitchen while we escaped down the stairs. The house was equipped with a water sprinkler system that would handle a localised fire set off by the perfume bomb. In reality I didn't trust the makeshift device to do more than set off a sweet-smelling flash, but it would have been enough to make the killer duck for cover, giving us the opportunity to get out.

But Jorgenson whacked me over the head with the goddamn wine bottle, putting paid to those plans. He hit me hard enough that the bottle shattered, cutting a strip of flesh from my scalp, knocking me to the floor. I was disoriented for a few seconds, but not stunned to a point that I lost my senses. Marianne yelped in dismay, but didn't resist him as Jorgenson grabbed her wrists and dragged her past me into the hall. I made a grab at her but missed, not able to go after them because of my ignominious position on the floor.

Thankfully they turned to my right. If they'd headed for the stairs the killer would have shot them dead in an instant. In a crouch they ran along the hall. Bullets whacked the wall in their wake, but they managed to gain cover and were – for the moment – safe.

Leaning forwards, I hung my SIG over the balcony, shooting blindly at the man below. Then I swung back on to my knees, rolling backwards into the bedroom for fear of return fire. My gun was depleted of ammo, so I took the time to eject the magazine, tug a fresh one from my hip pocket and slam it in place.

I was just coming to my feet when I heard a dull *whumph!* from below. A nanosecond later I was racing across the room, head down, firing repeatedly at the window. The glass was double-glazed and resisted the bullets somewhat. Then I was driving forwards, arms folded tight over my head. For one frightening instant I thought I'd recoil from the window, but then I was through the shattered glass and sailing through space. Around me the air went searing hot and even though I shouted involuntarily all the oxygen was sucked out of my lungs.

The sound was deafening, like some angry god had stamped his feet. The concussion of the blast picked me out of the air and sent me somersaulting towards trees. If I'd struck the bole of one of the palms, I'd have split like rotten fruit. Luckily, I hit the hanging fronds first, my body was spun full-tilt and I caromed to the floor through rasping leaves that whipped me mercilessly. Then I slammed the ground with enough force that my internal organs must have gone as flat as pancakes.

For too long I lay there groaning. Glad to be alive, but in agony *everywhere*. It was probably no more than ten seconds, but to my stunned brain it felt like I was prone for a month. The rest and recuperation didn't help. When I finally clawed myself on to my knees, I had to hold that position while my brain tried to right itself in my skull. I needed to vomit, but all that came out was a thin stream of bile. I spat on the mulch to clear my mouth. My eyes were still rattling in my skull, but I saw my SIG lying a few feet away and trained response made me reach for it.

Struggling to my feet, I limped through the bushes, making my way round the building in hope of a sign that Marianne had got out of there alive. As I went I wiped the SIG clean on my sweater sleeve.

Jorgenson's house was devastated. The entire upper floor had collapsed; the roof was a burst open wreck pushing splintered joists skyward. Flames and smoke broiled against the sky. The condominium I'd leased next door wasn't in much better shape with the whole of the front of the building spilling out towards the parking area. The buggy I'd rented to get me here from the ferry landing was flattened beneath fallen masonry.

Two cash deposits I wouldn't be getting back.

There was rubble heaped everywhere. Thankfully there weren't any chunks of burnt flesh or bones poking from the mounds. Which didn't negate the possibility that Marianne was buried beneath the wreckage of the house.

Movement nearby caught my eye. A shadow moving away from me. Wearing a dark suit, neither Jorgenson nor Marianne. The killer, I thought, making his escape. I lifted the SIG, drawing a bead on him. But then I let the barrel droop. The figure had longish fair hair, whereas the killer's had been jet black. For all I knew this was an innocent passer-by caught up in the fury of the explosion.

Moving back to the side of the building, batting cinders from my hair, I sought the couple's exit route. The building was still standing here, even if the upper portion now boasted a view to the sky and crenellations that hadn't been there previously. At ground level I saw an open door, steps leading upwards. A service stairway down to the dumpsters stacked against the wall.

The sound of an engine caught my attention.

Spinning on my heels, I ran towards the boundary wall, hooked my elbows over the top and pulled myself up. As I cleared the top of the wall I looked down to where the promontory pushed out into Biscayne Bay.

No sign of Marianne, but Jorgenson was standing in the cabin of his boat. His face was smudged with dirt, but he looked like he'd escaped the explosion without serious injury. I could only hope that Marianne had fared equally well. I shouted to Jorgenson. My voice was lost amidst the crackling flames, the creaking of collapsing masonry, the thrum of the boat's engine. But Jorgenson looked my way.

Our eyes met.

Jorgenson snarled in my direction. Then the boat was swinging away from the dock, heading for open water. I felt more than a little inadequate. Especially when I caught a flash of pale blue sweater, and realised that I'd failed to get Marianne away from her abuser.

In my pocket my mobile phone vibrated.

Pulling it out, I looked down at the screen. Despite myself, I smiled.

YOU STILL ALIVE?

Pressing buttons, I returned the call.

'Hi, Rink. Where are you now?'

'Watching some kinda fireball from out on Biscayne Bay,' Rink said. 'Don't tell me that was your doing.'

'Not responsible,' I reassured him.

'But as usual you're smack bang in the middle of it.'

'Who, me?'

Rink laughed. 'Glad you're OK, Hunter. Did you get Marianne away?'

'Afraid not,' I said. 'Something else went down here, Rink. But at least the girl is safe. We can pick her up later.' Then I told him about the killer, and what he'd done.

'Sounds like one desperate son of a bitch,' Rink offered. 'Any idea who he was? Why he was there?'

'I overheard a little. Sounded like a real sadist: he wanted Jorgenson to pick which of them died first.'

'Ah, just your typical whacked-out freak with his own agenda, huh?'

'He came across like a psycho killer, Rink. But there was more to it. He was a professional. He wasn't there just to get his kicks. He'd been sent by someone who wants Jorgenson and Marianne dead.'

'But they got away?'

'Yeah. And when this asshole realises he missed them, he'll be back.'

And we'd be waiting.

CHAPTER 11

The destruction of Jorgenson's home was all over the news before I even woke up. I was greeted by the early-morning paper slapped down on my chest by my big buddy, Rink. It had the desired effect of rousing me from troubled dreams where I was engulfed in flames while a demon tittered at me from behind a wax mask. Sitting bolt upright on my impromptu bed, I found it was the couch in the front office at Rington Investigations. Took a few seconds of head shaking to recall the mad flight from Baker Island, dodging police and Coast Guard boats so that I wasn't pulled in as the cause of the conflagration.

Feeling the effects of the evening before in every muscle and bone, I stretched, yawned, then decided I had to get my butt in gear. I could give in to the discomfort, or I could work the kinks out of my aching limbs.

When my eyes were able to focus, I scanned the newspaper. The press had given the explosion all the due of a planet-smashing meteor strike. Speculation was the order of the day. Rescue teams were sifting through the wreckage, but as yet no bodies had been discovered. That simple fact gave us a little breathing space. I threw the paper down and accepted the coffee that Rink held towards me.

The coffee was strong, the rich aroma invading my nigh-empty skull. It was the kick I needed. My injuries were superficial, grazes and scratches, the occasional bruise, but thankfully my bones were intact. The bullet graze on my shoulder hurt like a bitch, but it was more burn than open wound. The gash in my scalp had required stitches, and my last memory from the early hours of this morning was Rink coming at me with a tube of super glue, a needle and some cat gut. Probing the wound, I decided Rink was no Florence Nightingale, but he'd pass first level at sewing school.

I'd suffered a ride on an explosion, and a crashing fall through a window, but Rink didn't look to be in much better shape than me. He had dark smudges beneath his bloodshot eyes like he'd been peeping through keyholes all night. Can't have got much sleep, I surmised.

Sometimes Rink seems to read my mind. He nodded me through into his office. His glowing computer monitor cast a cold light on the walls of the otherwise darkened room; it made me feel the chill of the air-conditioning unit. I cupped my mug of coffee in my hands, savouring the steam on my face.

'Been surfing all night, trying to get a handle on who this killer for hire is.' He sat down wearily, his shoulders sinking.

'You look like you could do with some of this.' I held my mug up to him.

'Had a gallon of the stuff already,' he said. He tapped on the keyboard, brought up his email account. 'Been speaking to some people in the know about these kinds of things.'

'Find anything?' I asked. I could tell by the slump of his shoulders that he hadn't.

'Diddlysquat on the shooter. But there's a guy here says there's been a bit of a power struggle going on in the Jorgenson empire. Since Valentin announced his illness, and his impending retirement from the business, people have been jostling for position. Bradley is in pole position for taking over the business, as well as the family fortune. Couple of second runners not too happy with the situation. They don't think that the company is in safe hands with Brad. Apparently he hasn't the head for business his pa and grandpa had.'

'You think one of them would go as far as putting out a contract on Bradley? Bit extreme, isn't it?'

Of course, there maybe wasn't anything extreme about it. Richard Dean had set me on Jorgenson's heels because he was a little too liberal with the amount of contact he was laying on his daughter. Billions of dollars into the equation, I didn't doubt it warranted half-a-dozen hit men sent his way.

Rink said, 'There is any number of members of the "make-Brad-dead" club. Seems he's pissed off a lot of people. Mainly family.'

'What about?'

82

'The girl. Marianne Dean.'

'What? The way he's been treating her?'

'Yeah,' Rink said. 'But not how you mean. According to some of his nearest and dearest, he should be shot of her. They don't think she meets the high expectations demanded of one in their social circle. He treats her like a princess and they ain't too happy about it.'

'According to her father, Bradley treats her like shit. Beats her and practically keeps her a prisoner. You saw the police report, Rink.'

'Saw she had a bashed-up face, but nowhere where it said Bradley was responsible.'

'The witnesses denied it, too. But if you remember, the gossip was that Bradley beat her after some bad deal went down.'

'Someone beat her, that's for sure.'

'What're you saying, Rink? That it could've been another one of these disgruntled family members? They beat Marianne so they would get their way with Bradley. Maybe to force him into their line of thinking?'

'Could have been,' he said, dismissive. It wasn't like him. He closed down his emails, not meeting my eyes. There was something wrong with him, that was for sure.

'You should get some sleep, Rink.'

'No time for sleep,' he said, sounding a little like his old self.

'Nothing we can do for now. We don't even know where Jorgenson and Marianne are, let alone the killer.' Getting up and leading the way out of the office, I hoped that Rink would follow me. He didn't.

'Rink?'

He lowered his face. What is it about men that they don't want to show any weakness? He was my best friend, for Christ's sake. His pain was my pain. I moved back towards him.

'What is it, Rink?'

He coughed. Another male thing. His big fingers, capable of throttling a bullock, trembled over the keyboard. Rink was afraid of something. But I doubted that it had anything to do with hired killers or the dysfunctional state of the Jorgenson family. I'd been there when Rink was going into battle. Like the rest of our Special Forces unit, he'd practised the art of compartmentalisation – as had I – and could shove that fear somewhere where it didn't inhibit his ability to function. Like the rest of us he could use that fear to galvanise him. Make him a more efficient soldier. Rink's reticence now, the trembling in his hands, stopped me in my tracks surer than all the bullets ever fired my way.

'I should go to San Francisco, buddy,' Rink said.

Rink's parents currently lived in San Francisco. The wheels of trepidation began to churn in my gut.

'Tell me, Rink. What's happened?'

'My mother.' His eyes closed slowly and it was all the explanation I required.

'She hasn't . . .'

'Died? No, not yet. But she is very ill.' Rink started shutting down the open windows on the computer. 'She's had a heart attack. I should go to her.'

Immediately I said, 'I'm coming with you.'

Rink shook his head, looked at me with sparkling eyes. 'We have a job to do here, Hunter. There's a girl out there who needs us. There's a chance we can still save her.' There was a long pause, filled only by Rink's harsh breathing. 'It's maybe too late to save my mom.'

CHAPTER 12

Dantalion was on his way to Neptune Island further up the coast. It wasn't really an island, but a long finger of land separated from the mainland by a marshy inlet surrounding the Inter-Coastal Waterway. At the northern end, a causeway gave access to the island, the causeway constructed so that it was a permanent route and not governed by the tides. At the southernmost tip the coastal highway crossed the inlet on a suspended bridge that attracted weekend naturalists and bird watchers who parked on the bridge to view the wildlife on the estuary below.

It wasn't a densely populated region of Florida.

In fact, one family practically owned sole rights to call Neptune its own.

For three generations the Jorgenson estate had claimed much of the land that straddled Neptune's Atlantic shoreline. Since the late 1950s the family had purchased, acquired or built twelve family houses on the land. Each house was distinct in itself, but all were enclosed within a single walled estate that stretched almost three miles down the coast. At intersections every four hundred yards, access was gained by gates that were under twenty-four-hour surveillance. CCTV cameras were mounted on tall poles between each gate, so there was nowhere along the three-mile stretch where an intruder could gain entry without a swift visit from the armed security who patrolled the grounds.

On the coast side, men in boats patrolled night and day, and enforced an exclusion zone of almost a quarter of a mile off shore.

Some would think that the security measures were extreme. But the Jorgensons were implicitly tied to the military, and their secrets were protected almost as though they were a principality that the US military depended upon for its survival.

Dantalion had no worries about getting in. He was too good at his job to doubt himself.

Last night hadn't gone to plan, but he wouldn't let that dent his self-belief. At the end of the day, he'd successfully completed his mission. Killed the targets and then some. It was just a pity he hadn't been able to look into Bradley Jorgenson's face at the end. He always liked to watch the final grains of life sift away like sand in an hour glass.

He would have preferred to see the gunman dead, too. His unwelcome arrival had spoiled his plans for torturing Jorgenson. He'd been looking forward to killing the girl in front of him, then putting a bullet into each of Jorgenson's limbs. Lastly he'd have gut-shot him, made him squirm in his own spilled innards while Dantalion revealed who it was that wanted him dead. It would have been beautiful.

He was driving a truck. Blacked-out windows helped keep the sun off his exposed limbs, but there was another motive. CCTV observation would be kept to the minimum. The truck would be spotted, yes, but not the driver. He could drive by; scout the perimeter without alerting anyone to his identity. Unconcerned, they wouldn't be ready for the visit he'd pay them this evening.

Before arriving at the Jorgenson estate, he pulled into a layover, parking the truck beneath a copse of trees. Afforded shade, he lowered the window and peered across the marshlands that stretched towards the Atlantic. A flight of birds streaked through the pale blue sky, heading south, as if they had a premonition of what was to come.

On the passenger seat next to him, Dantalion laid his book of lists. He was tempted to look at it. Go over the numbers in his head, try to match them to the people he had killed over the twenty-two years he'd been engaged in the murder trade. The first few numbers were easy to recall. First, his abusive uncle. Second, his school friend Tyler. After that things grew a little foggy. The faces tended to meld and swirl in his mind. A week ago he'd murdered Caitlin Moore, her husband *and* child. That one stuck in his mind. He regretted having to kill the little girl, but she'd woken from the mild dose of sodium amatol he'd injected into her. Couldn't leave a witness who could describe his appearance, could he? Shame really; after he'd promised Caitlin that her daughter would be safe.

Then there were those he'd killed on yesterday's mission.

The boat owner was collateral damage, but he was still given a number. Two bodyguards, a maid, Valentin and Bradley Jorgenson and Marianne Dean. Last, but not least, the assassin sent to kill him after the job was done. Dantalion touched his thigh where the gunman's bullet had nicked him. The guy had been good, but not as good as he was.

He would show his client the folly of sending someone second-rate after a master killer.

From his deep pockets he pulled out his BlackBerry. Bringing up the internet, he deftly keyed in numbers that would put him in touch with an associate of his. In coded message Dantalion enquired as to successful completion of payment for his services. Was not happy when informed that the client had reneged on the arrangement. Positive confirmation of death had not been announced.

'What is wrong with these people?' he asked out loud.

After he'd fled the scene of destruction he had to use all his cunning to avoid the police and fire department personnel who had arrived en masse. The fire wouldn't have taken that much damping down – once the propane tanks were secured and isolated in the adjoining properties the task of sifting through the rubble would have began. They'd be pulling out charred corpses by now.

OK, give them a little time. Florida's bravest had a difficult job to do.

Charred corpses often took time to identify.

But it was annoying that the client hadn't the belief in him to accept that he'd done *exactly* what he agreed. Just in a more dramatic fashion.

There was, of course, another reason why the fee had not been delivered to his account.

The client had sent a killer after Dantalion. Why pay money to languish in an account as dead as the man with the codes to access it?

Dantalion would show Petre Jorgenson the error of such thinking.

CHAPTER 13

What surprised me most was that Bradley Jorgenson didn't run directly to the police. He was a man of power and could have demanded that the weight of the entire force be thrown into finding who had been responsible for the attack on his home. Instead, he seemed reluctant to cooperate with the officers on the case, stonewalling and throwing up barriers in the form of highly paid legal advisers to allow him immunity from the ensuing investigation.

It wouldn't last, but for now Jorgenson and Marianne Dean were in hiding and refusing to answer any questions.

In some respects their refusal to talk was a relief. I didn't want to spend half the day answering questions and denying allegations that I was anything other than a concerned citizen who had tried to intervene during a murder spree. Marianne could easily have dropped me in it by talking about our meeting in the garden before the killer's arrival. That would have shown that I had more than chance involvement. Some could even read into my presence at the scene something that wasn't true:

foreknowledge of what was about to happen. In some schools of thought, that would make me an accessory to the crime, and I'd be seeing much more of the inside of police stations. At the very least my movements would be curtailed, and I would be useless to Marianne. There'd be no way I could save her if I was locked up in Dade County Penitentiary awaiting trial.

Not that the police would immediately link me to the Joseph Evans who'd taken out the lease on the adjoining property, but once the federal government became involved – and for a case of this magnitude it would – my fingerprints would throw up an interesting connection to certain military records. With my background, my proximity to the scene, my name would raise more than a few eyebrows. There'd be no talk of coincidence. Christ, I'd be lucky if the entire shit storm wasn't blamed on me.

Rink shut down his office, and we travelled across country in his Porsche Boxster. The Ford Explorer would have been more comfortable for two big guys, but I'd had to abandon it last night at Miami Beach. Could be that by now the vehicle was in some chop shop in SoBe and I'd never see the SUV again.

We cut across country and skirted Bartow, then a series of low-lying lakes and open grasslands with the occasional outcropping of pine, ending up at Fort Pierce where we picked up Route 1 south. On our left was a peninsula that hugged the coastline, separated from the mainland by an open stretch of tidal sands.

Another hour or so would get us to the gated community on Neptune Island.

We were on our way to confront Bradley Jorgenson.

The decision had been made to lay all our cards on the table. Speak to Jorgenson. Brush the punk off if he stood in the way of freedom for Marianne, if in fact that was what she wanted.

I'd begun with the doubts after seeing how she'd clung to him when she thought they were about to die. Her words in response to the killer's demand that Jorgenson chose who died first.

'*Mari,*' Jorgenson had said to her, '*I'm sorry I dragged you into this, babe.*'

'*Not . . . your . . . fault,*' she'd whispered back.

At first I hadn't taken much notice. I was more concerned with what the killer had to say for himself, but thinking back I remembered the softness of her voice. No hint of vehemence or even resignation. She'd meant what she said. They sounded like the words of someone deeply in love. Certainly not someone fearful of the person she spoke to.

Then there was Rink's hint that everything might not be as clear-cut as it seemed, that perhaps Marianne's injuries were down to another person with a reason to hurt her. Witnesses said that Jorgenson had been arguing with someone. A family member perhaps? Shortly afterwards Marianne had been taken to an accident and emergency unit for treatment for her injuries. Two and two were put together. Maybe the witnesses weren't so great at counting.

Then there was the small matter of the hit man.

The killer had arrived at Jorgenson's home on Baker Island at someone's bidding. He was intent on killing not just the heir to the Jorgenson billions, but also Marianne. And when push came to shove Bradley had gone out of his way to protect his girl. I was still pissed off that he had cracked me over the head with the wine bottle, but I couldn't really blame him. I was just another man with a gun placing his woman in danger. If the roles had been reversed, I'd have done the same, and a damn sight more.

Rink was very quiet on the drive over. He had more on his mind than what our impromptu visit to Neptune Island could stir up.

His mother, Yukiko, was possibly dying. He should have been with her for her final days, but he'd chosen to be here with me. If I'd had my way he'd have been on the first plane out to San Francisco. But I knew how Rink's mind worked. Men of duty accept their lot without question.

There's an old samurai adage that when it rains the warrior continues to walk up the centre of the road. His path is set, and he must not deviate from it. The untrained run for cover and get soaked anyway by the water pouring from the eaves of the houses they seek shelter beneath. The warrior knows that he will get wet, so allows

94

fate to take its course. He cannot stop the rain, so he accepts it.

At a service station outside Port St Lucie we stopped to refuel, then ordered takeaway food at a diner on the site. The cheeseburger that I'd wished for last night had never materialised so I ate this one with the gusto of a starving man. The fries went down well, too. While I carried my greasy wrappers over to a trash can, Rink made a telephone call he'd been dreading.

Andrew Rington was of Scottish descent. In his thinking all this samurai shit could take a back seat when it came to family. His clan mentality dictated that there was nothing more important than family ties. I was with him on that one. Rink had inherited his size and build from Andrew's side of the family, but his mindset was definitely that of his mother. Duty would prevail, and his father would come round to it. But he'd likely bawl Rink out before coming to that conclusion.

When I got back to the Porsche, Rink had done speaking. I'd picked the furthest trash can I could find, and hung about watching the gnats buzzing round it for more than five minutes. Who knew what anyone watching me would have thought? Amateur entomologist, I'd have told them.

'How's Yukiko?'

'Hanging in there.' He ghosted a smile, but it was too laden with sadness to be anything but a front.

95

'She's a tough lady. How's your father handling things?'

'He's a tough guy,' Rink said. This time his smile held more spirit. Maybe I was wrong about the balance of genes that made up Jared Rington. For a second there he looked – and sounded – the double of his dad.

Living in Little Rock, Arkansas, Hitomi Yukiko was only five years old when the Japanese Imperial Army declared war on the US by launching an attack on Pearl Harbor. The little girl named 'Snow Child' was interned along with her parents at Rohwer, a Japanese-American *relocation camp*, by the very people who for two generations had been her neighbours. Following the devastation wreaked upon the Japanese mainland by the payload of the Enola Gay, the Hitomi family might have been forgiven for fleeing back to their ancestral land with a curse on their lips for the USA. Except they were US citizens and did not want to leave their home. Yukiko was seventeen when she met her husband-to-be, Andrew Rington, a Scottish-Canadian serviceman returning from the Korean War. Five years later they married. Yukiko bore three children: Yuko, a girl who died shortly after birth, Ronald, a son who would later die while serving in Kuwait, and then, at an age when she might have been content with nursing memories of the girl she'd lost, she birthed Jared. Both Yukiko and Andrew cherished their baby boy.

They still did.

As much as Rink cherished them in return.

I had a feeling that, down the line somewhere, Rink's decision to stay and help me would come back to haunt him.

'Told my father I'd be there as soon as we got finished with this,' Rink said.

I laid a hand on his shoulder.

'OK, Rink, let's get it done, then.'

CHAPTER 14

Neptune Island was more than a home to the Jorgenson clan; it was also an integral portion of the coastal highway that ran all the way up from Jupiter City to Hobe Sound. The mega-wealthy family might have purchased the island, but they couldn't stop the flow of traffic up and down the coast. The route provided an alternative to the I-95, the picture perfect tourist route, so at certain times of the year was packed with holidaymakers travelling along the coastline between Miami and Orlando. On the sandbanks and dunes that made up much of the coastal lands, holidaymakers would often camp out, wandering down on to the beaches and searching for sea turtles in the shallow tropical waters. Overnight camping wasn't permitted on Neptune Island, but there was no law against people stopping for short spells at any of the layovers next to the road.

Slightly further to the south and west tropical palms and trees such as mahogany and gumbo-limbo were prolific, but here on the Atlantic shoreline the predominant trees were the usual oaks, pines and willows. Much of the forests had been cut down to make way for the highways and towns that sprawled up the coast, but out on Neptune some copses had survived. Grass dominated, in the form of waist-high sharp-toothed saw-grass. Sporadically, the occasional limestone outcrop, formed hummocks of higher ground where the indigenous wildlife made its home. Holidaymakers, cameras in hand, would traipse through the grasses in hope of snapping pictures of raccoons, marsh rabbits, and – if they were truly lucky – bobcats.

Dantalion had no interest in wildlife, but in the guise of a bird-watching tourist, he had free rein to conduct surveillance of the Jorgenson compound without fear of discovery. He was only one of approximately a dozen tourists he'd seen armed with high-powered binoculars. He had dressed appropriately for the scene in a cream hat and dark glasses. His shirt was a gaudy Hawaiian number, designed, by the look of things, by a disciple of Jackson Pollock on a serious LSD trip. Pants were long khaki shorts, and on his feet he wore a pair of shabby deck shoes. Hydrocortisone cream was liberally applied to his exposed arms and shins, but was in keeping with others he'd seen with smears of high factor sun cream on their lily-white skin. He blended nicely with those first- or second-day Europeans arriving in the belting sun. Over one shoulder he carried a bag that bounced uncomfortably on his hip with each step. Inside was his 90-two Beretta, a half-dozen spare ammunition magazines and his book of numbers.

The bullet wound he'd taken to his thigh caused him to limp. But that was good, added to the disguise.

He didn't look at all like a killer.

At its southernmost tip, the island was artificially raised up to support the road bridge that then arched on towards the mainland. Under the structure of the bridge, Dantalion walked, his deck shoes disappearing beneath the silt. There was a family out on the tidal sands, turning over rocks, a child hoisting a trophy in the air with a shout of glee. The trophy squirmed in his hand, chitinous legs working furiously, and the little boy dropped it with a squawk of alarm. The family laughed at him as he ran away to avoid the crab's fury.

Dantalion paid them only minimal attention. He wasn't one for human interaction. Human beings were beneath him, good for only two things. Doing his bidding and paying him money. Correction, there was a third thing they could do for him: they could die in agony and fear.

Momentarily he considered pulling out his gun and shooting the entire family. Their laughter grated on his bones, reminding him of all the spiteful laughter he'd had to endure growing up. What saved them was that he wasn't in a counting mood. The formula for writing their individual numbers wasn't the most simple of processes, and one that demanded concentration. Didn't want to spoil his list with incorrect calculations.

Away from the shadows of the bridge, he walked again in direct sunlight. He could feel the prickle on the back of his neck, and his calf muscles felt like someone was holding a blowtorch to them. Sand stung where it adhered to his skin. He pushed into the tall saw-tooth grass. If anything things got worse. The grass snagged him and made tiny itching cuts in his flesh. Enough to send him insane.

But he wasn't insane. He was a professional.

He didn't give in to mild discomforts such as these.

In the past, he'd stoically taken the beatings doled out by the older kids. Smiled at them when they were too exhausted to strike him again. Enduring many hours in hospitals, he hadn't once complained. He accepted the reality of his existence. From birth to death, existence is measured in a series of chapters governed by various levels of pain, some greater than others. Some are easy to recognise. Birth is a screaming, howling experience. Growing, stumbling, taking the knocks in life; all are forms of physical, mental and emotional torture. There is loss and then there is grief. Then you die, and it's a lucky one who doesn't perish in agony. In comparison to some things he'd put up with, pressing on through the grasses was akin to bliss.

He was a professional.

He wasn't insane. Fair enough, his penchant for killing probably was tied to a psychopathic quirk, but he wasn't mad in the sense that other killers were mad. He was not a deviant who killed for the pleasure of collecting trophies, or for sating his need for sexual dominance over a weaker creature. He did not flay the hide from women to make himself a housecoat or lampshade and he did not keep the petrified remains of his mother locked up in an attic then run around in her clothes slicing up nubile young women.

He killed because that was what he was good at.

He killed because it paid him well.

He killed because he had a strict purpose.

The others, those that he personally chose to kill, were merely a by-product of his assumed persona. It didn't take a talented assassin to drive by a victim, poke a gun out of a window and shoot a man dead as he stepped down from his front porch. Any half-assed idiot with a gun could do that. But such actions quickly got them caught, or killed. Dantalion murdered in a fashion that was more thoughtful, planned to create impact. The style of his killings mimicked the actions of a deranged serial killer, not of a hired assassin. It wasn't always apparent who his intended victim was. They were lost among the body count. Law enforcement and FBI VICAP teams were scratching their heads, searching for elusive maniacs that would never be identified with him.

Plus, the randomness of the deaths made his clients fear him. It added to his mystery and ensured that his reputation as a master of his craft guaranteed full and prompt payment. No one wanted to chance upsetting him. They knew where that would get them.

Most of his victims were collateral damage. But they served his purpose well. Success bred success. The more he killed, the more often he was sought out. The higher the fee he could set.

He had no reservations about killing those innocents he chose. They were mere props for the theatre of his schemes. Also, he did share the blame around. Everything shouldn't be ladled on his conscience. He allowed his victims a choice. Who dies first? How do they die? If they pointed the finger at their loved ones, then so be it, it was out of his hands. He was only the tool that completed *their* wishes. It was fucked-up reasoning, he accepted that, but it was a coping mechanism he embraced. It relieved him of the burden of guilt and allowed him to continue doing what he did best.

No, he wasn't insane.

Crazy men don't know they are crazy. And neither do they question their actions.

Psychopaths don't deliberate over death the way he did. They certainly don't share out the glory. They keep it all to their greedy selves.

Crazy men do sometimes take on personas. But so do hired killers. They never use their real names. Not in a craft that demands anonymity and mystery. Jean-Paul St Pierre wouldn't bring the clients running to pay high fees for his services. When in his teens he'd shed his old Mississippi beliefs, he'd turned to esoteric books and lore for the incarnation of the professional killer he would become.

In the Book of Enoch he'd found the perfect match. Dantalion, one of the angels cast out of heaven by Gabriel and the army of God. The panoply of the Fallen were numbered. The seventy-first spirit was Dantalion. He was a great and mighty duke of Hell. According to legend, he appeared in the form of a man with many countenances, all men's and all women's faces. For one as androgynous as he, and with his talent for disguise, what better physical description could there be? The angel Dantalion was said to know the thoughts of all men and women and carried them in a book; he could change them at will. This modern Dantalion also had the knack for bending people's resolve and for jotting down the sum of their lives within his own book. He had the power of life and death over them.

Crossing the grasslands, he paused to bring the binoculars to his eyes, looking like every other bird-fancier in the region. Then he casually swung his view past the turreted gate on the Jorgenson estate wall. Near to the shoreline, this gate wasn't used daily – possibly not even yearly. It was a relic from almost half a century ago, a sally port down to the coast, long before the suspended road had been built nearby. He could imagine the folk from simpler times wandering out of their gardens on to the beach here. Perhaps carrying a picnic basket and a blanket. Maybe Valentin Jorgenson had enjoyed boyhood playtime on this very portion of the beach. Before he was moulded into the successful business man who would continue the legacy started by his own father. Before the cancer that blighted him in his last few months. Before Dantalion put some well-placed rounds through him last night.

A wrought-iron gate barred progress into the grounds. It was in need of a coat of paint, and the corrosive sea winds had turned the gates, and the chain and padlock holding them in place, rusty. A sign was riveted to the wall next to the gate. NO ENTRY WITHOUT PERMISSION – PRIVATE PROPERTY.

Like that was going to deter Dantalion.

A fortunate occurrence presented itself. A rare snail kite soared through the sky and perched on the wall near to the gate. Dantalion, binoculars fixed to his face, walked closer. Studying, studying. Not the bird. He could see that the lock would be easily shattered by a 9 mm round from his Beretta. He could be inside in seconds.

The bird streaked away. Dantalion wandered away, too.

But he'd be back.

CHAPTER 15

'We're here to speak to Bradley Jorgenson.'
'Name?'
'He doesn't know my name.'
'Then he isn't expecting you?'
'No, he wouldn't be.'
'Then you'll have to make an appointment through his office. You have the contact details?'
'No, I don't.'
'Then, I'm afraid you won't be able to see him. We are currently experiencing unwanted attention from the media and I have express orders to send everyone though Mr Jorgenson's press office. Good day, sir. Please move your vehicle so it isn't blocking the access drive.'

The intercom was switched off, the active green light dying. I leaned away from it back into the Porsche and looked across at Rink. His eyebrows jerked but that was the sum of his contribution.

I pressed the buzzer again.

'Sir, I already told you . . .'

I didn't listen to the guard's words. I swung open the car door and went up to the gate. Peering up at the CCTV camera above it, my hands clenched by my sides, I shouted, 'Speak to Jorgenson. Tell the ungrateful son of a bitch that Joe Hunter is here. He'd have died last night if it wasn't for me.'

Turning back to the buzzer on the intercom, I pressed my finger to it. Kept the button depressed. Somewhere on the property the buzzer would be shrieking in protest, probably sending the guard insane.

The tableau held for the best part of two minutes.

Then from within the compound I heard the grumble of approaching engines. Letting go of the buzzer, I said into the speaker, 'Now that wasn't so difficult, was it?'

The guard didn't respond. Maybe he was in one of the two dark silver sedans approaching the gate.

The sedans drew to a halt on the road beyond the gate. Four big guys with guns under their jackets got out. They eyed me coolly, the way a pack of jackals would challenge a lion. Together they could likely bring me down, but not one at a time. Rink got out the car and stood beside me. The odds now tipped the scale firmly in my favour. Rink's presence often had that effect.

One of the guards, a self-appointed delegate, stepped forwards. He was a man edging fifty years old, but he still retained a hard body and steady eyes. His brush cut indicated he was ex-army as did his straight back and staccato movements.

'What is your business here?' he demanded.

'None of yours,' I told him.

I wasn't interested in any of Jorgenson's hired guns. Looking past the man to the second sedan, I called. 'You can see me, Bradley. Same guy from last night. You would have died if I wasn't there. The way I see it, you at least owe me a couple minutes of your time.'

I waited and the man with the brush cut continued giving me dead eyes. After what seemed to be an hour, but was only half a minute, the driver's window slid open. The driver didn't say anything. To Brush Cut he just inclined his head in silent communication. Then the second vehicle began reversing up the drive. There was a turning circle twenty paces back and the sedan swung around and back up the road.

'You'll have to step back from the gate,' Brush Cut said.

About to argue, I felt Rink's fingers brush my wrist. One of the other guards had gone over to a box on a pole. He pressed a button and the huge gates began swinging towards us. We were forced to take a couple of steps back to avoid being swatted aside.

'Come with us,' Brush Cut commanded.

'We'll bring our own car.' Rink's tone said he'd brook no argument.

Brush Cut looked at Rink. Then at me. He sniffed once, then turned away, indicating that the others should get back in the car. Only the man at the gate controls waited.

Back in the Porsche, Rink drove through the gate and past the sedan. He pulled into the turning circle, waited until the gate guard was back in the sedan and it had gone past us. Then we followed.

'Well, that was easier than we thought,' I said to Rink.

'Could be taking us somewhere less public to shoot us,' Rink said.

We followed the sedan along the road, came to a collection of houses, almost a village community in itself. I thought they must be on-site accommodation for the large number of staff that had to be employed on the estate. At its highest point, Neptune Island was only a few yards above sea level. The ground swelled at its centre then quickly dipped down towards the shoreline. The houses built just above the shoreline were large and impressive, more like the stately homes from back in the UK than any I expected to find on the Florida coast. They were set at intervals of perhaps a quarter-mile apart, like the forts the Roman Empire once built to guard their frontiers.

The sedan angled towards the largest house of all. It would only be about fifty years old, but the architects must have drawn inspiration from Victorian times. A bird's-eye view would have seen an immense sprawl of red slate roof, shaped like a capital 'H'. My angle showed me a three-storey wing at either side, attached by a cross section that had windows extending from the roof-line to a yard or so above the ground. The windows were like those seen in cathedrals, but without the coloured glass. Kind of excessive, however much money you had to waste.

The silver sedan I assumed had held Bradley Jorgenson was already there, now empty. The driver was sitting on the hood of his vehicle. His arms were crossed, one hand nonchalantly dipping into the folds of his jacket. A second man stood on the far side, and he was a lot more obvious about the way he held an Uzi sub-machine gun braced across his stomach. The second sedan pulled up next to it, leaving room for Rink's Porsche between the two of them.

Brush Cut and his three companions climbed out of their vehicle, circling the Porsche like sharks. They were all holding sidearms.

Climbing out ourselves, we were clear on our intentions. Our guns remained out of sight and we showed our empty palms. Brush Cut pointed a Glock 17 at my chest.

'You can drop the posturing,' I said to Brush Cut. 'We're not here to cause trouble. We're here to help Jorgenson.'

'We don't need any help.' Brush Cut waved us towards the house with a jerk of his gun. 'We can handle things.'

Beside me, Rink grumbled to himself. He wasn't the only one bemoaning how amateur these guys were. What kind of bodyguards allow armed men to bring a vehicle directly up to the house where their principal is in residence? We could have a bomb under the hood for all they knew. Despite their guns, I was pretty sure Rink and I could draw and fire and all six of them would be dead or incapacitated in seconds. Any other time, I imagined Rink would have laughed in Brush Cut's face. But Rink wasn't in the best of moods. Neither was I.

'Where's Jorgenson?'

'Inside.'

He made it sound like an order, but that's where we wanted to be at any rate. We walked quickly towards a large wooden door, causing the others to stumble into a ragged skirmish line behind us. They were like children falling in behind the toughest kids in school.

The door swung open before we reached it and we were greeted by another couple of rent-a-punks. These two were your typical intimidators, men mountains with shaven-heads, broken noses and tattoos on their depressed knuckles. I brushed by them, not intimidated in the least. It's not guys with smashed-up faces that you have to fear, it's the unmarked ones; the ones who win all the fights. Sounds a little arrogant, but neither Rink nor I has the face of a second-rate pug.

Jorgenson was waiting for us in a huge room shelved floor-to-ceiling with a library of books to rival a university for knowledge. A cursory glance showed me that most of the titles were in northern European languages. Jorgenson was sitting behind a huge mahogany desk, elbows splayed, his chin resting in his hands. He watched our entry with a look of bored resignation.

'You made it out the house, then? I thought I saw you looking over the wall afterwards.'

'Yeah, I made it out. With no thanks to you,' I said. 'Didn't help being crowned with a bottle just before the place went up.'

He sat up a little straighter. His palms fell open. 'I couldn't be sure whose side you were really on.'

'I wasn't the one shooting at you.'

'You were about to burn down the house.'

'I think that's a little academic now,' I pointed out.

A shadow crossed his face. 'They still haven't found my father.'

Brush Cut and one other had followed us into the room. The rest all stood in various poses of menace in the hallway.

'Relax, Jorgenson, will you? If I was going to kill you I'd have done it by now.' I held his gaze and he finally gave a nod in return. He waved the pack away, but indicated that Brush Cut and the other man should stay handy. I said, 'Better if we spoke in private.'

'You haven't killed me yet,' Jorgenson replied. 'Doesn't mean you won't.'

Rink laughed sardonically, 'You think these frog-giggin' assholes would stop us?'

'Hey!' Brush Cut said. He stepped up close, realised just how big Rink was and faltered. Rink turned his head to regard the man as though he was something he'd tracked in on his boots.

112

'Try it, buddy,' Rink said. 'Go on. I'm in the right mood for slapping someone down.'

Jorgenson smiled at the testosterone-charged atmosphere. 'Mr Seagram is a highly regarded executive protector. He came from the Marine Corps with top recommendations.'

'Hurrah,' Rink grunted. 'What did you do in the service, Seagram? Cook?'

'West Point,' Seagram stated.

Rink sniffed, unimpressed. 'Yeah, they have cooks there. Decent cooks, I'll give you that.'

Seagram looked like he'd been slapped. But I could tell his mind was caught in flux. Rink had insulted him and paid a compliment in the same breath. Rink grinned, showing he was just ragging him. It was one of those forces things where all soldiers put down anyone who wasn't in their own troop. Seagram moved away, at a loss as to how to respond.

'Are we all finished now?' Jorgenson asked.

'We haven't started yet,' I told him.

'That's true. I don't even know who you are.'

'Where's Marianne?'

'Why do you want to know?'

'Because we're here more for her than for you.'

'Can I ask why?'

'You can ask.'

He shook his head. 'And you are?'

'I'm Joe Hunter.'

'What about him?' Jorgenson looked at Rink.

'*He* can speak for himself,' Rink said. 'My friends

113

call me Rink. But you can call me Jared Rington.'
He turned and shot a wink at Seagram.
'Mr Rington to you.'

Seagram hissed something under his breath. He
turned his back on us and went to lean against the
bookshelves. The other man, who'd remained silent
throughout, blinked rapidly, looking from Seagram
to Jorgenson. He was a whip-thin man with spiky,
sandy-coloured hair and freckled face. He wasn't
long out of high school, judging by his fresh face.
Looked like he wished he was back there.

'What's your interest in me?' Jorgenson asked.

'Zero. It's Marianne we've come about.'

Jorgenson's lips twitched down. 'Marianne doesn't
know you either. She told me about speaking to you
in the garden. But she says that she'd never seen
you before that. Is that true?'

'Do you doubt her?'

'No.' Jorgenson stared into my eyes. 'I love her.'

'Tough love,' Rink muttered.

Jorgenson snapped his gaze on Rink. Colour
flushed up from his throat, making his cheeks a
dapple of red blotches.

'What does *that* mean?' he demanded.

I leaned one fist on his desk. Time to interject,
I thought. Rink wasn't in the best frame of mind
to lead the negotiations. 'Forget it,' I told him.
'What I'm concerned with is what happened last
night. The man at your house was there to kill the
two of you. We're committed to protecting
Marianne. Now, you say you love her. If that's the

114

case, you will want Marianne to be protected. Seems to me that we're on the same agenda.'

'We don't need you,' Seagram said from the far side of the room.

'You don't?'

Jorgenson said, 'I trust my staff to protect us.'

'You shouldn't. They opened the gate to men who they know nothing about, allowed us to carry guns inside. We parked a car outside that could be packed with Semtex for all they knew.'

Jorgenson nodded along with my reasoning. But then his finger came up and wagged in my direction. 'But that was after I'd viewed you on the security system. I recognised you. Like you said earlier, if you were going to kill me, you'd have done so by now.'

'Fair enough.'

'I take it you have some kind of offer in mind?'

'Not interested in working for you, if that's what you're thinking.'

Jorgenson shrugged. He acknowledged Seagram. 'I'm happy with who I have already.'

'But I do want to speak to Marianne. If she wants us, then we will work for her.'

'And if I don't allow that?'

'Then we're going to have a problem.'

CHAPTER 16

Back in his truck, Dantalion headed north. Following the boundary wall of the estate, he scouted out other entry points should his first plan fail. The wall was twelve feet tall in most places. Nothing as obvious as razor wire had been installed, but he had the feeling that pressure pads would be laid along the top and numerous more sown inside the perimeter. They could prove a problem, but not insurmountable to someone with his skills. The CCTV cameras weren't too much of a concern either. A well-aimed shot would put a camera out of commission. A system with so many cameras would be prone to occasional malfunction; by the time a maintenance crew had come out to investigate, he'd have been in and out again, his business done.

He had more to worry about than cameras and pressure pads. He could hear distant barking. The estate was guarded by patrol dogs. It would take a master magician to spirit himself in and out of an enemy stronghold where trained attack dogs were running loose. Sometimes he wished his assumed identity came with all the trappings of the original

Dantalion. Dark angels have nothing to fear from dogs. Being a mere mortal still, he'd have to come up with a contingency.

He took out his BlackBerry, checked for messages. Nothing new. Just the same old message from his associate about the non-arrival of his fee. One hand on the wheel, he thumbed in a request, then sent the email spinning through cyberspace.

Eyes off the road for a split second, he almost missed the occupants of the car passing him on the other side of the road. However, something subliminal grabbed at his mind, made him glance at the Porsche Boxster in a moment's admiration for the vehicle. The small, sleek beauty was the black of glistening tar. The driver was of no concern; he was a muscular brute with straight black hair and tawny skin. There was a livid scar across his chin that was as white as Dantalion's entire body. No, it was the passenger who caught his attention.

He wasn't as big as the driver, rangy of build rather than muscular, with the broad shoulders of a swimmer or gymnast. His short brown hair had only the faintest hint of grey at the temples. It was the kind of face that could blend in with a crowd, but the intensity of his eyes would set him apart. Women would love those eyes, men would fear them.

Dantalion cursed under his breath.

The gunman from last night.

'How the fuck did you survive *that* explosion?'

But then the Porsche was by him and he was left wondering if perhaps he'd been wrong. He hadn't

117

got a good look; maybe the man in the passenger seat merely bore a passing resemblance to the man who'd almost killed him.

His hand crept to his thigh. The bullet wound was a constant ache radiating through the entire muscle, up his hip to his spine. He'd cleaned and dressed the wound, but it obviously hadn't been enough. It was a worry, but nothing that would stop him. Conversely, he'd been fortunate: If he'd been standing another few inches to the right, the gunman's bullets would have found a more fatal target than his leg.

Whoever that man had been, he couldn't possibly have escaped the exploding building. Dantalion had heard him retreat into the bedroom just as he had brought flame to the lighter. There had been only seconds before detonation.

No. The would-be assassin was as dead as everyone else in the house. He was already numbered in Dantalion's book. Just below Bradley Jorgenson and Marianne Dean. The numbers never lied.

Still, he looked for a place to turn, and then spun the vehicle around and pushed the truck after the Porsche. The man had the eyes of a killer. Even if he happened to be an unfortunate doppel-gänger, Dantalion had to find out. Perhaps he'd even have to kill the man.

Almost a mile later, Dantalion drove by the main entrance to the Jorgenson estate. He was intent on catching up with the Porsche and almost missed the vehicle parked outside the entrance gate. The two from the Porsche were talking to some of Jorgenson's security men who were standing on the far side. He only got a fleeting glance and couldn't be sure if it was the same man from yesterday. He had his back to Dantalion and his clothing was different. One thing he did notice though; Dantalion recognised one of the security men. The one with the brush cut. He'd been one of the men with Petre Jorgenson yesterday. One of those who'd feigned interest in the statue of Christopher Columbus at Bayside Park in Miami.

Doing the math in his head, there was only one answer. Brush Cut had been with Petre. His client had asked him to kill Bradley and Marianne Dean. A mystery man had turned up, almost killing Dantalion. A mystery man who bore more than a passing resemblance to the hired killer who was now talking to Brush Cut. Ergo, Dantalion had definitely been set up to die by Petre.

He turned the truck round.

Sped back northward.

He pressed the button to lower the window. Pulled free his Beretta, hanging it out of the window.

It didn't take a talented assassin to drive by a victim, poke a gun out of a window and shoot a man dead as he stepped down from his front porch. Any half-assed idiot with a gun could do that. Dantalion murdered in a fashion that was more thoughtful than that, planned to create impact. But every now and again a good old drive-by shooting was just what was required.

He slowed down and held the gun steady against the window ledge.

But he was too late.

The Porsche was already inside the compound, following a silver sedan. Other men were climbing into a second silver sedan. One of them was Brush Cut. A single guard was standing next to a control box, and the gate was swinging shut. Dantalion pulled the Beretta back inside, just as the guard glanced his way. Dantalion gave the man a nod, a tourist enjoying the drive. The guard didn't even notice.

Opportunities like that one didn't present themselves too often. He'd missed it. But this evening he'd make his own opportunities and this time he would not miss.

CHAPTER 17

'Who are you?'

The same question kept being asked of me. I suppose this time I owed more explanation than simply giving my name and that I was there to help. Marianne deserved as much.

'My name is Joe Hunter.'

'So you weren't lying.' I didn't quite catch her meaning, and she went on. 'Yesterday when you introduced yourself, you told me you were called Joe.'

'I wasn't lying about the rest, either.'

'That you were there to help?'

We were in a room adjacent to the library. Rink was keeping Bradley, Seagram and the third man company. I only hoped his surliness didn't provoke a confrontation before I could reassure Marianne of our good intentions.

She'd changed since I saw her last.

She had on black trousers and pumps, a pale cream blouse. But that's not what I meant.

She looked different.

Her light brown hair was loose, full of body as though recently washed. Her skin was pink and she wafted a scent that was more delicate fragrance of soap than expensive perfume. I guessed her shower had been long and very hot. Her flight from the house on Baker Island would have meant her clothes were tinged with the reek of smoke and dust and debris. But that wasn't what she was trying to scrub away. You could wash all you wanted, but you also had to expunge the memories from your mind. It sometimes took that to remove the stench after witnessing violent death.

She was perched on the edge of a desk, her feet swinging in space. Her arms were crossed beneath her breasts. Her body language was in conflict. The swinging feet were those of a young innocent girl, but the folded arms said she was now much wiser than her years, and understood the need to protect herself. She'd experienced something that most adults never have to go through, never mind a child. She had survived where she should have died, and she was suddenly feeling her mortality weighing on her as heavy as the collapsed house she'd so narrowly escaped.

'How did you know that . . . that monster was coming?'

'I didn't,' I said. 'I was there for another reason.'

She stared down at her feet. They were still now.

'My father?'

'Yes. Your father asked me to bring you home.'

'I don't want to go home.'

'I understand. You're an adult now. You want to live your own life.'

She shook her head slowly. 'That's not what I meant. I don't want to leave. My life is here now. With Bradley.'

'You don't have to be afraid of him. If you want, I'll take you away from here now.'

Marianne gave a small laugh. It wasn't humour, though. Not relief. 'Afraid of him. Yes, you could say that.'

'I won't let him hurt you again,' I promised.

'If you take me home, there will be no way to stop him. You couldn't be there all the time. He'd get to me sooner or later.'

'What has he done to you, Marianne? To make you so afraid? I saw the police photographs of your assault. Why didn't you go through with an official complaint then? This would all be over now. You'd be free of him.'

Marianne gave me a look that assured me that she had grown way beyond her years even before the terror at Baker Island.

'Love,' she said. 'It doesn't matter that he hurts me, *I love him*. How could I have him arrested and charged? It would destroy him. I couldn't live with that.'

'Men who hurt women don't deserve your love.'

'No, maybe they don't. But I can't help my feelings. I can't turn my back on him.'

There was a knock at the door. Jorgenson entered without waiting for a reply. When he saw my face he faltered. It took all my will not to grab him by the throat and throw him through the nearest wall. As it was I clenched a fist, considering that a gut punch wouldn't be out of order. Marianne saved him from punishment.

She hopped down off her perch and went to him. She hugged him, tilted up her face and he kissed her sweetly on the tip of her nose.

'You OK, babe?' he asked, giving me a hooded glance over the top of her head.

'I'm fine, honey.'

I had to turn away.

Love's blind, they say. Must also be an anaesthetic.

Rink came in the door, followed by Seagram.

'What's going on, Rink?'

'Been explaining to Bradley what we think is going on. About who could have sent the hit man after him. Bradley has agreed that we could be helpful in stopping him.'

'We're here for Marianne,' I reminded him.

'Marianne's with me,' Jorgenson said.

I nodded once, a curt lifting of my chin. He could see the anger in my face and wasn't so sure that it would be a good idea to piss me off.

He went on, more conciliatory, 'But Mari's safety is everything to me.' He said to her, 'If it's OK with you, babe, I'll let them stay.'

Marianne looked at me. Her confidant. 'I trust them.'

'Then we'll stay.' I looked across at Rink. Concern for his ailing mother must have been gnawing at him, but he agreed with a lift of his shoulders. Then I studied the room, the huge windows. 'This place isn't safe. We should move somewhere less vulnerable.'

Jorgenson followed my gaze. The view was phenomenal. Open sky and open sea. 'What's to fear?'

'Boat out on the water. Any half-decent sniper could shoot you from half a mile out,' I explained. 'But that isn't what I was meaning.'

'So what do you mean?'

Flicking a glance over Seagram, I said, 'Not now. We'll speak again later. First I want to get Marianne somewhere a little safer.'

'My room would be OK, wouldn't it?' Marianne volunteered. 'I've things I can be getting on with.'

'How many men have you got in the house?' I asked the question directly of Seagram.

He didn't have to think long. 'Eight including myself. Then there are five staff members.'

'Unlucky thirteen,' Rink offered.

'Round them all up, Seagram. Tell them that no one goes near Marianne until this is over.'

'Wait a second,' Seagram said. 'Who put you in charge? I'm head of security here. I decide what happens.'

'No,' Jorgenson put in. 'I decide what happens. Hunter is right. The man who tried to kill us last night was in disguise. He could be anyone. Who knows? He could already be in the house.'

'I know all of my men personally,' Seagram said in outrage. 'I can vouch for each and every one of them.'

'You care for your men,' I said. 'That's good. If you want to save their lives, you keep them the fuck away from Marianne's room. That goes for you as well.'

There wasn't anything subtle in the threat. It was a full-on challenge. I expected him to back down, and he did. He turned and walked away quickly. Back in the hall, I could hear him shouting angrily at his men. I paid him no further concern. Seagram was an asshole, and things would be much better if he kept out of the way.

'He can see to your personal safety, Jorgenson. I have no objections to that. But where Marianne is concerned, it's down to us. If you happen to be with her, then, so be it. We'll protect you too.'

'I'm seeing my legal advisers in an hour,' Jorgenson said. 'They've arranged a meeting with the police. I have to explain what happened at Baker Island.'

Complication.

'It's up to you, but I'd deny that I was there. You were here on Neptune last night, and Marianne was with you.'

'You expect me to lie?'

'For the time being.' Marianne was looking at me with her mouth partly open, wondering if she'd made the wrong decision in trusting me. I said to her, 'If the police believe that you were here, their investigation will be hampered, sure. But they aren't going to stop this killer. They aren't going to stop the person who hired him. All that will happen is that more strangers are allowed into

126

your home. The killer could infiltrate the building and get at you. Also, it will be impossible to keep you out of harm's way if you have to go into Miami to be interviewed.'

Jorgenson jammed his hands into his trouser pockets. 'My father died. Shot dead in cold blood. How do you expect me to lie about that? I was there and saw the man who did it. So did Marianne. You did. We're all witnesses.'

Jorgenson stared at me, almost a mirror image of Marianne in his open-mouthed incredulity.

'You're right. But our eyewitness testimony isn't worth shit. The killer was in disguise. He will look nothing like the man we describe.'

'How do you know it was a disguise?'

'Something I saw but didn't realise at the time. There was a pale smear on his chin. At first I thought that it was dust, but I've been thinking about it since. I now think that he had darkened his skin. The pale patch was his natural colour. His hair isn't black either.' I remembered the person in the dark blue suit stumbling away from the wreckage of the house. At the time I thought it was an innocent caught up in the blast. I'd held back from shooting him for that very reason. 'The killer had black hair, but it had to have been a wig. Really he has longish blond hair.'

'So tell the police that.'

'Won't help.'

'The police will give us all the protection we need.'

'No, they'll only give the killer more opportunities to get at you. It's better that we do it my way. This man doesn't know that I survived the blast. He doesn't know about Rink. He isn't expecting us. We'll be able to get him.'

'What if you don't?' Marianne asked. '*What if he gets you first?*'

'That's when you go to the police and tell them everything.'

CHAPTER 18

Hobe Sound in Martin County, Florida, has a strange history. In the early quarter of the last century, the movie industry was big news in Florida. The goal of the Olympia Improvement Association was to develop Hobe Sound to build a permanent movie production centre and town in the style of Ancient Greece. For a short time, Hobe Sound was renamed Picture City. A hurricane in 1928 put paid to the plans, devastating the area and putting an end to the land boom, and the hopes of OIA came to nothing. Their legacy remained only in the names of the streets: Zeus, Saturn, Mercury, Apollo, Athena.

Strange names were nothing new to a man who went by the name of a fallen angel, but even he would have drawn the line at the Downtown Demeter Plaza. He was sitting on a terrace outside a coffee shop called Pots and Pans – complete with a welcome sign depicting a life-sized satyr blowing on a reed pipe, and the day's specials chalked across his midriff. Pan pipe music played from tinny speakers above the door, but it sounded more Peruvian than ancient Greek.

He put up with the place out of necessity. His associate had arranged the equipment for his assault on Neptune Island, and would deliver it here within the hour. In the meantime, he sat gritting his teeth, drinking coffee as strong as sump oil, and moving with the shadows under the parasol over his table.

It was late afternoon but it was still edging ninety degrees Fahrenheit, and under his voluminous coat sweat was trickling down the small of his back and pooling on the vinyl chair he was sitting on. He was uncomfortable and the wound in his thigh was screaming in protest. He wasn't very happy.

Banyan trees with their weirdly twisted trunks and branches blocked the traffic noise from nearby Athena Street. Against the harsh afternoon sunlight they looked like the silhouettes of deformed giants. The chatter of tourists and locals was muted, as if the heat leached all energy, making speech above a whisper too difficult.

He watched the people in the mall, conscious of the glances he received in turn. Here, under his parasol, he stood out like a candle flame in a dark pit. He didn't like being so visible, but at the end of the day he wasn't going to kill anyone here. So long as they turned off that damn piped music!

A fat man approached him. He had on wide flannel trousers and a black shirt with embroidered flames writhing up the sleeves. Sweat stood on his forehead like mountain dew. He carried a backpack. Dantalion acknowledged his associate. The fat man thought he controlled Dantalion, but Dantalion knew otherwise. He was simply the mule who carried Dantalion's supplies.

The man sat down, the chair legs squealing under his weight. He dropped the backpack at his feet, pushing it further under the table with a couple of none-too-subtle kicks. Dantalion hooked a strap with an ankle and pulled the bag the rest of the way. If felt heavy.

'You want coffee, Gabe?'

Gabe Wellborn swiped at his forehead with the palm of his hand, scattering droplets on the table-cloth. Dantalion scowled at the damp patches, then up at the man's sweaty face.

'Or would you prefer something a little colder?'

'Appreciate it, Dan.'

Dantalion beckoned to a waiter. The man came over as though he had all the time in the world and wasn't about to waste any of it.

'Coffee for me and whatever my friend is having.'

'Soda,' Gabe said. 'Ice. Lots of it.'

The waiter didn't bother scribbling the order into his book. Bad form, Dantalion thought. Then he wandered inside to fetch their drinks. He'd be back in about fifteen minutes, judging by his lack of urgency.

'You have what I asked for?'

Gabe nodded. 'In the bag. EMF meter. Gen-Three night-vision goggles. Sound suppressor and ammo for a ninety-two Beretta. Ketamine, plus delivery system, just as you asked.'

'Thank you.'

'Be careful, Dan. You're familiar with the suppressor and ammo; I don't have to tell you they're illegal. I wanted to bring the drugs to your attention. Ketamine's become the party drug of choice. If you're found with it, the police will have you down to the precinct quicker than you can think.'

'The police have never taken me before, Gabe, why the concern now? Any way, ketamine's an animal anaesthetic, isn't it?'

'Originally, yeah, but that doesn't stop crackheads shooting up with it. It's used these days as a human antidepressant, strictly prescription only. Has some serious hallucinogenic side effects if the wrong dosage is administered.'

'Don't worry, Gabe, I won't be using it on humans.'

'Mind if I ask you what you do want it for?'

'If I told you I'd have to kill you,' Dantalion quipped. From the shocked look on his face, Gabe didn't get the joke.

'That's your business, Dan. I just thought I could give you a nod on the correct dosages you'd need.'

'Enough will be enough.'

'Planning on a ghost hunt?' Gabe asked. 'Electromagnetic field meter. Night-vision goggles. They're standard equipment for paranormal researchers these days.'

'There might be a few ghosts around after I'm done,' Dantalion told him. 'Yours for one if you don't stop asking stupid questions.'

Gabe stopped the questions. He knew when to keep his mouth shut when he was around *Dan-fucking-talion*.

The waiter returned. He placed the drinks down on the table, slapped down the check. Dantalion scattered a few dollar bills in his direction. The man clucked his tongue. Reached for the notes. Dantalion resisted breaking his arm. That would make the lazy fucker a bit faster on his feet. When the waiter had retreated to a place where he could study his fingernails, Dantalion leaned towards Gabe.

'What's the latest news on Baker Island?'

'Rescue crews are still sifting through the wreckage. They haven't released official numbers – or names – of those they've found dead yet. There's a lot of media speculation, they're throwing names around like rice at a wedding. It's all guesswork 'cause they've nothing firm to go on. Bradley Jorgenson's refusing to speak to the police. I'm sure he'll be subpoenaed before long and then he'll have to come clean.'

Dantalion was engaged in lifting his coffee cup to his lips. Some of the coffee slopped down his coat, leaving a stain like a month-old knife wound. 'Wait a minute . . . *Bradley Jorgenson*'s refusing to speak?'

'Yeah, he's got some top-dollar attorneys holding off the cops with a verbal smokescreen. Of course that'll only go on so long; doesn't matter how much money he has, the police are conducting a homicide investigation and—'

Dantalion slammed down his cup.

'I killed Bradley Jorgenson,' Dantalion hissed. 'Have you forgotten, Gabe?'

Gabe blinked rapidly. He slumped backwards in his seat, gaining distance from the anticipated lunge he could see building in Dantalion. It never came. He hoped that Dantalion – despite his jokes – valued his associate's help too highly to give in to base anger. Emboldened by that assumption, Gabe said, 'Not according to CNN. They say that he's currently at his home on Neptune Island.'

'And the girl? Marianne Dean?'

'Yeah, she's with him.'

'Son of a bitch!'

Dantalion stood up swiftly. He ignored the pull in his wounded leg. Anger overrode the agony.

'I guess that's why the client was remiss in making payment?'

'I guess so,' Gabe said. 'Sorry, Dan. I thought you knew.'

'No, Gabe, I didn't know.' He reached into his pocket, toying with the spine of his book. Withdrew his fingers and wiped them on his coat. The book had lied to him. The numbers were all wrong. 'But it looks like I'm going to have to do something about that.'

So, Jorgenson and Marianne had both survived the explosion. As had the damn gunman who'd been sent to kill him. Now they were all making pow-wow at Neptune Island. Suddenly he wasn't

134

so clear on how many enemies he was going to have to kill.

'You have access to a thermonuclear device, Gabe?'

Gabe sniggered. 'You're joking, right?'

'Do I look like someone with a sense of humour? There are a lot of people on Neptune Island about to die. Maybe every last one of them.'

Gabe gulped his soda in one continuous slurp. Smacking his lips, he said, 'Can't get you a nuclear missile, but call me if you need anything else, Dan.'

Dantalion stooped low, hooking the backpack with one hand.

'I've everything I need right here.'

He walked quickly away, leaving Gabe to sweat a lot more.

CHAPTER 19

Jorgenson's people conducted a background check on us. Rink came back fine. He had a private investigator's licence and his business was registered at the address in Tampa. On the other hand, my own legend was a tad more difficult to come up with. I told them they'd just have to take my word for it. No one argued.

Jorgenson left with an entourage of vehicles, heading down to Miami Beach to meet with his legal advisers, and then with officers from Miami PD's homicide department. His father's body had been pulled from the wreckage, but unlike those on the ground floor, his corpse wasn't so burned or torn to shreds by the blast: it was obvious he'd been shot.

Marianne stayed with us. Just the way I wanted it.

Whatever it was that she had to get on with, she was doing it in her bedroom. I'd conducted a cursory sweep of the room, checking that an intruder couldn't gain access, and had told her to keep the blinds closed so she didn't offer a target to anyone outside.

'We should move her,' Rink told me. He'd said the same thing about a dozen times previously.

'I agree.' I'd also said the same thing numerous times.

'So what are we waiting for?'

'Marianne doesn't want to move.'

'So we convince her.'

'She won't budge. Despite everything, she loves Bradley.'

We were sitting in the hall on the second-floor landing. Marianne's room was about three doors up. We could see the entrance to her room, but we'd placed ourselves so we could guard the main stairs and also see the door that led to a secondary stairwell further along the hall. Seagram's men were keeping well out of our way.

'While Bradley's outa the way, why not snatch Marianne, and have done with it?' Rink demanded. 'She'll get over it. When she comes to her senses and sees what an asshole he is.'

'Two things, Rink. We've made ourselves public coming here. Bradley would scream kidnap. We'd be hunted down by law enforcement, despite our good intentions. Plus, I'm beginning to think that Richard Dean hasn't told us everything. Neither has Marianne.'

'It's not safe here,' Rink said.

There were armed guards in the grounds, armed guards in the house, more CCTV cameras than the Big Brother house. But he was correct.

'I'll speak to her again,' I offered. 'But we have

to respect her wishes, Rink. I know we're looking at her like she's a child, but she is eighteen years old. She has her own mind, and a right to make her own decisions.'

Rink rolled his shoulders. 'She isn't thinking with her head, though. She's smitten with Bradley. She's got herself into a position where she's afraid to walk away. She'll take the violence from him, twist it round, blame herself. Try harder to be the good little wife. You know how these things work.'

I did. I'd seen it too many times. Women too afraid to walk away for fear of losing everything they'd worked so hard to achieve. Not realising that whatever they did, they'd never be *good enough*. They'd be caught up in the circle of domestic violence that spun on through their lives until one day he wouldn't stop hitting her. Sometimes that was when the woman finally broke. She'd pick up a knife and jam it between her abuser's shoulder blades. Or the man would hit her too hard and that would be that. More women were killed by their intimate partners – or other family members – than by all the strangers or serial murderers in the world.

'I'll speak to her again,' I repeated.

Rink stood up. Walked along the hall. He checked the door to the secondary stairwell. Still locked. He walked back to the head of the main stairs. Peered down them. Turned and came back. It made sense to stay vigilant, but Rink was conducting a patrol just to be doing something.

It wasn't like him. Rink could sit in the same position for hours on end without giving any signs that he was anything but an inanimate feature of the landscape. On seek and destroy missions we'd often be dropped miles from our targets. We'd make our way in, find an observation point, then sit tight while gauging enemy strengths and weaknesses. Once we were conducting surveillance on a terrorist training camp in the deserts of Libya. Rink took point and dug himself in less than twenty yards from the enemy base. He was there undetected for seventy-three hours before we launched our assault and wiped the bastards out.

His unease had nothing to do with our current mission.

'You shouldn't be here, Rink.'

He looked down at me. 'None of us should.'

'You know what I mean, buddy. You should be in San Francisco with your family.'

He nodded slowly, his gaze staring off to somewhere very distant. 'You're family, too.'

'OK.'

I didn't say another word on the subject. The decision was Rink's.

'Maybe we should draw on a few contacts, see if we can find out who this hit man is. We know him, we know his MO. We'll have a better idea of how to stop him.'

'I'll get Harvey on to it.'

Harvey Lucas was our friend out in the Midwest. He was an ex-Army Ranger who now ran his own private investigations outfit in Arkansas. He'd been an invaluable ally during a case we'd been involved with last year. He'd backed us up when the bullets were flying, and he'd got the job done. He was also damn good when it came to gathering the kind of information not generally in the public arena.

'I'll leave you to it. I'll go and speak to Marianne again.'

Rink brought out his mobile phone and hit a hot key.

I knocked on Marianne's door.

She answered it immediately. Almost as if she'd had her ear to the door. Her hair was pinned up again, and she'd changed her clothes. Tight blue jeans and a pale yellow sweater that bared her shoulders and the upper swell of her breasts. Her neck made a long sweeping curve towards the cream skin of her chest. I couldn't help a quick glance.

Marianne caught my look and she stirred uncomfortably.

'Come in.' Her arms folded, and I couldn't help but notice they went above her breasts this time.

'Mind if I ask you something?' I said as I followed her into the room. It was a well-appointed room, but I was more conscious of the delicate perfume that hovered in the space. The scent of her shampooed hair and freshly scrubbed skin. She'd been showering again. I felt a little awkward. A little like a father who is used to walking into his young daughter's room unannounced, until that day when suddenly he realises that *this isn't a child any more.* She's a woman that I don't recognise! After that he always knocks and hesitates in the doorway, shucking off the offer to enter.

'What would you like to know?'

'Your necklace,' I pointed out. 'I noticed it was missing.'

Her hand crept up to her throat, fluttered there like the beating wings of a butterfly.

'In the photographs you were wearing a small cross on a chain.'

'My mother's necklace,' she offered. I saw a shadow flit behind her eyes.

'You aren't wearing it now.'

'No,' she said. Her voice went to a whisper. 'It got broken.'

'It couldn't be fixed?'

'I . . . I don't have it any more.'

She didn't want to speak about it. I guessed it had been torn from her throat during the assault. A sore subject that she didn't want to acknowledge, let alone revisit. Quickly, I changed tack. 'It's not safe to stay here, you do realise that?'

'I'm not leaving without Bradley.'

'Bradley can come with us, but I think that it would be safer to take you somewhere that isn't associated with the Jorgenson family.'

'Not home.'

'No, Marianne, not home. Somewhere that can't be connected to you.'

'Why is this man after us?'

'Truthfully? I don't know.' I wondered how much of my suspicions I should lay on her. Decided that she had a right to know. 'There's been a suggestion that some of Bradley's family resent the fact that he's been named as sole heir to the business.'

'He has the right,' Marianne said. 'His father handed it on when he was too ill to continue, just as his father did before him.'

'I've no problem with that. But from what we've been able to gather, his father had two brothers. They also have children. They believe that they have been as instrumental in building the family business as Bradley has. They think that it should have been shared equally among them.'

'I know all of his cousins. Jack and Simon are brothers. Then there is Petre. He's the eldest. I can't believe that they would have anything to do with harming either Bradley or me.'

'Petre would stand to inherit the business if anything happened to Bradley?'

'Yes . . . but . . .' She shivered involuntarily.

'Envy among family members is nothing new,' I told her. 'Under the surface even the closest of siblings can be concealing a deep-seated hatred. It can stay hidden for life and taken to the grave. Sometimes it erupts into anger and violence. Especially where huge amounts of money are concerned.'

'And you think Petre may be responsible?'

'Petre doesn't like you, does he?'

'No.' I saw her fiddle again with the non-existent cross. Wondered why she wouldn't just come out with it. She asked, 'Do you think Petre would really go that far?'

'Could be any one of the cousins. Or all,' I said. 'Maybe I'm wrong and it's none of them. Regardless, there is a man who has tried, and will try again, to kill you and Bradley.'

'When he came to the house last night, he shot Bradley's father. He didn't know who Valentin was. That doesn't sound like someone working for any member of the family.'

'Maybe he knew,' I pointed out. 'But he just didn't care.'

'But why kill the man whose wealth is the bone of contention? Surely that only speeds up the process of dropping it into Bradley's lap?'

'Good point,' I conceded. 'Perhaps the killer has nothing to do with any of Bradley's family. Maybe it's got nothing at all to do with the business. Can you think of anyone else who would want the two of you dead?'

'No,' she said, but I could tell she wasn't being truthful. Something about the way her fingers again went to her throat, seeking solace from the missing crucifix, told me so.

CHAPTER 20

Dantalion was under the same bridge on the same beach, but the family with the crabby kid had long gone. The sun was a bloody slash on the western horizon. Out to the east, the first stars were twinkling in the purple evening. Above him the sky was a brown-yellow colour where day fought night, but was rapidly losing ground. Dantalion wished that night would get on with it, sucker-punch day, and then stamp it into surrender. He needed the darkness. It was his greatest ally.

He was sitting on a hummock of grass, his feet sunk in sand. Around him lay the flotsam cast up by the sea, sun-bleached twigs and the cast-off shells of crustaceans. There was also the ubiquitous plastic bag, dropped by someone careless. A soda can, ferrous-red around its lip, was buried to the shoulders in the sand. Between Dantalion's splayed feet was the backpack delivered to him by Gabe Wellborn.

From the bag he pulled out the sound suppressor. The one he had used last night was useless now. Suppressors didn't have an infinite lifespan, each successive shot robbing them of their effectiveness.

He screwed this fresh one into place on his specially adapted Beretta. He disengaged the magazine from his gun, inserted a new one, slid the loading mechanism to place a round into the firing chamber. He then fed a round into the magazine so that he had the full seventeen-round load ready to go.

Placing the gun across his left thigh, he reached back into the bag and took out a second gun. This wasn't nearly as effective a man-killer as the Beretta, but as he'd said to his associate, '*Don't worry, Gabe, I won't be using it on humans.*' The gun looked like something patched together from a plumber's offcuts. A pipe and valve and a canister. A simple trigger mechanism was the only item that looked as though it had been gleaned from a genuine firearm. It was a dart gun powered by compressed gas and could deliver the ketamine cartridges over a space of fifty yards.

Next came the night-vision goggles. They were advanced Generation Three goggles, military grade with image intensifier capacity, bright source protection and wide exit pupil design. They came with a fully adjustable, padded head rig to allow hands-free operation. With these in place he would have the ability to move through the darkness as though it was high noon. His enemies would be blind to his presence even when he was standing in front of them.

Last out of the bag was the EMF meter, a device for measuring electrical and magnetic fields. This particular device was distinct in its very wide frequency response and sensitivity. Any pressure pads or trip wires hidden in the grounds of the compound would set off an audio sounder not unlike the Geiger counter, increasing in intensity the closer he approached the hidden alarms.

The sun was almost down now. Under the bridge the shadows had thickened and swarmed around him like furtive confederates. He slipped out of his coat, bundled it and placed it into the backpack. In went his hat and sunglasses and he strapped the goggles on to his head, flipping up the dual-tubular-optics so that he could still use his own vision for now. He was dressed in close-fitting sweatshirt and cargo pants – the type with numerous deep pockets – tucked into laced-up boots. In the daytime Dantalion dressed in white or cream clothing, but his current garb was as black as the night folding around him. He holstered the Beretta on his hip; the wound in his thigh made it too uncomfortable to carry the gun in its normal position. Extra magazines were fed into the deep pockets on his left thigh. The EMF meter had a clip and he fixed it to his belt. He swung the backpack across his shoulders and cinched the straps tight. Lastly he picked up the compressed-gas gun and inserted a ketamine-charged dart into it, then thumbed the canister control.

He straightened, took a couple of steps so he could peer from under the bridge towards the gate he'd reconnoitred earlier. He couldn't make it out in the dark, not until he slipped the goggles in place. Twinkling green light played on the interior of the goggles. Now he could clearly see the dark bulk of the boundary wall on the horizon to his left.

Ready now, he set off, keeping low so that he was nothing but an amorphous shape against the swaying grasses. Earlier he'd picked his way painfully through the tall grass, but now he went more swiftly. The sunlight on his delicate skin was no longer an issue, and the cargo pants staved off the prickling edges of the grass stems.

Cars moved along the coastal highway, their lights streaking across the elevated bridge like a flight of UFOs. The sound was hushed by the fall of night; even the Atlantic made only the faintest of whispers where it caressed the shoreline.

Dantalion made his way through the grasslands, coming to the wall slightly east of the gate. Using the magnifying capacity of the goggles, he studied the CCTV camera mounted over the gate. It was angled away from him. Seemingly static, as though the controller within the grounds was taking a nap. The likelihood was that with a system of a large number of cameras, the controller rarely used this one. Wasn't much to look at during the dark hours. He'd probably be concentrating on the traffic outside the estate, or taking voyeuristic peeks into the bedchambers of the Jorgenson women.

Dantalion decided against shooting out the

camera. Whereas a malfunctioning camera along the wall near to the road wouldn't be of immediate concern, a broken camera at this remote corner of the grounds could call for immediate investigation. He scanned to the right towards the beach end of the wall, saw that the wall ended in a right angle, but that a tall fence extended out across the sand and disappeared into the Atlantic. The gate remained his best choice for entry unless he wanted to swim a couple hundred yards.

He tested the rusty chain and lock, found that they were still very strong in spite of the corrosion. Taking out his Beretta, he aimed at the lock. Fired once. Fired again. The lock shattered, but it was a task to twist it out of the links and unwind the chain from the metal bars. All the while he kept a discreet eye on the CCTV camera, anticipating it swinging his way. It never did.

Hauling one side of the gate towards him, he slipped through the gap. Then he tugged the gate shut. Immediately he took out the EMF meter and switched it on. Lights danced across the top of the device as it ran through a calibration sequence. He cupped a hand over it to smother the lights. It made a soft *beep!* Then a green pinpoint held steady. Ready to go.

Beretta back in its holster, he held the dart gun in his right hand, the EMF meter in his left, sweeping the ground as he advanced. Through the enhanced lenses of his night-vision goggles the nearest houses were black-green hulks, but lights from within the rooms were exaggerated, causing flare that looked like cold flames. The heavens above were afire with twinkling stars. Mist off the Atlantic swirled like translucent phantoms.

'Planning on a ghost hunt?'

Gabe Wellborn's attempt at humour came back to him. Dantalion smiled. It was as if he was traversing a haunted landscape. He recalled his own words: 'There might be a few ghosts around after I'm done.' Everything going to plan, his lists would be corrected, and there'd be further numbers to add.

Keeping close to the beach where the tall grass was left to nature, he continued past the first few structures. He needed to walk the best part of a mile to reach his destination. He had plenty of time, so he wasn't frustrated by his slow pace. Just because he hadn't yet come across hidden security devices didn't mean that they weren't there. He was vigilant with the EMF meter, and scanned with the goggles in continuous arcs of vision.

Almost twenty minutes later he ducked down among the reeds. A motor launch was creeping through the shallow water, a searchlight sweeping the beach for interlopers. The boat continued to the south, and Dantalion came out of his crouch, moving inland now. The long grass gave way to a low wall, behind which was a manicured lawn, and beyond that a statue-dotted garden.

The EMF meter finally warranted the effort of bringing it. The clicking started the moment he approached the low wall. Dantalion searched for the source of electrical disturbance: a motion detector mounted on the wall itself. Further along would be a second motion detector. A laser beam was fired between both contraptions, and anything breaking the beam would set off an alarm inside the house. It was a sneaky alarm, designed to catch out anyone stepping over the wall. Wouldn't stop him if he vaulted over the top of it. Which was exactly what he did.

If the security-conscious Jorgensons were clever they'd have placed pressure pads just inside the wall where a person jumping over the motion detector beam would be caught out by the secondary appliance. But Dantalion knew that dogs roamed the grounds after dark, so any pressure pads weren't practical. Being pragmatic though, he swept the lawn in front of him. The EMF meter remained silent. He moved forwards, looking for cameras. The house in front of him was huge. Cameras stood out from the roof line, but the two he could see scanned the areas at the sides of the building. Other cameras were mounted above the grand entrance door, but these were trained on the threshold itself, and he wouldn't be going in that way.

Staying out of the visual arcs of the cameras, he moved close to the building; its left wing extended out from the entrance portal. He crept up to it, keeping below the line of the windows, and then used the angle of the building to move directly beneath the CCTV camera. It would have a wide lens, but he doubted that he'd be visible when pressed directly to the wall; the cameras were positioned to spot anyone moving towards the building, not actually against it. He drew the Beretta, stretched upwards and fired a single shot into the camera housing. Sparks showered and the camera swung lazily to one side, then dipped in the final throes of its mechanical life.

Dantalion sped along the side of the building. At the far corner, he paused, peeking around the back of the house. Glad that he'd brought the ketamine, he lifted the gas-powered gun.

The dogs were penned in a compound. It was too early for their handlers to start their patrols and the two German Shepherds were lying with their heads on their paws, staring back at the house with a patience that had to be seen as virtuous. Dantalion took aim, vectoring in the slight breeze, the loss of velocity of the dart over the intervening space. He checked the gas pressure, flicked it higher. Aimed again. He squeezed the trigger and the gun gave a soft bark. In response both dogs' ears twitched. One of them yelped, swinging up from its crouch, inspecting the tasselled object embedded in its rump. Within the next second the dog dropped to the ground, one paw scrabbling uselessly at the earth. Dantalion had charged the dart with enough ketamine to fell a buffalo, or to give a dozen crackheads the trip of a lifetime.

The second German Shepherd was confused by

the conflicting stimuli. It had heard the gun discharge and duty bade it set off a racket, but it also watched its pack mate fall to the ground and moved to inspect it. Dantalion shot the second dog. The dart struck it just below its left shoulder. Angrily the dog turned on the stinging missile, trying futilely to pull the barbed dart from its flesh. It collapsed mid-snap.

Dantalion hurriedly slung the gun over his shoulder, came forwards drawing his Beretta. Beyond the dogs was a space where cars were parked. He moved among them, tempted to shoot out the tyres, but deciding not to. He would need the ammunition for something more important.

CHAPTER 21

Bradley Jorgenson returned from Miami looking worn and harassed. Immaculately presented when I'd seen him earlier, he now looked as unkempt as if he'd spent the night on a park bench. He was pale, his reddish hair dark with perspiration and standing up at weird angles as though he'd been pushing his sweating palms through it. His trousers were rumpled and moisture dampened his shirt beneath his armpits and at his lower back. His tie was askew, and the top button of his shirt was open.

Marianne went to him like he was a hero returning from war. He held her, and they cooed to each other. It would have been sickening if it wasn't for the context. Bradley's father had been brutally murdered, after all. I couldn't deny him the measure of comfort.

'We're going to have to make some decisions,' I told him when they finally drew apart.

Jorgenson nodded in resignation. It was as though the return to Miami had brought the enormity of what had happened yesterday to the forefront of his mind. Someone had tried to kill him and Marianne. In doing that the killer had murdered four others – one of them his own father – destroyed a multimillion dollar house, and would have killed the two of them if I hadn't shown up. This killer wasn't about to stop. When he discovered that his targets had thwarted him he'd come again. Who knew what lengths he'd go to this time to achieve his aim?

'The police didn't believe I wasn't at the house on Baker Island. Witnesses saw my boat. I'm under suspicion.' Tears sprang into his eyes and he turned away. He batted at his face with his hands, scrubbed them up and through his hair. When he turned back to me, he said, 'We can't leave the house. My attorney agreed to that and I can't go against the agreement. If I run away it'll look like I'm guilty.'

'Stay here and you'll die.'

'I can't run.'

'You can,' I said. 'And you will.'

Taking Bradley by the elbow I led him to the far side of the room. Marianne made to follow until Rink interposed himself between us. While she was distracted, I pushed Bradley through the open door and into the en-suite bathroom.

'Let's get a couple of things straight,' I said. To spare Marianne, I kept my voice low. 'I don't like you, Bradley. In fact, I'm struggling hard not to put a bullet in your skull. You're scum in my estimation. Do you understand?'

His mouth fell open and the blood drained from his face, leaving mottled patterns in his flesh.

He tried to step away but my fingers dug into the nerve at the back of his elbow. He squirmed against the pain, but was unable to escape.

'I don't like what you did to Marianne. Not one bit. Normally I treat men like you as the shit you are. I scrape you off the sole of my boot. But the truth is, I believe that there's someone out there who means Marianne more harm than you've already done her.'

'Marianne?'

'Shut it! Let me finish.' I leaned in, placing my mouth very close to his right ear. 'I came here with the intention of taking Marianne away from you. I'm still going to do that.'

He began to shake his head and I grabbed his arm even tighter, probing for the radial nerve. When I'd gained his compliance, I added, 'And you're going to give me your blessing.'

'What do you mean?'

'You are going to persuade Marianne to come with me. She's smitten by you, afraid to go against you. I want you to tell her it's best that she goes somewhere safe until this is over with.'

'You're not taking her back to her father?'

'I'll take her where I want, but no, I won't be taking her there.'

His shoulders relaxed a little. Was that relief in his eyes, I wondered. I said, 'The man who tried to kill you last night will come again. I can guarantee you that. It would be best if you went somewhere safe as well.'

'The estate is like a fortress,' Bradley said. 'Where would be safer than here?'

I snorted out a laugh. 'If I'd wanted to kill you I could've done it any time I pleased. The man from last night was good. He could get to you too.'

'I'll strengthen my security, bring in more men.'

'The killer could be among them for all you'd know.' Leaning close again, I whispered in his ear. 'Take my advice, Bradley. Don't strengthen your security. Strengthen your options. Take some of your most trusted men and get the hell away from here. Go somewhere you can't be found – it's the only way to stay safe.'

'Why do you care about my safety? You've just made it clear that you don't like me.'

'You're right, Bradley: I don't like you. The only reason I'm interested in keeping you alive is for Marianne's sake. Things are bad enough; I don't want to have to contend with a distraught woman grieving for her dead lover as well.'

Letting him go, I watched him work his sore arm. There was a scent coming off him that I recognised as fear. The patches under his armpits had grown.

'Where will you take Mari?'

'I can't tell you that.'

'Why not? I—'

'If the killer gets to you he could make you tell him where she is. Do you want that, Bradley?'

'No. No, of course not. I . . . I . . .'

'Love her?' My mouth twisted into a knot around the words. 'If you do love her, you'll let her go.

156

The most important thing in the world to you should be her safety.'

'It is.'

'Then we're in agreement?'

He nodded acquiescence.

I shoved him towards the door. 'Go and do it, Bradley. Convince her.'

He paused, looked back. 'I will. But there's something that you've got wrong, Hunter.'

'Yeah? What would that be?'

'Whatever you were told, you're wrong about me.'

'We'll see.'

He pointed a finger at me. 'Ask her. Ask Mari, and she'll tell you.'

'Put the finger down, Bradley, or I'll break it,' I snapped. He dropped his hand to his side, but the challenge remained in the set of his shoulders. I shook my head at him. Pathetic bastard didn't frighten me. 'Marianne will only tell me what you've ordered her to say.'

He exhaled. 'Believe what you want. But you'll learn the truth in the end.'

'Yes, Bradley, I will.'

CHAPTER 22

antalion is a great and mighty duke of Hell. He knows the thoughts of all men and women, and can change them at will. Nothing can stand in his way. Or so it was written in the fabled Book of Enoch.

After sedating the dogs, he'd walked through the rear entrance unchallenged. In a vestibule he'd come across a man sitting reading a newspaper and had shot him in the throat. Then he'd moved on. At the front of the house was another man in a small room that was in darkness but for the glow from numerous CCTV monitors. He seemed to be dozing, and Dantalion killed him without his victim even coming awake. Next he'd checked the opposite wing of the house where he shot two guards in the back. The plush carpets had absorbed the shock of their landing.

And then he was moving up the stairs, intent on the task he'd set himself. The numbers in his book required correction and there was only one way to achieve that.

Numbers are the building blocks of equations,

he reminded himself. Equations are formulae with a strict resolution. They gave him the answers to his existence.

Answers. That was why he was there. He wanted answers.

At the head of the stairs he heard the murmur of voices from within a room to his left. He took a spare magazine out of his pocket, ejected the one from his gun that was half depleted, and fed in the fresh one. He racked the slide. Continued up the stairs with new resolve. He moved along the hall towards the bedroom. The tugging sensation in his wounded thigh was a reminder of what mistakes can cost. There would be no mistakes this time. He entered the room, the gun levelled at chest height.

And found himself staring down the barrels of five guns pointed directly at him.

'Ah, Dantalion. We've been expecting you. Please come in,' said a familiar voice.

He didn't look at Petre Jorgenson, instead he looked at the fat man sitting behind the armed men. The fat man wouldn't return his gaze.

'You betrayed me, Gabe?'

Gabe Wellborn shifted in his chair, looked to Petre for support.

Petre took a step forwards, his gun pointed at Dantalion's midriff. 'Best you drop the weapon.'

Dantalion kept his gun exactly where it was.

'If that's your choice,' he said. Then he allowed the gun to lower to his side.

'Put the gun on the floor and kick it away,' Petre ordered.

'No,' said Dantalion.

'Then we'll shoot you and you'll never know why you had to die.'

Dantalion dropped the Beretta, kicked it from him with the side of his foot. 'Explain.'

Petre approached Gabe and placed a hand on his shoulder. Squeezed reassuringly.

'Mr Wellborn has done us all a great service.'

'He has?' Dantalion twisted the corner of his mouth into a sneer.

'Yes.' Petre looked at him oddly. Nodded at the night-vision goggles. 'Are you going to take off that ridiculous contraption?'

Dantalion made do with flicking up the dual tubes so that they stood up from his forehead like a ram's horns. Symbolic in its own way, but lost on all the others in the room. Petre waved a hand. 'Take a seat. We may as well be comfortable.'

'I'll stand.'

'OK, but I insist that you are searched for weapons. You can lose the dart gun, for a start.'

Dantalion allowed two of the armed men to strip the gun from him, then the backpack. His Beretta was scooped off the floor. One of them, a tall, thin Cuban, brushed the book concealed beneath his sweatshirt. Dantalion grasped his wrist. 'You don't touch that! Nobody touches that.'

The man pulled his wrist free, but it was an effort. Dantalion's spindly fingers held more

160

strength than his emaciated frame would suggest. The man looked at his boss for direction.

Petre said, 'Leave it.' Then to Dantalion, 'I take it that's the book you showed me at Bayside Park. Mr Wellborn has already explained to me how important it is to you. You may keep it, Dantalion.'

'I was going to.'

The armed men moved away, giving him space so they could hold him in their line of fire without blocking the other two guards. Petre sat down behind a desk. He laid his Glock 19 on its top within easy reach of his hand.

Normally, the position of power is held by the standing person. It forces those seated to look up at them, see them as the dominant figure. It didn't seem to perturb Petre Jorgenson, he appeared at ease. But then again, the illusion of Dantalion's dominance was severely compromised by having four automatic weapons aimed at him.

Dantalion looked from Petre to Gabe. He blinked very slowly. 'You betrayed me, Gabe. How could that be a great service?'

Gabe swallowed.

But it was Petre who answered. 'Mr Wellborn was concerned about your intentions. He believed that your decision to come here was not based upon professional logic, but on some misguided notion of revenge. Revenge is never good for business.'

'My decisions are never misguided,' Dantalion said.

Petre folded his hands, tapped his little fingers on the desk top. 'OK. So let's call it misinformed.'

Dantalion didn't reply. The tapping set off a tic on his jaw line.

Petre continued, 'Mr Wellborn – as you know – is an asset to both of us. He brokers deals, organises payment, supplies necessary equipment and intelligence. After he spoke to you earlier, he contacted me. He feared that you were acting irrationally. When you heard that your targets had survived last night, he believed that you might do something to rectify the situation. I applaud that; you have pride in your work. But he also gained the impression that there was an underlying problem.'

'You could say that,' Dantalion grunted.

'You thought I'd reneged on the deal?' Petre steepled his hands against his lips. 'I can see how you might have come to that conclusion. But it wasn't the case, I was merely awaiting confirmation.'

'Yes,' Dantalion said. 'Confirmation that I was dead.'

The skin on Petre's brow creased. 'Why would you think that?'

'My words when we spoke at Bayside Park.'

Petre sat back in the chair. He shook his head, a smile on his tanned face. 'I took them as the words of someone bolstering his negotiating position, not as a direct threat. I hear similar comments day in and day out at all levels of my business.'

'It's one thing receiving veiled threats from *ordinary* business associates,' Dantalion pointed out. 'Quite different when dealing with a professional killer, wouldn't you agree?'

Petre put up a hand, as though waving away Dantalion's words. 'Nevertheless, I did not take them seriously. Your credentials are superb; I had no doubt that you would deliver. I never perceived you as a threat to me.'

'So why send a man to kill me?'

Petre rested his hands in his lap. At ease. Nothing to hide. 'I didn't.'

Dantalion glanced round the room, taking in the positions of the other armed men. They too had visibly relaxed. Their guns were still aimed at him, but only loosely.

'How do you explain this man turning up, then? He was prepared for me, almost got me. Only I happened to be better than him.'

'Mr Seagram. Please come in now,' said Petre. Dantalion made a quarter turn, watching as the man with the brush-cut hair walked into the room. He skirted Dantalion so that he was standing next to Petre's desk. Petre raised his palm, giving him the go-ahead. 'Explain, Mr Seagram.'

'The man's name is Joe Hunter. He's freelance.'

'So you hired outside the network.' Dantalion directed his comment at Petre, who lifted his shoulders in a 'so what?' gesture. Dantalion wasn't in Petre Jorgenson's network either, so this was no major surprise.

Seagram said, 'He wasn't hired by us.'

'Don't lie to me,' Dantalion said. 'I saw you talking to this Hunter earlier. At the front gate.'

Seagram made an apologetic nod towards Petre. 'No offence, sir. My allegiance lies here, but *officially* I work for Bradley Jorgenson. I was with Bradley when Hunter and his partner turned up at the front gate. Unannounced, I may add.'

'So it was Bradley who hired him?' Despite his misgivings, Dantalion could see how that could work.

'No.'

'No? Then who?'

'Like I said, Hunter is a freelance. Our best guess is that it was Marianne Dean's father. Hunter's there to protect Marianne.'

'How would her father know I was coming?'

'He wouldn't,' Petre put in. 'Hunter turning up was a coincidence, that's all. He has come here for reasons of his own.'

Dantalion gently stroked the book beneath the material of his sweater.

Seagram went on; 'There is no love lost between Bradley and Hunter. However, Bradley's doing what he is told. Hunter's moved in and practically taken over the security arrangements in the house. Him and his partner, some asshole who goes by the name of Rink.'

'Two of them. Is that all?'

'I'm still in charge of security, whatever Hunter thinks,' Seagram said, his face rigid. 'I command all the others in Bradley's house. I can ensure that there is just the two of them.'

Dantalion looked away from the man. He was a disgrace, a turncoat with no honour. Check Gabe Wellborn into the same box. He returned his attention to his client. This was a man who desired his own cousin dead. He was no better than Gabe or Seagram. But for one important fact. He was the man with the money.

Petre Jorgenson spoke now, 'Thanks for your input, Mr Seagram. Best you get back to Bradley before you are missed.'

After he was gone, Petre said, 'So how does this play out, Dantalion? Now that you know we are not enemies.'

'I'd be dead by now if you weren't considering some new arrangement,' Dantalion said. 'Double the money. Half up front for services already rendered. The remainder when I kill Bradley, Marianne and Rink. I'll kill Hunter for free.'

Petre nodded. Satisfied in part. 'How do we know that we won't be in this self-same position after you are done with Bradley and the others?'

'It wouldn't be good for business if I went around killing my clients, would it?' He gave a slow smile that would have curdled milk. 'Now, I see Gabe has his laptop with him. He can patch into your system, transfer the money across to my account. Once that's done, you can count me in. Deal?'

'Deal,' Petre said.

They didn't shake hands. Petre recalled the scaly touch of Dantalion's fingers.

'Five hundred thousand, now, Gabe. Five hundred on completion,' Petre ordered. Double again the price just requested. 'Call it a token of my sincerity.'

Gabe flipped open the laptop, and set to it with a speed that belied his bulk. Dantalion smiled inwardly. Not too bad a resolution when all was said and done.

'That's it!' Gabe said with a final flourish. 'The money has been transferred to your offshore account.'

Pointing to the man who held his Beretta, Dantalion said, 'I'll need my gun.'

The man looked across at his boss for assurance. Petre gestured assent, sitting back in his seat.

'Relax,' Dantalion told the guard as he accepted the Beretta into his hand. 'We're on the same side again.'

Then he shot the guard point blank in the face.

Hollywood glamourises gun battles. On screen there are bunches of men loosing bullets while remaining cool and objective throughout. Every bullet finds a mark in the bad guys, while the hero dodges and whirls and avoids injury. Dantalion didn't mind that scenario. He was the hero. The only man of honour in this pit of filth. But he was also a realist.

Gun battles are down and dirty. No getting away from it.

He would accept the risk of debilitating injury – even death – to get the job done.

One guard dead. Three with guns in their hands. Petre Jorgenson already reaching for his. Gabe just a fat useless lump in the corner.

Dantalion fired again. Not at anyone. He shot out the light bulb above his head. There remained enough light-spill from the hall that he could still be seen, but that was OK. He slammed shut the door.

The Cuban guard brought up his gun and fired. The bullet made a hole in the door that sent a shaft of light across the room. It was as good as a laser guide back to the man who'd fired the gun. Dantalion fired twice, both bullets striking the man's body. Droplets of blood rained through the narrow beam of light.

Bullets punched the wall next to Dantalion, but he was already moving, dodging and whirling and avoiding injury like the best that Hollywood could offer. Snapping the night-vision goggles over his face. Firing 9 mm ammunition at the guards. One he got in the head, the other in the chest. Then, with no more than five seconds gone since he'd killed the first guard, he moved across the room towards his client.

Petre Jorgenson fired.

Dantalion felt the displacement of air by his left ear, realised how close the bullet had come to taking his head off. He shot back and his bullet didn't miss. Petre slumped back into his seat, the Glock 19 falling across the desk and on to the floor at Dantalion's feet.

Petre Jorgenson wasn't dead. Not yet. Dantalion had deliberately shot him in the gut. The man would last, but his final minutes on earth would be in extreme torment. Petre screamed.

So did Gabe Wellborn.

He knew exactly what was coming.

'You betrayed me, Gabe.'

'No. I didn't betray you. I got you the money, Dan. You would have blown everything if it wasn't for me!'

'You're right, Gabe. I thank you for that. But don't call me Dan.'

He shot Gabe between the eyes.

Turning back to Petre Jorgenson, he levelled the gun on the man's face. Petre couldn't possibly see him in the dark, but he would know how close death hovered over him.

'We made a deal,' Petre croaked.

'I made a deal to kill the original targets. You can rest assured that I will do that. I did not make a deal not to kill you.'

'Bastard . . .' Jorgenson hissed. 'Not . . . good . . . business . . .'

'To kill my client?' Dantalion exhaled. 'You're right, Petre. Except I haven't killed my client, have I? I made a choice. This was personal. I *am* the client.'

He shot Petre Jorgenson in the heart.

By now the suppressor was almost useless. The sound was very loud. An exclamation mark to this latest chapter recorded in Dantalion's book.

CHAPTER 23

Seagram came in the room yelling.

We were in the downstairs library again. Me, Rink, Marianne and Bradley. I almost shot the security man as he burst in. I thought he'd lost it and had gambled his lot on a mad charge into the room. But then I saw the terror on his face and the blood on his hands.

Some professional, I thought scornfully. Ex-West Point? Made me wonder if Rink's estimation of the man had been about right, except cooks aren't normally upset by the sight of blood.

Marianne had been against the idea of splitting up from Bradley, but the combined effort of the three of us had convinced her that it was in her best interests. Probably more persuasive was my argument that Bradley would be safer without the added worry that she could come to harm or – worse still – be used against him. She was just gathering up the last few possessions she couldn't do without when Seagram burst in.

'What the hell?' Rink intercepted the older man, barring his way with one hand. Seagram twisted, tried to get by and Rink grabbed him round the

170

neck, spinning him into the crook of his elbow and giving his throat a squeeze. The pressure of Rink's corded muscles could easily have throttled the security man within seconds, but that wasn't the intent. Rink only held him, hissing into his ear, 'Calm down, Seagram. You're good to nobody like this.'

The blood on his hands wasn't his own. Neither were the smears on his trouser legs. But to look at him, you'd think Seagram was mortally wounded. His face was pale and his lips had a faint blue tinge to them. He was shivering uncontrollably. Shock, I decided.

Rink manoeuvred Seagram to a chair, pressed him down into it. 'Now, tell us what's going on.'

Hands twisted together, shivering wildly, Seagram looked past Rink. Bradley had moved to cover Marianne, but when he realised there was no immediate danger, he crept closer to Seagram. He also asked, 'What's going on, Seagram?'

Seagram moaned.

In the end, Rink lost patience. 'Call yourself a fucking soldier? Suck it up, man. You're a goddamn disgrace.'

The older man's reaction was to slump, his head going into his hands. His knees shuddered with the fear coursing through his frame, making the chair creak with each movement. Sounded ear-piercing. Enough to make my mouth flood with saliva.

Rink grabbed at him again, forcing the man's head up by gripping the longer hair at the front of his brush cut. 'Goddamn it! Do I have to beat the freakin' words outa you?'

Finally Seagram appeared to take stock of where he was. Colour swept through his features like a morning tide racing to shore. He reached up, batting at Rink's hand. 'Get off me, for Christ's sake!'

Rink released him, took a step back. He held his hand ready to smack Seagram should the necessity arise.

Seagram rocked back in the chair. He turned his hands palms out like a magician about to perform sleight of hand. To Bradley he said, 'This is Petre's blood.'

Petre Jorgenson. Recalling Marianne's earlier words, I knew that Petre was the name of Bradley's eldest cousin. One of those she couldn't believe would have anything to do with harming Bradley or her. Maybe she'd been right.

'Is he hurt?' Bradley asked.

Judging by the amount of blood on Seagram, the way he was reacting, the question was pretty redundant. But to be fair, the same words had been on the tip of my tongue. Instead, I changed the emphasis, 'Is he *dead*?'

Seagram's face twisted into a leering gargoyle's. He stared at the floor as if the answer to some great riddle could be found within the weave of the carpet. When he looked up, he had a touch of mania in his eyes. 'They're all dead. Every last one of them. Murdered by the same man who's after you!'

Behind me I heard Marianne moan. Bradley, too. Rink and I took out our guns.

'Tell us what happened,' I demanded.

Seagram shook his head. It wasn't in denial; he was trying to regiment the words in his head. That, or come up with a plausible lie. I've dealt with too many self-serving assholes in my lifetime not to recognise another when I saw him. I guessed the story he was about to unfold would be only partly true. As long he was honest about the important details, I didn't mind. We could deal with the lies at another time.

'Don't be mad at me, Bradley,' he began. 'I only went to speak with Petre out of concern for you. You haven't been getting on that well lately but . . .' His eyes flickered once to Marianne, then back to Bradley. 'But I thought that he could help. He has his own security team, and if we pooled our resources—'

'There'd be an even bigger bunch of amateurs running around the place with guns,' Rink offered.

Seagram's face darkened. But he ignored the insult. 'When I got there I could hear talking upstairs. I couldn't see any of his staff around, so I made my way up to where Petre has his office. Suddenly there were guns going off. The door slammed. There was more shooting. Then silence. I'm ashamed to say that I didn't immediately go into the room to help, but my first loyalty was to you. I thought about running back to raise the alarm then and there.'

173

'Very noble,' Rink said. I could see he was buying Seagram's tale about as much as I was. The only part that rang true was that he didn't try to help.

'What was I supposed to do?' Seagram asked. 'I had no idea who was in the room. No idea of the numbers or the fire power. I waited. Hid myself. That's when I saw a man come out and run down the stairs. I was going to follow him, stop him, but I realised that Petre maybe needed help.'

'Petre was dead?' Bradley asked.

Seagram looked at his hands.

'I tried to save him. But it was no good. The man had shot him twice. He was gone.'

'Who else? I asked.

Seagram looked at me as though I was a stranger.

'Tell me,' I ordered. 'Who else was dead? Numbers specifically.'

'Petre. Some computer geek I'd never seen before. Four of Petre's guards.' He made as if to wipe his hands over his mouth, but then realised they were covered in blood, and scrubbed them down the front of his trousers. 'There were others, too. The security staff downstairs were dead. At least another four.'

'So a man kills ten people single-handedly?' My question was pure rhetoric; I was weighing up the ability of the man, not questioning the figures.

'Perhaps more,' Seagram said. 'But that's how many I saw.'

'Weapons?'

'Just a handgun, I think.'

'You saw it? Describe it.'

'I didn't get a good look.'

'Useless,' Rink said.

'What did *he* look like?' I asked. 'Tell me about him.'

Seagram chewed his lips. It was like he wanted to tell but also to hold something in reserve for later. Like it was his 'get out of jail free' card.

'White male. Mid thirties. Tall but thin. A hundred and fifty pounds at most. Dressed like a cat burglar.'

'Anything else?'

'Yes. He had on night-vision goggles.'

'And he managed to shoot dead five men in that one room?'

'In the space of seconds,' Seagram confirmed.

Damn good shooting, I had to give him that.

'We have to leave,' I announced. Marianne didn't appear so reluctant now. She took a couple of steps towards me, and I nodded her on. Took her hand in mine. 'Don't worry. I won't let him harm you. I won't let anyone harm you.'

She flicked a glance at Bradley, her lips pinching. They clung together.

'How long since you saw the killer?' Rink asked Seagram.

'Ten . . . fifteen minutes, I can't be sure.'

'How far away is Petre's house?'

'Two down. Maybe a little over a half-mile.'

'So he could already be here.'

'I was inside the house a few minutes after he left. But I drove, he was on foot.'

Rink shot me a glance. We'd both caught something very obvious in Seagram's words. But we let it go.

'Seagram,' I said. 'Among your supplies, do you have any Kevlar vests?'

He thought a moment. 'Yes. I think we do.'

'Go get them.'

'There's one at least.'

'Then go get it.'

'I should be here with Mr Jorgenson,' he said. 'To protect him.'

'Punk!' Rink called him. 'Tell me where the fucking thing is and I'll get it.'

'No,' Seagram made an attempt at regaining face. His eyelids were flickering wildly, so his words didn't do the trick. 'I'll get it. You make sure Bradley is safe.'

'Just get the vest, then get back here,' I snapped. 'Round up any of your men that aren't already dead.'

Seagram got up from his chair looking unsteady on his feet. He moved towards the door, faltered, grappled with his shoulder holster to pull out a gun. A Colt Mark III .38 special. Double action revolver. The famous law enforcement gun. It looked large and cumbersome in Seagram's shaking hand.

He ducked out the door, disappearing along the corridor to our left. I turned to Bradley. 'After this is done, you should take a serious look at the calibre of staff you employ.'

Bradley frowned. But he wasn't thinking about the ineptitude of Seagram. He'd lost his father. Now a cousin had died. The Jorgenson family was dwindling fast, and he was wondering if he was going to be next.

Not my problem, I decided. Marianne was the only reason I was there. Bradley should thank his lucky stars that I hadn't killed him at the first opportunity. Rink's suggestion of waiting until Bradley's back was turned then spiriting Marianne away maybe hadn't been a bad idea after all. She'd have been more angry than reluctant to go with us, but it would have saved us this latest trouble.

Might as well make the most of the situation.

'Bradley, you're going to help us get Marianne to safety,' I told him.

Then I related the rest of my plan.

By the end, everyone was in agreement.

Seagram returned with the Kevlar vest.

I gestured to Marianne.

'Put it on her,' I said.

Seagram reared up. 'But that's for Mr Jorgenson.'

'Shut up, Seagram, you asshole!' Bradley said, and the man just took a step up in my estimation. Bradley snatched the bulletproof vest, turned and held it out to Marianne. She accepted it like he'd just gone down on one knee and presented her with a diamond ring.

The vest was designed for a man, not a young woman, so was rather big and clumsy-looking on her. But it had adjustable Velcro straps. I stepped in close and cinched them tight.

'I can barely breathe,' Marianne said.

'You'll breathe less if a stray round makes its way between the vest and your body,' I pointed out.

She turned back to Bradley and he smiled at her. Touched her chin. She tilted her head and kissed his palm. Sweet.

'Let's get moving,' I grunted.

'Sheesh! Thank fuck for that,' Rink said.

CHAPTER 24

The night-vision goggles were an encumbrance now that Dantalion was close to Bradley Jorgenson's house. Lights had come on all over. Floodlights spilling out from the building like it was the finale of a rock concert. Bugs swarmed in the beams, making swirling patterns around the floodlight housings.

'Good move,' he whispered. The people inside knew he was there, and what he'd come equipped with. They were trying to take away the advantage of his goggles by making the area as bright as day.

With old-type goggles a sudden intrusion of light could strike the lenses and momentarily blind the wearer. These Generation Three goggles didn't have that problem. They had integrated flare protection to combat such a thing. Still, with the bright lights surrounding the building, the contraption did feel a little redundant. He took it off. Dropped it on the ground next to him. Moved towards the house.

His Beretta was in his right hand; Petre Jorgenson's appropriated Glock 19 in his left. The extra firepower wouldn't go amiss.

Dantalion had still been outside Petre's house

179

when Seagram had come running out. The man looked ready to vomit. His face was white. He'd jumped into a silver sedan and streaked off towards Bradley's house. He should have shot the man when the opportunity was there, but he'd decided to wait. He regretted that decision now. With Petre gone, Seagram would be Bradley's boy again. He would spill everything. That meant they knew Dantalion was coming, and were setting themselves up to defend the house.

Hunter and Rink.

He hadn't heard the names before. Not associated with his line of business. They had to come from some other discipline. The only yard stick he had to measure their ability with was how Hunter had fared the night before. He'd done well – credit where credit was due. The man had stopped him killing his targets, had shot him in the leg, and then survived an explosion that should have put anyone in a casket. He had to assume Rink would be as good.

He'd better be very careful here on in.

Careful but not cautious.

Caution breeds fear; fear builds an inability to act. Lack of action would kill him.

He crept forwards.

This house was very similar in design to that owned by Petre Jorgenson, in the form of a sideways 'H'. Dantalion had decided on the same approach as before: from the beach to the front of the house. To hell with the EMF meter, he didn't need it. They knew he was coming anyway. This time his advantage wasn't in stealth, but in full-on assault. Movement and noise. Shock and awe.

He came out of his crouch and ran.

From inside the front door a gun opened up in his direction. Dantalion swerved right, then left, bullets punching turf from the ground behind him. He kept moving, bringing up the two guns and firing as rapidly as he could pull the triggers. Three shots from each gun. A half-dozen high-velocity rounds into the partly open doorway.

Unaware if he'd hit the shooter or not, he continued to zigzag his way across the lawn, until he had the corner of the left wing between himself and the gunman. There he didn't stop. His painful leg wasn't a hindrance now. Adrenalin was a good anaesthetic, better than all the ketamine in the world.

He ran along the front of the building, stooped, but peering sideways through the windows. The rooms were deserted. He kept going. Came to the corner. The camera above him was swinging wildly, trying to get a bead on him, but he was below its arc of movement. The camera swung along the side of the building, just as he'd thought it might, and he immediately spun round, running back the way he'd come.

Alerted by whoever was controlling the cameras, the people inside the house had expected him to rush to the back of the building. But here he was approaching the front door again. The lack of bullets fired his way suggested he'd hit the person who'd been guarding the door earlier, or that his ploy had worked and the guard was even now rushing to the rear of the house to add reinforcement to the troops there.

Fortune favours the bold. Sometimes a full-on assault can achieve more than any amount of sneaking around. Bravery, or downright recklessness, had the ability to disarm the enemy.

Dantalion had never been of a timid disposition. He ran at the front door, lifted a boot and kicked the partially open door back on its hinges. He was through in an instant, moving sideways with his back to the wall as he probed the entrance hall for movement. Nobody. But there was blood on the floor, a trail of drops leading further inside the house. Stepping forward, he lifted his guns, one to the front, one to the side, exchanging positions as he moved along the hall, passing doorways.

Further back in the house he could hear voices and the thump of feet. The sound of a vehicle roaring to life. Dantalion was spurred on. He passed through a doorway and into the kitchen. The sounds were now further to his right, and he charged through the kitchen, seeking the far door. A shadow lurched into view and Dantalion fired. No time for differentiating one target from another when everyone in the building was a viable kill. If the man falling across the threshold was Hunter or Rink or Bradley Jorgenson, then so be it. In the event that it turned out to be none of them, well, that was all right, too. He'd get them soon enough.

When he gained the doorway he saw that his bullet had struck the man in the throat, and he was gagging on his own blood. The gun had fallen from his hand, but Dantalion wasn't of a mind to leave behind an enemy who might yet have the capacity to put a bullet in his spine. He shot him a second time, and the man's skull and brain matter spilled across the floor.

Another vehicle started. A lower roar, as the vehicle was driven away at speed. Dantalion cursed under his breath. He stepped into a second vestibule beyond the kitchen. There were three men blocking his exit. They turned on him even as he ran at them. He fired. They fired. A bullet tugged at his left arm – a searing pain – but he ignored it. His arm was still up and his hand was still pulling the trigger of the Glock 19. His mind processed these things without inhibiting his ability to perform. He continued towards the men, and they scattered, seeking cover. He shot one of them in the side and the man went to his knees. The other two had the sense to put the door frame between them. One on each side of the opening.

Bottleneck.

He couldn't go through the doorway without being cut down by the crossfire of the two guns. But it didn't stop his forward dash. He merely swerved, going left towards the window. He jumped, crashing through it, taking shards of glass and wood with him. He landed on his feet – his injured leg protesting but not giving in – and he spun, already firing both guns.

These were anonymous men. Not ones he recognised. But he killed them anyway, without discrimination. The man furthest away, who didn't have to turn round to fire, got off a shot, but it zinged away into the bug-filled night.

Dantalion ignored them; he was more intent on seeking out the two vehicles speeding away from him along the drive. The workers' village was a jumble of silhouettes on the near horizon, but neither car was headed in that direction. They were going for the exit gate out on to the coastal highway. Even if his leg hadn't been paining him he wasn't about to catch them on foot. He required transport.

A silver sedan was still parked in the area at the back of the house. The two making off were a second sedan and a Porsche. The three cars he'd seen at the gate earlier in the day. Dantalion approached the vehicle, wary that others might be lurking about. He stuffed the Glock 19 into his waistband, but kept the Beretta ready should anyone try to take him as he opened the car door. He leaned in, checking the rear seat, not wanting to be caught out by a silent assassin popping up and putting a bullet in the nape of his neck. No one there. He reached under the steering column, feeling around. It wouldn't be the first car he'd hotwired during his eventful life. Then he forgot that idea, reached instead for the sun visor and flipped it down. A bunch of keys dropped into his palm, one of them the new card-key type. Fate was on his side.

Getting in, he placed the Beretta on the seat beside him. He fired the engine, pulled away, swung the car in a tight circle and headed up the exit drive after the tail lights of the Porsche.

The car was this year's Lincoln Town Car, with V8 engine capable of 289 hp and complete with electronic traction control and an automatic rear suspension levelling facility. The vehicle was built with comfort in mind, but it was also built for speed and manoeuvrability. Dantalion could have done far worse.

Pushing the car up to seventy miles an hour, he felt the Lincoln respond beneath him. He floored the gas pedal and the car continued to pick up speed. The Porsche had a lead on him that he couldn't hope to close on this straight, but the electronic gate at the exit would slow them. He'd catch them there.

Behind him, pulling out from the blind corner of Jorgenson's house, came a fourth vehicle. It was driven without lights, and joined the procession of speeding vehicles without Dantalion noticing.

CHAPTER 25

Rink's Boxster was not as fast as the similar 911 Turbo Coupe model Porsche that I'd once had the pleasure of driving, but I couldn't complain. Not when it accelerated from nought to sixty miles an hour in under six seconds and had a top speed approaching 160. Ten seconds later I was up to a hundred and gaining on the sedan in front of me. I flashed my headlights, exhorting Seagram to greater speed, but he held steady and I had to slow down and follow at a moderate speed of ninety-five.

Passing the cluster of buildings that made up the homes of the estate staff, we kept going on our pre-planned route towards the highway. Glancing in my mirrors, I saw another car peel round in a circle and take up the chase. That would be the killer, then.

Beside me Marianne had her eyes closed and she was gripping the seat belt across her chest as she might once have gripped her crucifix at times of stress. It made me recall her words.

'My mother's necklace. I . . . I don't have it any more.'

I wondered who did.

One thing I was pretty sure of now. It wasn't Bradley Jorgenson.

When I'd been putting the fear of God into him earlier, he had explicitly denied ever harming Marianne and he'd been oddly convincing.

I'd originally accepted this job with the intention of taking Marianne away from Bradley. If that meant killing him, I'd even prepared myself for that. I'd been led to believe that Marianne was in a violent relationship – which the police photographs proved – but I now believed that it wasn't Bradley who'd done that to her. Domestic violence often hides behind lies and deceit, but in Bradley and Marianne I'd only witnessed genuine tenderness. He loved her the way she deserved to be loved. He hadn't hurt her. Her abuser was the person who now had her cross. Marianne hadn't confirmed who that was, but I had an idea. And if my suspicions proved true, he'd be made to pay.

First, though, I had to get her to safety. There was a far greater threat to her than the person who'd blacked her eyes and slapped her around – the crazy fucker who was third in line of this cavalcade.

We still didn't know who the killer was. But I had to pay him his due: the son of a bitch was good. He must have gone through Seagram's security team like a dose of salts. Otherwise he wouldn't be chasing us now.

Approaching the highway, I saw the brake lights

187

flare on the vehicle I was following. Seagram decelerating rapidly. I braked as well, cursing under my breath.

Marianne's eyes snapped open. Full of terror.

'It's OK,' I lied. 'Nothing to worry about.'

We'd a good lead on the sedan racing after us, but for one thing. The gate that gave exit on to the highway was closed. We should have thought ahead, had it opened from the control room back at the house. As it was, I saw Seagram jump out of the car in front and race to the control panel in the grounds. He stabbed buttons and was running back to the sedan even as the gate began its slow crawl outwards.

A noise like an angry hornet buzzed by my right shoulder and the windscreen starred. From somewhere behind me I heard the retort of a gun as the sound finally caught up with the supersonic bullet.

Out of the window, I roared at Seagram, 'Get that fucking car moving!'

Another bullet swept through the interior of Rink's Porsche and lodged itself in the fancy console. Rink was going to be royally pissed off, but that would teach him. He should have taken more time in selecting his wheels of choice, considering the business he was in. The Porsche's soft top was no defence against a hard-flung knife, let alone high-velocity rounds.

Back in the sedan, Seagram booted the throttle and pushed the heavy car through the opening gate. He blasted the front fender against the gate, knocking it flying, but also tearing loose a good portion of the wing. Half a million dollars' worth of car was nothing when the alternative was a swift and violent death.

As we'd agreed, Seagram swung the sedan to the right. Seconds later I went left, straight along the four-lane highway on the wrong side of the road. Two hundred yards on – and immensely thankful that no one had been heading along the road at that time – I powered the Porsche across the gravel bed separating the two carriageways and on to the correct side of the road. The Porsche spat gravel and sand as I accelerated away. On our right was the Inter-Coastal Waterway, and beyond it the lights of the mainland.

'Is he still following us?'

Marianne's words caused me to glance in the rear mirror.

'Yeah.'

'Dear God,' she whispered.

The killer had been given two options, right or left. He'd chosen to continue left. I'd have preferred it if he'd gone after Seagram and his passenger rather than me and mine. I was better fixed to protect my charge than Seagram was, but I'd rather have got Marianne well away from harm before turning on the bastard and showing him just who he was messing with.

Speed was my best weapon.

I pushed the Porsche up to one hundred and

fifty miles an hour. Just a little way behind, I saw that the Lincoln matched me for speed. Maybe it even gained a little. The driver hung his hand out the window. I saw the muzzle flash, but the bark of the gun was lost as we sped on.

I pressed Marianne down. 'Unclip your belt,' I told her. 'Get down in the footwell. Undo your vest and pull it over your head if you can.'

The trunk and seats wouldn't stop the bullets, but I guessed that the shooter would aim that little bit higher, shooting where he'd expect a hit. Comparatively safer than I was, Marianne would be very unlucky if a bullet found her. But that possibility wasn't out of the question.

The gun fired again, and sparks jumped along the door frame next to my elbow. I couldn't return fire, didn't have the angle. All trying to twist round and firing would achieve was a deceleration, possibly a high-speed collision with the bollards on my right, then a flipping, rolling, body-tearing wreck that would do more harm than the killer's bullets ever could.

I concentrated instead on pushing the car to the limits of performance. Technical specification of the Porsche Boxster boasts a top speed edging 160 mph, but I saw the odometer register 165, then 170, then 175. But the RPM needle was hovering dangerously in the red zone. Pushing the vehicle to these extremes could wreck the engine, but then again, so could the killer's bullets.

The road was preformed concrete, and every so

often a seam projected above the surface, causing a bumping noise to sound from the tyres. Rocketing along at high speed, the bumping rattled like a drum roll. The accompanying ting of bullets off metal and Marianne's yowls of fear made for an ungodly timpani.

Approaching the southern extremes of Neptune Island, I made out the sweep of the bridge that took the road across the Waterway. It looked like a humpbacked whale had breached the depths and would at any second flip up its gargantuan tail and send us flying into space. I pressed the Porsche on.

The Lincoln couldn't match the Porsche for acceleration, but the heavier sedan was gaining along the straight. There was a slight sway on, the way it went from one side of the carriageway to the other, but that was more to do with the killer driving with only one hand on the wheel. He continued to shoot. This time he sent a volley of five bullets. Two of them lifted concrete shards from the road ahead, but three of them impacted the Porsche. None hit me, but I snatched a glance at Marianne. She looked up at me from beneath her Kevlar shield with big, round eyes.

'Hold tight,' I told her.

Then I stomped the brake.

The Lincoln was the much heavier vehicle, but I was counting on the killer's reaction to do more damage than the Porsche could. True to my expectation, he swerved. The front fender clipped the back of the Porsche, lifting us from the road for the space of a very long two seconds or more. I felt weightless, and a tiny portion of my mind expected the car to flip over and disintegrate in a billion pieces. Then the rear tyres found traction again, and I pushed the Porsche forwards, gaining distance on the killer, who had to struggle to control the Lincoln.

The daring manoeuvre bought us only a few seconds' respite from the bullets. But it had slowed the pursuit somewhat. We were now only averaging 140 mph.

The bridge swept upwards, then curved to the right. There was no meridian on the bridge, only collapsible plastic markers. A U-Haul truck went by on the other side. The driver swerved in dismay. Distractedly I wondered what he'd think of the Lincoln behind, with the gun poking past the door frame and raining 9 mm Parabellum ammo at me.

On my right, all that protected us from launching into the sea was a waist-high barrier. Every so often along the way, I saw evidence of where other cars had clipped the barrier, gouging paint but causing little other damage. I doubted they were doing more than twice the average speed when they'd collided, though. I swung the Porsche to the left, straddling the central markers of the two southbound lanes.

Behind us, I saw the Lincoln roaring towards our back end. When I braked, the killer had been forced to control his vehicle. Now he had decided that it was our turn. He rammed the Lincoln into the rear end of the Porsche, jamming us forwards. He rammed us again. I could feel some of the traction go from beneath me. I dropped a gear, pressed the throttle, surged ahead, taking control again. In response the gun came out of the window once more and another bullet went through the Porsche. The windscreen had had enough. It exploded, some of the glass collapsing inside so that I got a lap full of tiny, grainy squares. I closed my eyes to avoid the splinters and glass particles I felt on my skin.

It was little more than an exaggerated blink. But when I opened my eyes once more, the Lincoln was surging up alongside the Porsche on my left. It was scattering the plastic markers up the meridian as though they were ten pins, flattening them or throwing them into the air. I swung the Porsche at the Lincoln, but all that achieved was to lock us together momentarily. There was a squeal of buckling metal.

I got my first look at the man behind the wheel. I'd been correct about the pale smear on his chin. The guy had the face of a ghost. Or some other more evil, ethereal creature. His thin blond hair knitted a pattern over his features from the wind driving in through the open window, and I only caught a snatch of his eyes. Pale blue slits. But it was enough to see that he was as psychopathic as every other nutcase who killed for fun.

He nodded at me, as if in recognition.

Here, I thought, do you recognise this?

I lifted *my SIG* Sauer left-handed and fired at him, unloading half the clip as fast as I could pull the trigger. The noise inside the Porsche was deafening. I didn't hear my rounds smack his car, but I saw his windscreen implode. Sparks and particles of metal flew off the bonnet. Something burst in the engine and there was a gout of steam. No blood, unfortunately.

The Lincoln dipped on its suspension. He was braking. Then he was behind me and I couldn't see to shoot any more. A quick glance at the odometer showed me I'd decelerated almost forty miles an hour. But we were still travelling at over one hundred. It was insane. Something else – our collision had taken us back towards the barrier on my right. The wing mirror was snatched off and went tinkling into the darkness behind us. I jinked left, to get away from the metal barrier.

Now the Lincoln was nosing up to my bumper. He nudged the Porsche. We slewed. Almost had me with the PIT manoeuvre police patrol vehicles occasionally employ to stop fugitive vehicles. Unfortunately for him – very fortunately for us – his vehicle hadn't been in the optimum position to spin us out. But it did make the Porsche's back end swerve towards the central median, blasting more of the plastic markers out of commission, the front end juddering for traction on the concrete.

Marianne wasn't the only one yelling. I probably

had the edge on anger, though. I grappled with the steering, righting the Porsche, but the Lincoln was now alongside me, and this time the killer was directly in line with me. In his left hand I saw a Beretta 90-two. In the split second it took to register the make and model of the gun I also calculated my chances of avoiding the bullet aimed at my skull. Zero or nil. Take your pick.

He mouthed something at me, but I didn't catch it.

In one of those slow-motion moments of ultra-clarity, I saw his index finger caress the trigger. In reflex I started to duck. But, even in slow motion, the bullet wouldn't register.

CHAPTER 26

He'd lost count of the times he'd been back and forth over and under this selfsame bridge in the last day, but Dantalion had a feeling that this wouldn't be the last. Even after he finished Hunter and his unseen passenger, he was going to have to go back after the second vehicle that had headed off up the coastline towards Jupiter Island.

He'd recognised the dupe immediately the sedan had turned right, while Hunter had headed left. They were attempting to split his targets with the hope that he'd be frustrated and give up the chase. He wasn't the kind of man to back down, so they'd assume he'd continue hunting Jorgenson and Dean, but not until he rallied and got his act together. Likely they thought that would give them the opportunity to prepare for his next assault. They couldn't have expected that he'd chase one of them with unabated determination.

If Seagram had been telling the truth earlier, Hunter would be Marianne Dean's chaperone, so it was probable that the woman was in the Porsche with him. She was most likely hunkered down in the footwell so she made a smaller target. He didn't mind killing Marianne first. That had always been the plan, what he'd almost forced Jorgenson into agreeing to yesterday on Baker Island. And he definitely didn't mind killing Hunter.

It had been an exhilarating chase up until now. But it was time to end it. Dantalion saw his opportunity. Hunter was a damn good defensive driver to have controlled the Porsche after he'd rammed it into a sidelong skid, but in doing so he'd lost some of his forward volition. Plus he must have dropped the gun. Dantalion swerved round the Porsche and came parallel with the driver's door, smiling as his theory was proven.

Both Hunter's hands were back on the wheel, the gun out of sight. Dantalion lifted the Beretta. Aimed it directly at Hunter's face as it swung to look at him. The man didn't look alarmed, he just had a grim set to his jaw.

'Hello, Hunter,' Dantalion said. 'And goodbye!'

Hunter made a token attempt at saving himself, but a bullet would always be faster than human reaction.

He pulled the trigger.

And heard only an empty click.

'Shit!'

He was a man governed by numbers, yet he had to have miscounted. He was positive that there had been one last bullet in the gun.

Seventeen rounds. But then he remembered. When he'd reloaded, shoved in the fresh magazine, he hadn't racked one into the firing chamber as he had when first loading the gun. He hadn't miscounted. He'd made an error of gun craft.

A bigger error would be to dwell on the fact. He quickly traded the Beretta for the Glock 19. It was a matter of no more than two seconds, but as he tracked his vision on Hunter the man was no longer in sight. Neither was the Porsche!

Hunter had braked, and the Lincoln had sailed on by.

Worse than that, Hunter was now behind him lifting his own gun. Through the gaping hole in the windshield Hunter fired. The flash of the gun was like a strobe light. Bullets zinged through the Lincoln. Three missed, lifting padding from the headrest on the passenger seat. One of them scored a hot line along the flesh of his jaw just below his left ear.

It was like someone had hit him with a hammer and his mind flashed with scarlet agony. The pain was excruciating, sense-numbing. Darkness descended for the briefest of moments, and his hands slipped from the steering wheel.

And that was all it took.

In the next instant his mind was full of flashes and bangs, and he was rocked sideways, jerked upright, then slammed back in his seat. The volume of noise was horrendous and seemed to go on and on and on. Around him the Lincoln shuddered like a dying behemoth. Finally, he blinked, and silence surrounded him.

Stunned, he was only vaguely aware that the Porsche was now passing him, then in front of him, moving away at speed over the arch of the bridge and out of sight.

He was sitting in the driver's seat and both his hands were in his lap. He'd lost his grip on the Glock, and it was now somewhere out of view in the footwell. The partly inflated airbag that had erupted from the steering column didn't help. He wasn't concerned about the Glock. He could soon pick it up again. As with the Beretta. First he had to check that he was uninjured. Both arms were all right. His hands responded to the messages sent from his brain, fluttering up his midriff to find the comforting bulge made by his book beneath his sweater. His toes wiggled at command. His legs ached, primarily the one that was already injured, but he detected no broken bones. His jaw hurt more than anything. Tremulously, he lifted his fingers to check the wound. Part of his mind expected a gaping wound through which would project shattered teeth, but his fingers found only a groove in the meat itself. It oozed blood, but it wasn't going to kill him.

He looked out of the open window.

He had lost control and the Lincoln had collided with the barrier at the edge of the bridge. The metal barrier was mangled into a twisted heap. But it had done its job. It had stopped the Lincoln from sailing out unchecked into the Inter-Coastal Waterway. The front of the Lincoln hung a precarious two feet over space, only one loose portion of the barrier holding the sedan in place.

He laughed. There was a slight manic edge to the sound: realisation at how close the car had come to going right through the barrier and into the sea a long way below him.

But that was when he heard the roar of an approaching engine.

Swinging round to stare at the vehicle barrelling towards him, he had only a second or so to register the face of the driver. It was enough.

Rink, Seagram had called him.

Black hair, hooded eyes, livid scar across his chin.

Rink made no attempt at shooting him. Neither did he stop the car. He kept on coming and rammed the car into the side of the Lincoln.

Dantalion was rocked and slammed yet again. There was the rending of metal all around him. The front wheels went through the barrier and the car abruptly dipped forwards. Rink continued to force his vehicle against the Lincoln. Then the world tilted as the back wheels of the Lincoln were forced over the demolished barrier.

He barely registered what had happened.

All he saw was the solid black wall that reared into his field of vision. It approached him at speed and it was only when it was a few yards away that Dantalion made out sparkling highlights on the wall. A second after that he recognised the highlights for undulating waves casting back the reflections of his own headlights as the Lincoln hurtled down towards the sea.

CHAPTER 27

'**S**on of a bitch,' Rink sighed. 'There goes my no claims discount.'

We were in a beauty spot, but he wasn't interested. He was standing with his hands on his hips, surveying what remained of his Porsche.

We'd stopped at a parking lot on the northern side of the Jupiter Inlet, near to a terracotta tower over one hundred feet tall that served as a lighthouse to steer boats into Loxahatchee River. The beacon itself stood on a mound almost fifty feet tall, so it was a definite landmark that I'd been able to pick out. Rink arrived minutes after Marianne and me.

While Rink bemoaned the death of his pride and joy, we stood shoulder to shoulder. On the shoreline, we looked south, watching traffic zoom by on the Federal Bridge, and even more traffic on the A1a highway bridge beyond that. Across the water I noticed yet another marina, and found myself thinking that you couldn't live in Florida without owning a boat. I saw my first mangroves, but in the darkness they just looked like a bundle of twisted branches dumped on the water. Which, I supposed, was exactly what they were.

The lot was next to a visitor centre that served the lighthouse. Through the day the place would be a jumble of vehicles and bustling tourists snapping photographs. At this hour we were the only ones there. I'd parked the Porsche beneath a stand of palm trees so that it was hidden from the nearby road. Rink had parked adjacent to us. The big grey Ford Crown Victoria he had brought wasn't as bashed up as the Porsche, and hadn't been the target of numerous bullets. Nevertheless it did have a crumpled fender and one of the headlights was smashed. Any cop snooping around would immediately associate the two cars with the high-speed gun battle at nearby Neptune Island.

'What happens now?' Marianne asked.

'We take you somewhere safe.'

'But that madman is dead, isn't he? Didn't your friend say he rammed him right off the bridge and into the sea?'

'I did just that,' Rink said, coming over to join us. 'But he's not the only danger we have to contend with.'

'If he's dead, can't we just go to the police?'

'Not yet,' I told her. 'We still don't know who sent the hit man after you. Whoever did so could try to get at you again.'

'All the more reason to tell the police what's going on. Why do we have to keep running away? It's *him* who should be punished, not me and Bradley.'

'You're right. But we're not ready to get the police involved yet.'

'Why not?' she asked.

'They'd take you from us,' Rink explained. 'And we don't want that to happen. We're committed to protecting you and we can't do that if you're kept away from us.'

'I don't get it,' she said. Then she looked directly at me. 'Yesterday on Baker Island, you said you were there to help me, Joe. But I don't understand how you could have known that I was in danger. You aren't doing this for nothing. Someone is paying you. Who sent you?' Then she closed her eyes, shook her head. 'No. Don't answer. I know who it must be.'

So I didn't answer.

Marianne said. 'How could my father have known this was going to happen? No, wait . . . he couldn't have. He sent you to take me away from Bradley. I can't believe that he just won't let things go.'

Rink said, 'Doesn't matter who sent us. Or why. Truth is we're here, and that should give you peace of mind. We ain't going to leave you until we're sure this damn thing is over with.' He turned and scanned his Porsche again. His lips turned down. I looked at him. That was quite a mouthful from my usually imperturbable friend, and I guessed he was saying it for my benefit as much as Marianne's.

'Sorry about your wheels, Rink.'

He shrugged. 'S'OK. I was about due to trade it in anyway. C'mon, better get moving, folks.'

We weren't talking cars. Not as such. I was expressing my regret at keeping him away from his mum's sick bed. He was telling me that material objects didn't mean much to him. Ergo, his mind was fully on his mum and nothing would change that. Except getting this job done.

'Better take the Crown Vic,' Rink said. 'Porsche is done, you ask me.'

'We leaving the car as it is?' I asked. The Porsche was full of trace evidence, fingerprints, fibres, spent rounds, and would be tied to us even faster when a CSI team got to it.

Rink took out a petrol lighter and flicked back the lid. He turned the wheel and orange flame sprouted.

'Like I said, I was about to trade it in anyway.'

We drove away in the Crown Vic, the guttering inferno that once was a Porsche lighting up the parking lot. The flames were reflected on the hundred-foot lighthouse and bounced back off the lens at the top like a ghost-light.

Rink was in the driving seat. Both Marianne and I took up position in the back. She sat in a far corner, her legs pulled up and her feet tucked under. She hugged both arms round her knees. For safety's sake I'd made her put the Kevlar vest back on. It swamped her, the collar riding up almost to her ears, so that only the upper portion of her face from the tip of her nose was visible. Cute in its own way. Desperately sad in another. She was lost in her own thoughts, so I concentrated on what we were going to do next.

Rink had called our mutual friend Harvey Lucas. It was time to find out what he'd come up with. I had his number stored in my mobile phone and hit the hot key. Harvey picked up in seconds, his mellifluous tones rich in my ear. I put the call on to speaker so that Rink could catch what was said.

'You guys are up to your necks in it as usual,' Harvey said.

'Tell us about it,' I said. From the front seat Rink grunted agreement. He was navigating an interchange and taking us up and over the A1a highway bridge towards West Indiantown Road, crossing the broad Loxahatchee River inlet.

'Don't have much on your shooter,' Harvey said without preamble. 'Seems he's a bit of a ghost.'

'He is now,' Rink said.

'You got him?'

'Pushed him into the sea from a great height,' I said. The eternal sceptic in me wouldn't accept he was dead until I saw him laid out all white and bloated on a coroner's slab.

'So the heat's off?' Harvey asked.

'Not yet. Don't know how many other players we have,' I said. 'What've you found out about who hired him?'

'Nothing yet, but I have done a bit of digging around regarding the Jorgenson business.'

I glanced across at Marianne but she was lost inside her own head. She didn't even look my way, and didn't appear to be listening to the conversation. Thinking of other things: Bradley, for sure.

'Go on, Harve,' I prompted.

'You want the full history or just the potted version?'

I checked the charge on my phone. Down to two bars. 'Best just give me the main points.'

'OK, then.' Harvey paused, as though ordering his thoughts. Not that he needed to. I believed he knew exactly what he wanted to say. 'First off, you know the family business goes back three generations here in the US, right? Since Korea, Vietnam, and up to the modern day, the Jorgensons have been working hand-in-fist with the Pentagon. The partnership has been a rosy deal and brought millions – actually billions – of dollars into the Jorgenson coffers. Problem is, it seems that for the last half-dozen years Valentin Jorgenson has been ruffling a few feathers. On both sides. His company has been responsible for the development and production of vaccines for the use of the military. Well, you remember the fuss following Desert Storm, don't you? Gulf War Syndrome, it was sometimes referred to. Soldiers returning from war complained about debilitating problems brought on by the inoculations they were given before going out there. Well, Valentin wanted no part of the fallout from that. Seems like old news now, but with the current rumblings in Iraq and Afghanistan, there are new questions being raised in Congress about the chemical soup our troops are being fed these days.'

'The chemical soup that the Jorgensons are supplying?' I clarified.

'One and the same. The Jorgensons certainly don't have a monopoly on government supply, but they do develop some of the vaccines. Valentin didn't want any involvement in the same kind of scandal that went down first time round, so, basically, he's pulled the plug.'

'And the other Jorgensons aren't happy?' I thought back to when Bradley had defended his father in the room at Baker Island.

Harvey said, 'His ethical decision could cost them billions in lost revenue.'

'You're saying *could* cost them? So the contracts haven't been terminated yet?'

'No. As in all businesses, Valentin hasn't got the ultimate say. Has to be a majority agreement. He has had some stiff opposition in the form of his partners.'

'These being his nephews and son?'

'Yeah.' Harvey sounded like he was riffling through papers. 'Petre, Simon and Jack. His son, Bradley.'

'I'm guessing that Valentin had a majority share in the business?'

'No, just over the quarter mark.'

'So how come he was outvoted? Oh, wait, I get it. Bradley?'

'Yeah, Bradley's vote went his cousins' way. Between them they own a little over seventy percent of the vote. With Bradley on their side, the decision was made to honour their agreement with the government.'

'So why, if that's the case, is someone trying to

kill Bradley? Are you saying that our shooter might belong to some group opposing the supply? Some Gulf War Syndrome support group?'

'Not at all,' Harvey said.

I was relieved by Harvey's answer. I had some friends from back in the day who had suffered badly on their return from Desert Storm, could sympathise with them in a big way. Didn't really want to go up against anyone with the same fundamental belief that I had on the subject. Apart from the fact their decisions could mean death for innocents like Marianne. For that I'd fight them tooth and nail.

Harvey went on: 'Bradley has changed his outlook these past few months.'

'He's gone across to his father's way of thinking?'

'He has. Valentin was dying – you knew that, huh? – and he had recently bequeathed his share of the company to Bradley. Added to his own shares, that gives Bradley a majority sway. He hasn't done it yet, but when Bradley takes over, then the military contracts will be dropped. It'll cost the company billions of dollars.'

Marianne was rocking in place, humming that same sad tune I'd first heard in the garden at Baker Island. Suddenly I knew where Harvey was going with this.

'Someone has Bradley's ear? That's what you're suggesting?'

'His opinion changed round about the time his new girlfriend came on to the scene.'

I noticed Marianne's eyes flick my way but she didn't add anything. Neither did she argue.

'It's starting to make a little sense now,' I said. 'So Bradley has gone against his cousins, and that's pissed them off? If Bradley is killed off then they inherit his voting power. They keep on with the billions that the government are happily handing them.' I again looked at Marianne and saw that her eyes had closed. Confirmation of my theory. To her I said, 'And that's the reason the killer wants you as badly as your boyfriend? You're the reason that Bradley has changed his way of thinking.'

She didn't answer, but her nose dipped below the neckline of the bullet-proof vest.

From the front, Rink asked, 'Where are you now, Harvey?'

'Where I said I'd be,' Harvey said.

'OK, buddy, we'll see you in a short while.'

'Gotcha, Rink,' Harvey said.

'Keep on digging in the meantime,' I added. 'See if you can find out anything on the shooter. You might want to listen in to what's going on at Neptune Island. By all accounts, the crazy fucker paid Petre Jorgenson a visit before he came for Bradley and Marianne again.'

'Reading between the lines, I take it that Petre didn't survive?'

'No one survived,' I said. 'Except some pussy that goes by the name of Seagram. Bradley's bodyguard. Maybe you can do a little digging on him, too. West Point's a good starting place.'

'Leave it with me.'

'Thanks, Harvey.'

'Pleasure.'

I clicked off the phone, pushed it in my pocket.

We'd come off the highway on to surface streets. Nice enough area. Low single-level houses with pretty gardens. No one around as though people here lived only for the sun and dissipated when darkness fell. On our right was a tributary of the Loxahatchee. The water was slow and still. I wondered if alligators sometimes crawled up out of the river and wandered these lonely streets. That would explain the lack of domesticated animals prowling through the night. There were no cats, no dogs, but then again, there were no alligators, either.

We had agreed to meet Harvey up at Hobe Sound. That meant taking a circuitous route back up past Neptune while avoiding the coast road. There'd be an army of law enforcement personnel converging on the Jorgenson estate by now and I didn't want to run a cordon of blue lights. The only way I trusted that Marianne would be safe was if she stayed with us. OK, it appeared that Petre Jorgenson was now shaking hands with his murdered uncle, and it would take a very lucky man to survive the fall from the bridge into the sea, but that didn't mean that other attempts wouldn't be made on her life. It didn't take a rocket scientist to work out the probability that Petre and the shooter were in cahoots. Something

211

had happened between them that had left Petre dead. But that didn't mean all our enemies were done with. There were still two cousins alive who had reason to wish both Bradley and Marianne were out of the picture.

CHAPTER 28

Following our detour round the back streets of the suburbs of Jupiter, Rink found a slip road that took us to the Florida Turnpike, where we picked up the 95 north. He drove on through the darkness in silence, and eventually we arrived at a motel on the edge of Seabranch Reserve State Park. Here I saw my second lot of mangrove, as well as sand pine and scrubby flat-woods and many other trees I didn't recognise. Wild buckwheat and fetterbush grew interspersed among the trees and the wild sandy hummocks that the Atlantic had moulded into weird shapes.

Harvey's rental was in the lot outside the motel entrance. It was a Ford Explorer, not unlike the one I'd been forced to abandon down at SoBe. For our purposes it wasn't the most discreet of vehicles but it was still less conspicuous than the bashed-up Crown Vic. Rink pulled into the parking lot and I accompanied Marianne towards the room that Harvey had booked. Rink drove off again, heading for the nearby state park on a short errand to get rid of the Crown Vic. Maybe it would turn up one of these days when the shifting and

213

squeezing of the earth's crust forced it out of the depths of the mangrove swamp like a corroded leviathan rising from the depths.

The motel celebrated the local Native American Hove culture, but spoiled it somewhat with a fake totem pole, copied from one I'd seen a few years ago commemorating the great Chief, Seattle, in the Northwest city of the same name. The totem pole was mid-centre on a swathe of grass in front of the motel reception. Standing nine feet tall, it almost dwarfed Harvey Lucas where he leaned against it. Almost, but not quite. Harvey is a huge man. He doesn't have the musculature of Rink, but he's still a physical specimen that would make most men envious. He stands well above my near six feet. His skin is so black and sleek that he looks like he has been carved from jet by a master sculptor. On his broad shouldered, slim-waisted frame, clothes hang on him the way clothes are meant to hang. At forty years old he could give men half his age a run for their money on the football field, as well as a lesson in style.

We greeted each other the way old soldiers do. A masculine hug of the left arm, our right hands hooked together at our thumbs, a bump of chests.

'Looking good, Harve.'

His jeans and shirt weren't that different from mine, only he looked like he'd just stepped out of a Hollywood gossip magazine, while I looked like something that people gossiped about – for all the wrong reasons.

214

He touched the wound in my scalp. Shaking his head in amusement. 'I see that Rink's been practising his field dressings on you. Never could see straight, that one.'

I'd forgotten about the slash on my head. But now that Harvey mentioned it the damn thing reminded me it was still there with an itch that demanded scratching.

'Brought some supplies with me,' Harvey said, nodding over his shoulder towards his room. 'Better get that cleaned and apply some antiseptic cream. Don't want it getting infected.'

'What're they going to do if it does? Cut my head off?'

'Sure would be an improvement,' Harvey grinned.

Marianne was standing in our shadow, looking up at Harvey as if he was a demi-god who'd come down from Mount Olympus on a cloud. There was trepidation in her gaze, but not a little awe.

'You must be Marianne.' Harvey held out his hand.

'Mari,' she answered shyly.

'Mari,' he repeated, and he took her hand in his, giving it a gentle squeeze. Her smile made her look like the girl I'd seen in those first couple of photographs.

She said, 'You're not what I . . .'

'Not what you expected. Yeah, I know. You thought I was gonna be as ugly as these two brutes you've been stuck with?' He shot me a wink and I grinned behind Marianne's back.

'Joe isn't ugly,' she said, and that made me grin

215

even more. I should have maybe defended Rink, but to some he did seem like he'd be more at home dressed in skins and wielding a club. Then there were others who found his rugged face and scarred chin attractive; the epitome of the bad boy look.

Harvey asked me, 'How is Rink?'

'Holding it together.'

'He shouldn't be here.'

'Tell me about it.'

Harvey turned back to Marianne. He touched the shoulder of the Kevlar vest. 'Come on, girl. Let's get you inside and out of that fashion disaster, huh?'

The motel was the type that has a stand-alone reception with rooms located in adjacent wings. It was constructed like a loose crescent, the parking lot nearest the road, then the grassed area with the faux-totem pole, and the rooms curving round on either side. Harvey had rented the room furthest away on the right-hand horn.

It was a standard room in a standard motel. Twin beds. Couple of chairs. A desk. A credenza with a pay-per-view TV sitting on top of it. Instructions for dialling up porn on a card on the wall. Harvey's laptop computer was plugged into a socket on the wall and was resting half-open on top of the nearest bed. A partly open door on the left showed a glimpse of a standard bathroom. Marianne's eyes widened, but then a shadow crossed over them.

'I've checked it out,' Harvey told Marianne. 'No

creepy-crawlies. Shower's hot and the towels are clean. Why don't you go ahead? Make you feel better.'

Marianne agreed with a slight nod of her head, then walked towards the bathroom, tugging at the straps of the vest. She dumped the heavy vest by the open door, then slipped inside. I heard the locks engaging. Not that she'd need them with us there, but it made sense. She was shutting out the horror of the last couple of days. I suppose that we were as much a reminder of that horror as anything else that had happened.

The shower went on.

Harvey closed the door to the outside.

'Got anything for us, Harvey?'

He picked up a bag, delved inside it and tossed me a tube of antiseptic cream. 'That for starters,' he said. Then going over to the laptop he pushed open the screen and tapped a few buttons. 'Plus this.'

There was a profile photograph of a fat man on the screen. Then a portrait. Then a profile from the opposite side. Police mugshots, all of the same man. He had dark hair in sweaty fringe on his forehead. His jowls were blotchy with broken veins, and his eyes were the type you normally see on bloodhounds. He was smiling, but it was just bravado for the camera. His eyes weren't smiling. They were fearful.

'Dead for a start,' said Harvey. 'He's one of the guys shot dead inside Petre Jorgenson's house.'

'Got a name for him?'

'Gabriel Wellborn. Goes by Gabe. Not the kind of character you'd normally expect to move in the same circles as the Jorgensons.' He held his hand at shoulder height. 'On the social ladder, the Jorgensons rate a nine.' He dropped his hand way down. 'Gabe Wellborn scores a minus two if he's lucky.'

'So what's his deal?'

'Officially? He has a web design business. Small potatoes, not so many clients. Just a front, if you ask me.'

I nodded. 'Unofficially?'

'Go getter.'

I didn't catch his meaning. Not at first. Then I said, 'Go get me this, go get me that?'

'Yeah,' Harvey said. 'You want something, Gabe's your man. Particularly if the thing you want is illegal. Guns, drugs, underage sex . . . you know his type.'

'Maybe there is an argument for justifiable homicide. Pleased to hear he's dead,' I said. Then, 'These things he gets for people, does that include killers for hire?'

'Unconfirmed rumour. But, yeah. He's been on and off the FBI radar for years, but they haven't been able to make anything stick. He recruits through these soldier of fortune sites that have sprung up all over the web. Takes on mercenaries who are after a quick buck. Very discreet operation. All coded to protect their anonymity. Works for anyone who can pay, not just a select clientele.'

'How is his operation run?'

'I spoke to an FBI contact. It's only a theory of theirs, and up until now they've been unable to prove it. It's so simple it goes way beyond sophisticated.'

'Usually the way. Hide in plain sight and people don't see what's right under their own noses. So, how is he doing it?'

'All via the web. Untraceable URLs are used. Hosting by ex-Eastern Bloc companies. Firewalls that would rival Homeland Security. Until now, the FBI have been unable to crack it. His employees use disposable cell phones with internet connections to keep in touch. Gabe gives them their instructions under the guise of a fantasy role playing game based upon the war between heaven and hell.'

My snort of derision was like the air brakes on a taut-liner. 'And he's the Archangel Gabriel, no doubt?'

Harvey smiled. 'Got it in one. But what about the others?'

'Named after the fallen angels?'

Harvey patted me on the shoulder. 'See, I knew there was a reason Rink took you on as his business partner.'

'Got a name for the shooter yet?'

'Nope. But I got this.' He started pressing keys on the laptop. The screen changed to a list of names. They were all picked out in magenta, underlined. Shortcuts to web pages, I guessed.

Alphabetical, beginning with Amdusias and ending with Zagan. Weird names from a forgotten language or a cheap sci-fi movie. There were eighteen names in all.

'Names of all the fallen angels?'

'Not all,' Harvey said. 'There are many more than this. I lifted this list from the FBI. These are all names assumed by the players in Gabe Wellborn's game.'

'So we could be up against this many shooters?' I asked.

Harvey shook his head. 'No. You don't have to worry. Only one of these assholes has been active in the recent months.'

With a manicured fingernail he tapped the screen.

'Dantalion?' The name tasted like bile in the back of my throat. 'What do we know about him?'

Harvey double tapped the blue line under the name and the computer flickered between screens. First came words written in flame. They said:

> The seventy-first spirit is Dantalion.
> He is a great and mighty duke, who governs
> thirty-six legions of spirits. He appears in
> the form of a man with many countenances,
> all men's and all women's faces. Dantalion
> knows the thoughts of all men and women,
> and can change them at will.

Next, I saw a stylised painting of a man in a long white coat. His skin was white and he had flowing white hair. He held an open book in one palm and a sword in the other. I stared at the face. Androgynous, it could have been male or female. Beautiful but cruel. The eyes were like slivers of arctic ice.

I'd seen that creature before. Not so beautiful, but even more evil. Right now it was lying at the bottom of the sea with a Lincoln sedan as its tomb.

Or that was my hope.

CHAPTER 29

First came weightlessness as the Lincoln fell through space.

Then a crushing force as it slammed into the water.

Next came pain.

Hopelessness.

Bubbles frothing, red flashes across his vision.

Weightlessness again as he sank.

And blackness.

The blackness was complete.

Then there were bubbles again and the taste of salt on his tongue. Not salt from the sea but salt from his blood. Sanguinary and bitter, like sucking on a copper spoon.

He tried to move. But the weight of the world was on his shoulders, like Atlas of the fables. No, not the world, just the roof of the Lincoln. But it felt as heavy as the planet.

He blinked, trying to make sense of his thoughts. Now there was salt water and it made his weak eyes smart. He rubbed at them, realised that he was fully submerged, and gave up. Instead he groped for something tangible to hold on to. He found a circular bar, his confused mind eventually recognising it as the steering wheel of the car he was trapped within. The steering wheel was below him, almost at his knees. It took him a moment to realise that the car was standing up on end, nose down. Bubbles raced by through the gloom, and the surroundings were getting darker by the second. The car had not yet come to rest, it was still sinking. The smashed windscreen, the open windows, had allowed the sea to rush in.

Good and bad.

Good because it meant that he wouldn't have to fight the pressure of the sea to open the door. When a car is submerged, fighting at the doors is a losing battle. Only when the pressure inside equals the pressure outside can the doors be opened. Advice under those circumstances is to sit tight. Allow the water to flood in while breathing deeply from the air trapped inside the body of the car. Lungs full and the pressure equalised, it is a simple task to open the door and strike out for the surface.

Bad because the water had rushed in on impact. The car was on a steep angle as it dove deeper and the bubbles were the oxygen escaping through the smashed windows and bullet holes. There was no air pocket.

Add to that the fact he was doubled over, ass lifted by the buoyancy of air trapped inside his clothing, head down staring through the smashed windscreen so that the rushing water battered his features, and he could be forgiven for panicking.

But Dantalion didn't panic. He was a professional. He was calm and practised.

That was the theory, at least.

Like many caught in a life and death predicament, he opened his mouth to shout. And all that did was empty his lungs of what precious oxygen was left to him. Then he was thrashing and pulling, and he was half out of the open driver's window. The car continued to drag him down, his legs caught behind the knees by the window frame.

He kicked and kicked and then he was free. But his lungs were screaming and there was a foggy blackness at the edges of his vision, even deeper than the darkness around him. He was tumbling in space, arms and legs pulling and pushing, but not moving him towards the surface. He didn't even know which way the surface was.

He had a moment of epiphany.

The single remaining headlight of the Lincoln pointed into the depths below him. The last few bubbles escaping his lips streaked upwards over his head. Follow the bubbles, he told himself.

He set off after the bubbles. It was a race he couldn't win, but he wasn't going to give in. He struck out after them, clawing handfuls of water.

He had no recollection after that.

His next conscious thought occurred when he was lifted from the water by strong hands and laid out on a pitching deck that even in his confused state he recognised as the bowed bottom of a small boat.

His vision swam.

The star-filled heavens were above him. And a pale grey blob that swam in and out of focus. Something like leather smacked against his face.

'You still with me, buddy?' a voice asked. 'Hey! Hey! Are you with me?'

Dantalion lifted a hand and grabbed the wrist of the man slapping his face.

'Hey, you're alive! You're all right?'

'I will be when you stop slapping my damn face!'

'Oh, sorry, buddy. I thought I was too late getting to you. I thought you were dead.'

Dantalion let go of the wrist. He dropped his hand to his waist, patting for the bulge. Found his book. He finally exhaled. Then he started coughing, and in reflex he rolled on to his side, vomiting sea water over the planks.

A hand patted him between the shoulder blades, then moved to his shoulders, supporting him through his final spluttering coughs.

'Easy now, buddy, easy,' said the Good Samaritan. 'You'll be fine in a minute or two.'

Through spittle Dantalion said, 'I'm fine now. You can lay off with the helping hand, goddamnit.'

But the man wouldn't listen; he helped Dantalion to his feet, letting him rock backwards on to a bench seat.

'I can't believe you survived that.' The man was standing with his legs braced, hands on hips as he peered upwards. Above him – way, way above him – was the dark underbelly of the bridge.

Mangled wreckage marked where Dantalion's Lincoln had been rammed through the barrier. A drop of more than a hundred feet. Bubbles still fizzed and popped ten yards out where his submerged vehicle continued to give up its final hold on the oxygen caught in its sub-frame.

Dantalion didn't have the strength to look any longer. He dropped his head between his knees, spitting out a long string of salty saliva.

'I saw it all, buddy. I'm your witness. I saw that lunatic hit your car and push you over the edge. He didn't even stop. Just took off like nothing was the matter.' The man turned to look down at his patient. 'What kind of madman does that?'

'Beats me,' Dantalion muttered. He regarded his benefactor.

The guy was about seventy but in good shape for his years, short and stocky, face bronzed by the sun but a deep blue in the dark. His hair was as white as Dantalion's but it was thick and wavy. He was of sturdy build, with thick forearms and bowed legs, wearing a T-shirt and shorts. Leather gloves. There was a fishing pole on the bow of the boat, forgotten now.

'What are you doing out here in the dark?' Dantalion asked.

'Night fishing,' the man answered, indicating the pole. 'Best time, if you ask me.'

Dantalion raised his brows. He wasn't the only one who preferred hunting in the dark. 'No argument from me.'

'Good job I was here,' the man added. 'Otherwise no one would have seen you hit the water. They wouldn't have pulled you out in time.'

Dantalion noted that the man's clothes were as wet as his own.

'You jumped in and pulled me out?' Dantalion stood up and extended his hand. 'You saved my life?'

'It was nothing,' said the man, accepting the hand.

'I thank you for that,' Dantalion said. 'I really do. And it pains me to have to kill you now.'

Mid-handshake the man jerked.

'Uh?'

Dantalion snatched the hand towards him, dropping his forehead so that it struck the man flush in the face. The sound was like a hammer smacking a watermelon. The man dropped on to his backside, hands going to his smashed nose. Dantalion's head swam. Not from the force of the blow but from the lack of oxygen. He had to suck in a couple of lungfuls of air before he felt strong enough to reach down and grab the man's arms.

'Now, in gratitude for your selfless help, I'm going to give you a choice.'

The man was heavy, his sturdy body a dead weight, not helped by the fact he was swimming in and out of consciousness.

'I'm going to give you a choice on how you die,' Dantalion explained. 'Fast or slow?'

'Go to hell,' the man slurred. He tried to pull

away from Dantalion. His hands were slick with blood and his knees weak. Dantalion let go of him. He fell to his knees, bumping along the bottom of the boat. Dantalion grabbed at the nape of the man's neck.

'So it's slow, then?' Dantalion asked. 'OK . . . *buddy.*'

He swung the man round on his knees, pushing his head over the side of the boat. The man tried to resist and Dantalion punched his free hand into the man's kidneys. He bent him over again, pushing now with both hands at the back of the man's head. Forcing his face under water. The man yelled in terror. Bubbles frothed. But not for long.

When he was still, Dantalion pushed him overboard. Held him submerged beneath the water with both hands. Counted to one hundred. Numbers, always numbers.

Then he gently prodded the man away from him, watched as he slowly sank head first, aimed at the place the car went down. Maybe the police would think that he was the driver of the crashed Lincoln and their search wouldn't be so exhaustive, giving Dantalion the opportunity to sort himself out. With that breathing space, he would soon be ready to complete his mission.

But already, above him on the bridge, other motorists had stopped. They were peering over the balustrade, looking down at him. He didn't think they could have seen what had just occurred between him and his would-be saviour, but it wasn't a chance he was about to take.

The boat was equipped with an outboard motor. He quickly set to it, pulling the starter cord. When the engine coughed to life, he sat down, aiming the prow towards the shoreline of Neptune Island.

He could hear distant voices. It didn't sound like shouts of accusation, more like concerned witnesses calling out for survivors. Dantalion didn't answer. He just angled the boat along the shoreline, heading further away, looking for where he'd left the truck.

He was angry.

Angry that Bradley Jorgenson had escaped.

Angry that Marianne Dean had escaped.

But more than that, he was angry that Hunter and Rink had got the better of him.

Worst was the seeping wetness at his waistline. His book was sodden. He dreaded what he might find. The book was precious to him, even more so the numbers written inside.

They were the sum of his life's work.

CHAPTER 30

Rink came back within the hour, looking more morose than ever. He had dark mud on his boots and spattered up the backs of his jeans. There were even droplets of mud sticking to his black T-shirt and on his face and forearms.

'Almost ended up in the swamp with the goddamn car,' he announced. And then he smiled, and it was good to see. It was the first ray of light through the cloud that had been hanging over his head since the news about his mother's illness.

He was holding his mobile phone cupped in his left hand.

'You've heard something?'

'Yeah,' Rink glanced round the room, taking in Harvey and Marianne, noting that they too wore expectant faces. 'Doctors have stabilised my mom and she's feeling much better. Must be; she's been giving my father a hard time for trying to pull me away from my work.'

I went over and held my friend.

'Thanks, Joe,' he said. It's not often he uses my given name; only in moments of tenderness like this. It means a lot.

Harvey came over too. He hugged Rink and they said their bit to each other.

Marianne didn't know what to do. She just sat down on the bed and put her elbows on her knees and smiled up at Rink. My friend, not the shy and retiring type around young women, went over and sat down next to her. Patted her on the knee and said, 'OK, Marianne. Now we can get on and sort out your problems.'

Marianne bobbed her head. Smiled sadly. Then she asked, 'Is your mom ill?'

'Yeah,' Rink didn't expound, but he didn't have to. The gravity of the situation must have been clear in our reaction to the good news.

'And she's all the way across the country?'

'Yeah.'

Tears welled in Marianne's eyes with the confirmation that there was still good in the world. Here were three men ready to put their own lives at risk for her, to push aside their own needs and desires to see to her safety. 'Thanks, Rink,' she whispered. Then lifting her head, she looked at me and Harvey. 'Thanks to you all.'

'Don't worry about it,' Rink spoke for all of us. He patted her on the knee again, then stood up smoothly and nodded at the door to the bathroom. Steam still pervaded the space beyond the open door. He indicated his muddy arms. 'Unless you've used all the goddamn hot water?' he said in mock anger.

Marianne smiled again, this time not so sadly.

'Marianne's safe for now.' Looking across at Harvey and receiving a nod of confirmation, I continued, 'Harvey can take her to the safe house. It's time you got on that plane, buddy.'

Rink shook his head.

'You aren't going to miss anything, Rink. Catch the red-eye out of Miami. You can be there and back again in a few hours. Go on. Go see your mother and father.'

'You sure?' he asked. All three of us made shooing motions, which got us a smile. 'Best get that shower then, huh?'

Meanwhile Harvey had been industrious with the computer.

'Hunter. Come take a look at this.'

He had the CNN news site on the screen.

It showed a story about the mysterious slaying of a young family. Nathaniel and Caitlin Moore, and their eight-year-old daughter, Cassandra, had been murdered in their home in the suburbs of Miami.

Yes, it was sad. A terrible reality in today's world where a family can be wiped off the face of the earth to appease one man's sick fantasy. It was exactly this kind of story that made me do the things I did.

'What're you getting at, Harvey?'

'You said the shooter used a Beretta 90-two,' Harvey said.

I remembered looking down the barrel and thinking how there was no way to avoid the 9 mm bullet headed my way. In that moment of epiphany I'd identified the gun. 'Yeah,' I agreed. 'This murderer used a Beretta, as well? Popular gun.'

'Taken singly, it wouldn't mean anything.' He tapped the screen. 'But a witness also saw a tall man with long white hair leaving the house in the early hours. Sounds like your shooter, doesn't it?'

More interested now, I leaned down, placing my hands flat on the bed to get a clearer look at the screen.

'Then there's this.' Harvey highlighted a block of text in the story so I could better read it.

'"The thunders of judgement and wrath are numbered,"' I read out loud. 'Written in Cassandra's blood on the living room wall. Jesus!'

'Sounds like your usual whacked-out religious freak,' Harvey agreed. 'Until I did a search on those words.'

He brought up another site he'd been holding in a bank along the bottom of the screen. A History of Enochian Ritual was emblazoned across the page.

'Black magic?'

'Goetic magic,' Harvey corrected. 'Something taken from a *grimoire* written hundreds of years ago by an Elizabethan astrologer named Dr John Dee.'

I'd heard of John Dee. He was the court astrologer to the first Queen Elizabeth. Purportedly he was also her top spymaster, and something of a legend among the security community. He went by the code number of 007; maybe there was no coincidence when Ian Fleming was developing his fictional James Bond character.

'I think I know where this is going now,' I said to Harvey.

He pressed a few more keys. A page came on the screen and there were the same words the murderer of the Moore family had scrawled on a wall in an eight-year-old child's blood:

> *The thunders of judgement and wrath are numbered.*

'It's a quote from the Book of Enoch,' Harvey pointed out. 'A line from the Bornless Ritual. Something referred to as a "Calling of the Aethyr". All mumbo-jumbo bullshit, I agree. But translated it refers to the summoning of a dark angel.'

'Dantalion,' I said.

Harvey's fingers tapped keys yet again, bringing up another link. A table full of weird symbols next to names and descriptions. Dantalion was eighth down.

'Shit,' I hissed.

'Shit about sums it up,' Harvey said. 'This guy's one crazy motherfucker.'

'But why kill a family? What have the Moores got to do with this?'

Throughout our discourse, Marianne had kept her thoughts to herself. But at the mention of the family name, I heard her croak. She stood up slowly and came to stand at my shoulder as she stared at the screen.

'Did you say *Moore?*'

I nodded to Harvey and he brought us back to the CNN screen.

Marianne's hands went to her mouth. 'Oh, dear God! Caitlin Moore was my teacher at Collinwood High School. It was Caitlin who introduced me to Bradley.'

Harvey turned off the CNN screen as Marianne dropped to the bed. Her hands worked down from her mouth and plucked at an imaginary crucifix at her throat.

'Back in 2002,' she said, her voice barely above a whisper, 'my brother Stephen was among the first Marines to be deployed to Iraq. There was a fear that Saddam Hussein had weapons of mass destruction hidden away and Stephen was one of those sent in to try to locate them.'

Uh-oh, I thought, having a feeling where this was going. Richard Dean had never mentioned having had a son. Neither had Marianne mentioned a brother before, nor that he was a soldier. Even when Rink had done a background check on Dean it hadn't come up.

'He was given inoculations to protect him from ABC warfare?' I offered, thinking back to how many times I had stood in a line baring my shoulder for a nurse or doctor with a huge syringe. Never questioning, just taking the injections as protection from the atomic, bacterial and chemical weapons that could be coming our way.

'Yes.' Marianne sucked in a ragged breath. Her next words were a little stronger. 'And it was pointless. As you know, these weapons were never found. Stephen came back from his tour sick. No one would accept that his sickness was as a result of the medication he'd been given. They still won't.

'They said it was psychosomatic. He was imagining his problems. Fatigue, a loss of feeling in his extremities, blinding headaches. It drove him to throw himself off a ten-storey building during an anti-war rally.'

'I'm sorry,' I muttered feeling awkward. 'It's a terrible thing to lose someone. Especially under those circumstances.'

'I miss him dearly. Five years have gone by and there hasn't been a day when I haven't thought about him.'

'Yet you're in love with the man responsible for his death?' I asked.

'Bradley isn't responsible. I don't blame him. Not one little bit.'

'It was medication developed by the Jorgensons that you believe caused Stephen's illness?'

Marianne nodded, then said, 'Mrs Moore was one of my teachers at school, but she was also a trained counsellor. She helped me after my brother's death. We shared common ideas on the wars in Iraq and Afghanistan. Our servicemen and women are dying needlessly and all for the wrong reasons.' She blinked, realising that I used to be one of those self-same service men, albeit with a different army, who had fought the same war as her brother. 'I'm very supportive of all our brave soldiers. I'm not against the military at all. I just wanted to do my bit to see our troops were given the respect they were due. I joined a protest group that Mrs Moore had set up to express our views.'

'You attended a meeting with the Jorgenson family?'

'Yes. That's where I first met Brad. He was very charming and he was open to our opinions. He was a good listener. We talked quite a lot afterwards.'

'And that was when you started dating?'

'Yes.'

'But your father didn't approve?'

'My father is still very angry. He hates Bradley. He blames him for Stephen's death, as much as he blames everyone else involved.'

'Maybe he has a right to hate Bradley. Your father showed me photographs of you,' I told her. 'One of you fighting off Bradley in the back of a car. It looked like he was molesting you.'

She shook her head in incredulity. 'Tell me any celebrity that hasn't had a similar photograph taken. We were just playing up to the cameras, Joe, giving the paparazzi something to get excited about. It was a prank. In hindsight it was a bad idea.'

'He showed me a police photo where you had been a victim of assault.'

Her lips pinched.

'Yes.'

'But it wasn't Bradley who beat you up?'

'No, of course not. Bradley loves me and I love him.'

Bradley had been telling the truth. Made me feel a bit of a shit.

'So who was it?' I asked. 'I thought one of his family could be involved. Petre, maybe.'

A quake ran the full length of her body. 'It was my dad.'

I'd already come to that conclusion. It was obvious, when I thought about it. I remembered our first meeting in the grimy roadhouse. As I'd walked away from the bar in Shuggie's Shack, Richard Dean had been fiddling with something that had flashed in the subdued light. Something metallic: her crucifix. He'd stuffed it into his pocket before feeding me a line of bullshit a mile wide.

'He came to Bradley's house to take me home. He accused me of betraying my brother's memory. Said I'd made myself a whore for my brother's murderers. He couldn't see that he was wrong, that Bradley was actually on our side and was prepared to cancel all contracts with the military.' Her fingers went to her throat, teasing the imaginary cross. She began to weep. 'He told me that I had betrayed our family. That my mother would be rolling in her grave. He tore my mother's necklace from my throat. When I tried to take it back he struck me. He was in a rage, and he struck me again and again. He didn't know what he was doing, he was just mad.'

'That's no excuse.'

'I forgive him,' she said. 'I still love him.'

Thinking back to when we'd first broached this subject, I'd assumed that she was referring to Bradley when she'd said similar words. She hadn't been, I saw now. She'd forgiven her father for his actions and his words. But Richard Dean hadn't forgiven anyone.

He had sent me here to take Marianne back to him under false pretences. He had another reason for sending me. I was supposed to stop Bradley coming after her. 'The balance will be paid as soon as I get the proof that Jorgenson is no longer a threat to me or any of my family,' he'd said. His meaning had been explicit. Stop him for good. Kill him.

That wasn't going to happen.

I was going to protect Bradley.

Then I would see to the problem that was Marianne's father.

Rink came out of the bathroom, whistling and scrubbing his hair with a towel.

He stopped and looked at us all.

'What did I miss?'

Where the hell do I start? I thought.

'Nothin' important,' I told him. 'Go and catch that plane, Rink.'

CHAPTER 31

There were only two things stopping Dantalion from immediately returning to the Jorgenson estate on Neptune Island.

First, he was unarmed. He'd lost both the Beretta and the Glock in the water. He didn't doubt that he could take a weapon from one of the two-bit guards the Jorgensons had in their employment, but then there was the second thing.

It was as if half of the Martin County Sheriff's Office had turned out, along with officers from Miami PD, and he was pretty sure that some of the men and women in stylish business suits were FBI. There were even officers from a Hostage Rescue Team in attendance, dressed in black jumpsuits, helmets and armed with assault rifles. Add to that the proliferation of CSI technicians, ambulances from Hobe Sound and Jupiter, and various other supporting agencies, and the estate was a no-go area for the foreseeable future.

Or was it?

A man of his abilities could wander among so many people who were not used to working together in such numbers and he would be missed among the throng. Hide in plain sight. Become one of them. Look like he had the right to be there.

Except he was soaked through and did not have a change of clothing. He'd dumped his backpack with his kit prior to the assault on Bradley Jorgenson's house. Though it freed him up to move more easily during the anticipated gun battle, he had never intended leaving his bag behind, expecting to be able to kill them all and return for his bag at leisure. But then came the high-speed car chase, his subsequent near drowning, and the termination of the fisherman. It wasn't until he returned to the truck and drove away – passing the first blue lights and sirens hurtling towards the island – that he'd recognised his error. Right now his bag and clothing would be in the hands of a CSI tech, sealed in an evidence bag and en route to the nearest lab for forensic examination. They'd find DNA, hair fibres and other trace evidence, but that didn't concern him. They'd tie the forensics to some of the hits he'd carried out, but that was all. They wouldn't be able to pin the evidence on him.

Not unless he was caught.

And that wasn't going to happen.

More worrying was the laptop he'd left at Petre Jorgenson's house. He didn't doubt that Gabe Wellborn had taken precautions to ensure that the transactions he'd performed through that computer couldn't be easily traced. But to be sure, Dantalion would have preferred to have destroyed the damn thing entirely after Gabe had transferred the halfmillion dollars into his offshore account. That account was a numbered account only, and the Bahamian bank that he used wasn't famous for bending to the demands of the American law enforcement community.

The FBI had some very clever computer wizards. No doubt about it, somewhere, someone would break the codes. It would show his history; maybe even lead back to his true identity. After that he would be forever on the run. Not that they would find him. Jean-Paul St Pierre would simply cease to exist.

On top of the money he'd already earned from previous jobs, the half-million dollars would make him a wealthy man. He could go anywhere. But that wasn't even a consideration right now. He still had a mission to complete.

He'd driven the truck north to get past any road blocks the police might put up. A little part of him had hoped to intercept Bradley Jorgenson on his return to the island, but he knew that there was a only a small chance of that happening.

Approaching Hobe Sound on the Southeast Dixie Highway, he looked for an appropriate place to turn off. He found it after a couple of minutes and angled the vehicle down a cross street that headed inland towards the Jonathon Dickinson

State Park. He was looking for somewhere secluded, a place he could rest up and consider his next move. Somewhere to dry out his book.

The road wound through a picture of suburban tranquillity. Beautiful houses in beautiful gardens snoozed away the night-time hours, at rest and at peace with the world. Inside families young and old would be sleeping, dreaming their dreams and murmuring in contentment. No one would expect a professional killer to come to Aurora Village, let alone take up temporary residence there.

The village ended abruptly, giving way to swamp and scrub lands. Irrigation – or more likely drainage – channels had been formed at intervals along the way, and he found himself on a dirt track and series of short wooden bridges. His tyres bumped over the wood, making a double thump like a faltering heartbeat. He could smell the swamp, the cloying odours of decaying vegetation and stagnant water, but thought the smell could be coming from his soaked clothes and body. Sea salt had invaded his clothing and his skin had begun to itch.

To his left he noted the squat silhouettes of buildings. Agriculture wasn't the largest industry here, but the buildings looked like some kind of farm. He found a turning off the track and drove the truck into it. It was little more than a series of ruts and potholes and he decided this probably wasn't the main route to the farm. Nevertheless, he switched off his headlights so that he approached in darkness. He didn't want to alert anyone to his arrival until it was on his terms.

He stopped the vehicle a hundred yards short of the buildings, turned off the engine and slipped out the door. He didn't close the door fully, only pushed it gently to. Then he moved towards the buildings at a steady lope. The bullet wound in his leg was knitting, but with each step it felt like his skin cracked open. Ordinarily such a minor wound wouldn't be a distraction, but now it made him chew his lips against the pain. The limp became more pronounced the nearer he got to the buildings.

In his black clothing, his face stark and smudged with blood, hair hanging in colourless ribbons, he felt like a B-movie vampire skulking through the night. Not a bad image – it would strike fear in the hearts of those he might come across. Fear would be his greatest weapon.

He scanned the buildings. Two were little more than lean-tos, while one was an enclosed barn. There were a couple of adobe-style outhouses and then a small, single-storey house. The house was adobe as well, more like those he'd seen in Santa Fe than those indigenous to this part of Florida. He was approaching from the back of the house, but he got the impression of large windows in all the rooms. Because of its remote location, with no discernible neighbours, the drapes hadn't been drawn when the occupants had retired for the

245

evening. The only light he could see was from a dull bulb in a porch at the rear door.

It was hot here through the day, so he could guarantee that the house was temperature-controlled by A/C units. For them to work to their best ability, windows and doors would be kept shut during the sultry hours of the night. Shut but not necessarily locked.

The obvious door to try would be the back door. People who lived and worked in the area of the outbuildings would use that door on a regular basis. The front door would hardly ever be unlocked. Still, he bypassed the rear of the property to fully reconnoitre the building. When he got to the front of the house, it was in darkness. His peek through the large picture window showed a simple living space with sturdy wooden furniture and an old-fashioned stereo built into a cabinet. Trinkets adorned shelves on the wall. Framed photographs lined one wall, but in the darkness he couldn't make them out. Portraits for sure; sons and daughters and grandkids, more than likely.

Continuing round the far edge of the building, he found a car port. It housed only one vehicle, a Dodge pick-up, dusty and scraped from hard toil in the fields. He found the door unlocked and opened it. No alarm. He wasn't expecting one: an alarm or central locking would have armed itself by now and made the doors secure. He searched the interior for a weapon, but there was nothing. He did note something, though. The driver's seat was misshapen and tattered, but the passenger seat was as smooth as the day it came off the assembly line. Only one person ever rode this vehicle. No Mrs Farmer to contend with inside the house. Whoever lived here did so alone.

He poked around on the back of the flat-bed, and came away with a large lug wrench from a box of tools. Heavy and blunt, it was a formidable weapon. He also took a screwdriver that he pushed into his waistband. It wasn't dagger quality but it could still be rammed through flesh if the need arose.

As he made his way past the front of the house the scene hadn't changed. The lights were still off, the living room devoid of life. He kept going, gained the back of the house once more. Gnats swarmed on the screen of the porch, seeking the light bulb within. Dantalion opened the screen very slowly so that it didn't squeak, then stepped inside, accompanied by many of the darting insects. Some of them batted off his features and clung to his hair and he shivered involuntarily. He wiped them away. He turned the door handle. Felt resistance. The person inside was security conscious after all. But that was a good thing, could mean he also had what Dantalion had come seeking.

He took the screwdriver out of his waistband, inserted it alongside the lock and levered against the frame, gradually forcing open the door. The lock was as much use as nothing when the door frame was made of weathered wood. He was happy that the noise of his breaking and entering was minimal, that it wouldn't have woken even the lightest of sleepers. He stepped inside. A utility area with a stack of laundry waiting for the iron greeted him. Chequered shirts and jeans, a pair of tan nylon trousers, socks and underwear of a conservative type. His assumption of a single occupant was taking on more validity. An older man, judging by the style of clothes. He picked up the nylon trousers – a fashion faux pas to anyone under the age of fifty – and checked the size. Not that he was planning on wearing them himself; he wanted to get a picture of the man he would have to kill. They were narrow around the waist, short in the leg. Small, skinny bastard, then? He selected one of the shirts and found that it was surprisingly bulky. Who was this guy, Dantalion wondered, a goddamn ape?

There was only one way to find out. He went through into a kitchen. It had only the most basic of utilities. Cooker and hob. Sink with a couple of neatly stacked dishes on the draining board. One cup ringed with coffee stains waiting to be washed under the faucet. A drawer in a cupboard disclosed silverware. Dantalion took out a heavy-bladed bread knife. It was better for stabbing than the screwdriver, and he kept it fisted in his right hand.

Moving towards the living area, he passed an upright vacuum cleaner standing in the hall. Ambient light came in through the front door so he avoided tripping over the pipe that lay at his feet like the coils of a boa constrictor. On his right now was the living room. He gave it only cursory attention, then turned to the door on his left.

He listened, an ear to the door.

From within came the tell-tale sounds of snoring. Just a light buzz, but it did appear to be from only one person. He tried the handle and the door swung silently inwards. He stepped inside and squared his feet on the carpet. The figure lying on his back beneath a sheet didn't even stir. Dantalion was a child of the night; his condition had ensured that, so he had no problems with the darkness. He could make out the man's sleep-relaxed features where they poked from beneath the sheet. Younger than he'd thought. The man had a shaved head and a thin moustache that hooked round the corners of his mouth. One shoulder looked muscular where the sheet had dropped away. Strong, farm strong, but maybe something to do with gymnasiums and heavy weights, too. Could be a handful in a hand-to-hand tussle.

A quick stab to the carotid artery would do it.

No. The man would wake, thrash about, his blood jetting around the room, growing less with each failing heartbeat.

Maybe not the best way to kill him.

Club him senseless with the lug wrench, then cut his throat? Less thrashing but still copious amounts of blood.

A single stab to the heart would be best. Very little blood if the heart died instantly. The only problem with that was he couldn't be sure of an immediate hit. The man had a sheet over his upper torso and it appeared one of his arms was draped across his chest. It would mean lifting the sheet to get a clear view. If the man woke up there would surely be a fight.

Choices, choices, Dantalion thought, always choices.

And with each choice a myriad tangents to choose from.

The man muttered in his sleep. Maybe some primal instinct was warning him about the presence of danger hovering so close by.

Maybe I should let him choose how to die, Dantalion thought.

But no. This killing wasn't for pleasure.

Dantalion lifted the lug wrench with his left hand. Brought it down in a sweeping arch. It struck the man's head on the left temple, making a deep depression in the skull above his ear. That could prove a killing blow in itself. The man's eyes shot open, but his pupils didn't contract, they stayed wide and bewildered. He didn't even see the knife that Dantalion drove through his chest. And that wound definitely did kill him.

Dantalion leaned over and flicked on the bedside lamp. Pearlescent light shone. He pulled back the sheet until it snagged against the shaft of steel protruding from the man's chest. Just left of dead centre. Dantalion smiled at his precise stab. But he still needed a gun. He was going up against men who had guns and he had to at least even his chances of a fair fight.

He checked the bedside table. No gun.

He checked the closet but found only more of those plaid shirts and jeans. Another pair of cream nylon trousers, too. These were sheathed in plastic, as though kept for best. He took them out and saw that the leg length was much longer than the worn pair in the utility area. These hadn't seen a trip to a seamstress yet. He held them alongside his own legs and found that they stopped a full inch above his ankles, but though he'd probably look like Pee-Wee Herman they would do at a push. He set them on the bed at the foot of the mattress. He selected the less gaudy of the shirts, pale blue with a white plaid. There was also a battered stetson on a shelf at the top of the cupboard. That joined his growing pile of clothes. He found socks too. He'd be going commando, however; no way was he going to wear the man's underwear.

He drew the knife from the man's chest, wiped it clean on the sheet, and then threw the remainder of the sheet over the man's ceiling-staring face. Taking the pile of clothes he went in search of the shower.

On his way he dipped his head into the living room. Glancing around, he noticed a wooden chest pressed up against the wall below the photographs.

Switching on the overhead light, he placed his supplies on a worn couch and approached the chest. It was held closed by a flimsy hasp and cheap padlock. One smack of the lug wrench was all it took to break off the lock. He threw back the lid.

He bared his teeth in a grin of pleasure as his eyes took in the contents.

CHAPTER 32

As dawn broke over the Atlantic, Harvey headed north-west towards Tampa. He took the Ford and he also took Marianne. Harvey was one of only two people on the planet that I felt easy handing the girl over to. The other, Rink, was already in San Francisco. He called to tell me he'd be on his way back as soon as his parents stopped hugging him. I asked him to hug his mum for me. For my part, I had another job to do. Several, actually, but all involving locating Bradley Jorgenson and delivering him to the safe house where Marianne would be waiting.

While I waited for my rental car to be delivered, I took a run through the state park. A tourist pamphlet in the motel room said that there were more than four and a half miles of trails through the swamps and hummocks of brush. By the time I was finished I'd have covered twice that distance. I needed the exercise. In my line of work you have to remain at a peak level of fitness. All being equal in other areas, it was always the man with the greatest endurance and conditioning who would win a fight. I pushed myself hard. My lungs laboured for the first mile, but then I settled into a rhythm and my breathing evened out so that I was running at a steady gait and my breathing came easy.

Finding myself on a stretch of sand overlooking the ocean, I stopped for a while. I watched the sun come up while performing a yoga 'sun salutation', stretching my muscles and limbering up. I dropped and pushed off two hundred press-ups and the same number of crunches. Then I spent ten minutes going through a series of prearranged patterns of movement that involved punching, kicking, and elbow and knee strikes. Nothing fancy; not karate or t'ai chi or anything so flamboyant. The moves I did were short and brutal and designed along the lines of a simple equation: minimum effort x maximum impact = devastating effect.

Sweating like a pig in a sauna, I ran back through the swamp, detoured so I completed the course again, then headed back to the motel room. My rental was waiting for me, and I signed an assumed name and showed the delivery guy a fake driver's licence courtesy of Harvey Lucas.

Taking the keys for the imported Audi A8 from him, I went inside and immediately checked that my SIG Sauer was where I'd left it inside a tissue box stuffed behind the TV.

Dripping from my workout, I went into the bathroom and turned on the shower. Then I stripped out of my damp clothes and stepped gratefully under the hot water. My muscles were pumped with blood from the exercise, and I relaxed under the steaming flow, working the kinks out of my body with a soaped-up sponge. When I stepped out of the shower my mind was back on the job.

I slipped into fresh boxer shorts and pulled on a pair of crisp denims that clung to my damp body. Shirtless, I retrieved my SIG from its hiding place and sat on the bed to clean it. I had rags and oil and I stripped down the gun so that I had all the working parts laid out on the bed. When I was done, I inserted a full clip, racked the slide so that I was good to go. Police forces the world over teach a method of safe gun handling. They absolutely will not condone carrying a gun with a bullet in the firing chamber. In case of lawsuits, that was. Or to avoid a fumbling cop shooting off his toes. I come from a different school of thought and practise a method called 'point shooting'. A bit like the quick-draw heroes from Western movies, I could draw, point and fire in an instant. The thinking behind the system was that there should be no natural wastage of time. And it would be a waste of a precious second if I had to rack a bullet into place before I fired. In that time I could already be dead.

The SIG I used was specially modified so that there were no safety switch or sights on the barrel to snag on my clothing. It was a steel-bodied blow-back model that barely recoiled in the fist. Handy when the 9 mm soft-nosed Parabellums it fired were a powerful enough load to stop most men in their tracks. I didn't want a gun that I had to constantly fight to control and to retarget after every shot.

Harvey had brought plenty of spare ammunition. He'd also supplied me with a military issue Ka-bar knife coated in black epoxy. Finally, there was a new pay-and-go mobile phone for use during the operation ahead.

I caught sight of myself in a mirror at the back of the room. Most people would see a taller than average man on his way to forty years old, but with the hard body of someone ten years younger. They'd see the short brown hair with only a hint of grey at the temples and the eyes that flashed between blue and green depending on my mood. They'd notice the tattoo on my right shoulder and wonder what it represented. Only if they looked close enough would they notice the story of my life etched into my skin in the form of a tapestry of scars that I'd picked up during fourteen years as a counterterrorism officer and the four years since. On my right pectoral muscle is a tiny white indentation where I was shot when on patrol in Northern Ireland. The scar where the bullet exited formed a puckered mass of scar tissue an inch or so from the tattoo.

I touched a more recent scar, running my fingers over the pink ridge in my chest just to the left of my heart. That was courtesy of a fight with an ex-Secret Service agent named Martin Maxwell who had taken to killing people and stripping bones from their corpses. The bones he took to Jubal's Hollow, his secret repository in the Mojave Desert. Maxwell, dubbed the Harvestman by the FBI, made a mistake when he took my brother, John. I hunted the bastard down and rammed one of those bones into his throat. He got me good, though, and it was pure chance that he missed my heart and found only the meat of my pectoral muscle.

Thinking of the Harvestman, I couldn't help but draw parallels between him and this latest maniac I was up against. Why was it that they had to take assumed names? And often from the Bible? Martin Maxwell had believed himself Tubal Cain reincarnated, and now I had some lunatic who thought he had fallen from Heaven with Lucifer and his crew. Well, he'd certainly taken a fall, rammed off the bridge at Neptune Island and sent to a watery hell in the sea below.

Ever the pessimist, though, I had to admit that I hadn't seen him die. He could still be out there someplace. With that in mind I pushed the SIG into my waistband at the back and felt around for fresh socks. I pulled on my boots – still dusty from my run – then slipped the Ka-bar alongside my right ankle. A plain black V-neck T, with a loose canvas jacket over the top of that. It was too warm for outerwear but I needed something to cover the bulge that my SIG made at the small of my back. I had a licence to carry, but not in my real name. Fundamentally the cops were on the same side as I was, but it wouldn't stop them running me in if they realised the licence was as bogus as the name on it.

A man of many resources, Harvey had already paid the bill for the room. But I still had to hand back the keys before leaving. Pulling all my belongings into a pile, I shoved them into a plastic bin liner and knotted the top. I slung them on the back seat on passing the Audi then went and deposited the key to the room through a flap provided. Then I got in the car, and headed back towards the Dixie Highway. I watched the totem pole grow small in the rear-view mirror as I pulled away.

The Dixie Highway went through Hobe Sound. It was still early, not yet eight o'clock, and the road wasn't so busy. There were only a few people out on the palm-lined streets. Out of Hobe Sound the road hugged the coast. A short distance later, I found the turnpike that allowed me on to the road that traversed first Jupiter then Neptune Islands.

As I drove I watched the boats sailing up and down the Inter-Coastal Waterway. The sea was turquoise against pale sand. In places I could see all the way to the bottom. The sky was equally clear with only a haze on the southern horizon that wasn't cloud but pollution from the cities of Miami and Miami Beach. A mile overhead a passenger plane headed out over the ocean, and

I imagined holidaymakers with glum faces as they took their last look down on paradise. They wouldn't think it was paradise if they knew what had gone on down here the evening before.

Arriving at Neptune, I slowed the Audi and pulled into a layover next to a picnic area. There were already families in attendance, but they were too busy enjoying the scenery and glorious weather to pay attention to a lone man making a telephone call. Harvey was driving so it was Marianne Dean who answered. She put the call on speakerphone so that the two of them could listen.

'I hope Harvey's treating you well, Mari?' I said, to keep things light between us. Purposely I used the name she wished to go by; a way of reassuring her that I was fully on her side.

'Don't worry, Joe, Harvey's being the perfect gentleman.' Her voice sounded musical, like some of the worry had been expunged from her soul. I only hoped my next question wouldn't send her two steps backwards.

'What has hit the news about last night, Harve?'

Harvey grunted. 'World War Three, the way the networks are handling things.'

'Anything specific?'

'If you're asking if the shooter has turned up, the answer's no. But some old guy was found floating nearby the crash scene. Unless he was unlucky and the Lincoln landed on him, I think Dantalion did the poor sap in.'

'What was he doing out there?'

'At a guess? Fishing. And before you ask, the water's too deep for wading; he had to have had a boat with him. Looks like Dantalion survived. Worse than that, he got clean away.'

We should have made sure. It's a pity Rink didn't get to put a couple rounds in his ugly face for good measure before pushing him into the sea.

But, the news didn't exactly surprise me.

'So he's still out there,' I said. 'But if we were right about Gabe Wellborn being his handler, then I'm guessing he's been cut free. He has no support network to back him up.'

'Has to be resilient enough,' Harvey said, 'surviving the crash and getting away. I don't think he's about to crawl away and hide under a rock someplace. He's probably got himself holed up somewhere and is planning his next move.'

'OK,' I said. 'This is what we're going to do. You go ahead with getting Marianne to the safe house; I'm going to try to get hold of Bradley. I don't trust that asshole Seagram to protect him. Only way that piece of shit would stop a bullet would be if he tripped over his own feet and fell into the line of fire.'

'Can help you there,' Harvey said. 'We spoke to Bradley a few minutes ago. Marianne guessed where he'd be. A motel they used to use when they were first seeing one another.'

In the background I heard Marianne saying something about their rendezvous all being innocent, that they'd only meet there then go on to some movie or bar.

'Where is he?' I asked.

'On his way back to Neptune by now. We caught him on his way out. Tried to convince him to keep well away but he wasn't having any of it.'

'Idiot,' I said.

'He has to be concerned,' Marianne said in his defence. 'Don't forget that we're talking about his home. His family.'

Yeah, I thought. The same family who were trying their damnedest to kill Bradley and her off. I went on, 'The place will be swarming with cops. It's not going to be easy getting in touch with him.'

Then Marianne chipped in, 'I can always give you his phone number.'

'He's carrying a cell?'

'No, I don't think so. We spoke to him on the motel phone. But if he's home I can give you a direct line through to his private office.'

'Sounds good.'

Marianne reeled off the number and I memorised it to put into my phone's address book later.

'OK, guys, I'll let you get on with your bit. I'll ring you when I know what's happening. Watch your backs. If this crazy is still out there we've no idea where he'll pop up next.'

'Don't worry,' Harvey said. 'Next time there'll be no mistakes.'

'Yeah,' I said. My own sentiment exactly.

'Take it easy, Hunter.'

'Yeah, look after Marianne.'

Marianne had her say. 'Please be careful, Joe. And bring Bradley safely back to me.'

'I will,' I promised and pressed the button to end the call.

Then I stabbed in the number that Marianne had narrated.

The ringtone came back at me. And kept on coming.

Deciding I was a little premature in ringing Bradley, I got out of the car and stretched my limbs. From where I was standing I could see the beginning of the Jorgenson estate. The wall that encompassed the landward side of the grounds was a smudge on the horizon. Beyond it I could just make out a hint of the first of the family homes beyond it. A steepled roof with turrets at each corner. But the heat haze was building, so the turrets could simply have been a play of the shifting light.

Quite a large number of tourists were about now. Some had brought blankets. Some had fishing poles and were wandering across the sand dunes that swayed with saw-tooth grass, heading towards the inlet. Others came armed with binoculars, and I thought that there was an inordinate number of ornithologists unless some pretty special birds lived hereabouts. A noisy group of college-aged guys played volleyball on a stretch of open sand. Some of them had bottles of beer in their hands and were posturing for the young women who watched them from their beach towels. I had no beer; I'd brought mineral water with me and I slaked my thirst directly from the bottle.

I should have thought to ask Marianne how far away Bradley's motel was. It would have given me a clearer idea of how long he would be on the road. I didn't even know which direction he'd be coming from. When they'd taken off last night, Seagram had driven north. But the motel could have been in any direction. My plan was to cut him off before he arrived back at the estate and take him back to Marianne. Then the problem posed by Dantalion's apparent survival could be dealt with without the encumbrance of someone I had to protect along for the ride. With that in mind, my obvious recourse would be to park up next to the main entrance gate, but that would likely bring the police down on me in seconds. They'd have been there all night, and there would be more coming and going throughout all of this day, and perhaps many more to come. A strange vehicle with a gun-toting driver would raise the eyebrow of any cop worth his salt.

I decided to wait where I was.

I had a good view of the road, and would recognise the silver sedan Bradley and Seagram had taken off in the night before. If by chance I didn't see them, I'd ring the number for his office on each quarter-hour. I hoped to have made contact by mid-morning at the latest.

While I waited I watched the traffic heading south. I didn't bother with those coming towards me, as none of them would have Bradley on board. Streams of vehicles drove by, some stopped at the layover, but none was a silver Lincoln. I tried Bradley's number. No answer. A quarter-hour and about two hundred vehicles later, and I tried it again. Still no answer.

I wondered if Seagram was clever enough to ditch the sedan and bring Bradley home in a less conspicuous vehicle. Something like an older model station wagon or the black truck with tinted windows I watched sail past. But then I recalled his panic from last night and decided he wasn't fully suited to his chosen career. He would drive the sedan back, because that was what bodyguards drove when they had an important passenger.

Trying the number again, someone picked up. A female voice. Officious. Cop, I thought, and hung up quickly.

It didn't surprise me that the police were in Bradley's office. They'd be trying to make sense of the mayhem that had gone down at two of Bradley Jorgenson's homes, plus that of his cousin Petre, and would quickly tie the family business dealings to the attempts made on their lives. Police officers would be going through the records in Bradley's office in an attempt at identifying who had attacked the houses.

I regretted standing outside the gate when we first arrived, challenging security by shouting

264

angrily at the CCTV camera. The cops would likely be reviewing those recordings right now. Two angry guys demanding entrance, obviously armed and pissed off, would be immediate suspects. Rink's image and mine would be flashing across country to the FBI VICAP HQ at Quantico to try to identify us from their store of mugshots. Not that they'd find us there, but someone with a bit of savvy might think to interrogate military records, and that would finally give us up.

Hindsight's a wonderful thing.

CHAPTER 33

The wooden chest in the dead man's living room disgorged its secrets.

It would have been nice to have discovered a cache of weapons but what he found instead were the makings of a disguise that could get him close to Bradley Jorgenson. Each item he lifted out was folded neatly, preserved within layers of tissue paper the way some couples preserved their wedding suits and dresses. Not that the man he'd killed in his bed ever appeared to have been married. Not to a woman at any rate. But he had been married to his career. The love and care with which he'd saved his uniform indicated that. As did the proliferation of photographs that showed him standing alone, or with groups of colleagues, proudly grinning towards the camera.

Dantalion wondered where things had gone wrong for the dead man. Perhaps he'd been injured, or had become sick, or merely grown jaded with the day-to-day, but he seemed to have taken early retirement from his career. He guessed that the man must have left on good terms, otherwise he might have destroyed his uniform in protest.

The uniform was complete. Even down to belts and equipment.

The only things missing were the tools of his office, but Dantalion believed a more thorough search would turn them up.

The trousers might present a problem, the man being shorter in the leg than Dantalion, but he saw a way round that. The shirts might be a little large, but he only had to fool Jorgenson long enough to take him out and then he wouldn't be concerned by how many people saw through the disguise.

First, though, he had to get out of his wet clothes. Take a shower. He had no hydrocortisone cream with him to salve his itching skin, but he hoped the dead man would have moisturising lotions of some kind in his bathroom. And he didn't know of a farm that didn't possess a rudimentary first-aid kit. Or weapons, he reminded himself. There were always guns on a farm.

He had a tepid shower. Not hot, his skin was too raw. Then he dried off with the softest towel he could find. He dabbed body lotion over the exposed areas of skin on his face and hands, but decided that the rest of his body would be fine as long as he kept covered up and away from direct sunlight. He found antiseptic cream in the same bathroom cupboard and cleaned his bullet wounds. The wounds on his arm and cheek were inconsequential. However, the one on his leg was particularly angry-looking, the flesh at the edges red and swollen like collagen-plump lips. He wondered briefly about the effects the infection could be having on his system. But he discarded the notion. Mind over matter.

Then he set to his hair with a pair of scissors, trimming the long strands into a crew cut. His hair was sparse and tufted in places, and he'd never survive a thorough inspection, but with the hat in place the haircut would suffice.

With the same scissors, he unpicked the hems on the trouser legs, letting them down a full inch. Not too bad, he thought, but tucked them into the tops of his boots all the same. With the shirt on, he folded the back over twice and tucked it into the waistband of his trousers, cinched it in place with a thin leather belt. On went a clip-on tie. The collar sagged a little, and he looked like someone who'd been on a drastic diet and hadn't gotten round to replacing his wardrobe yet, but over all he didn't look too bad. He pulled on the jacket and adjusted the wide-brimmed hat to a jaunty angle, admiring himself in a mirror on the bathroom wall. The mark on his jaw was only a graze, not that noticeable if he kept his chin tucked down.

He found a utility closet. Cleaning fluids and brushes and rags were stacked in boxes. On a shelf at head height he found a strong box. Next to it a key. When he popped the lock he found what he'd been looking for.

The gun was a Taurus 85, a five-shot revolver.

One of the .38 calibre specials worn by some law enforcement officers as a backup weapon. There were two rapid loaders filled with standard .38 bullets. This time he wouldn't be conducting a full-on assault on the Jorgenson estate, so ten rounds would be sufficient.

He couldn't find a holster, so assumed the dead man had kept this gun purely for home defence. Not that it had proved much use, locked in a metal container two rooms away from where he'd died. Dantalion loaded the revolver, then slipped it into his jacket pocket alongside the spare rapid loader.

Then he saw to the most pressing task of all.

His book.

When he opened it, he found that the sea water miraculously hadn't invaded the interior beyond a broad margin. Most of his lists of numbers were still legible. The ink had spread a little, causing an auric light effect around the figures, but that made the numbers seem ethereal and magical and somewhat to his liking. Only the final numbers troubled him. They told a lie. The three he'd written down pertaining to Bradley, Marianne, and Hunter held no power. He could offset that by entering the numbers of those he'd killed since: Petre Jorgenson, Gabe Wellborn and upward of half-a-dozen bodyguards, but that could throw off the value of the figures. The numerology system he used demanded that he be exact at all times. The three he'd already written down must die before he could tally the others' numbers.

In the pantheon of the Fallen, Dantalion is the seventy-first spirit. He is a great and mighty duke, who governs thirty-six legions of spirits. A legion is a subjective figure, whichever way you look at it. In ancient Rome, a legion was a division of soldiers numbering between three and six thousand. That would give Dantalion dominion over the spirits of between 108,000 and 216,000 people. However you approached those figures, it was an unattainable sum for any single killer without the power of an army behind him, or his finger on the button of a nuclear arsenal.

But numerology is flexible. Dantalion had found that by adding up each victim's personally calculated three-digit number, he was quickly approaching those kinds of figures. Once his targets were dead, and he added those from earlier, he'd only need another few victims to be truly treading in the original Dantalion's shoes.

He used a hairdryer from the bathroom to dry the book off. Inevitably the paper had warped along the edges, but again it added to the esoteric look of the book. He swathed it in cling film – just in case. The silver chain was tarnished, but that was OK. The antique look was all the rage. He clipped the free end of the chain to a belt loop and fed the book into his opposite jacket pocket.

Then he lay down on the bed next to the dead man and fell asleep. When he awoke, he ate food from the refrigerator. Not that he was hungry, but he had to keep up his strength. He chose some fast and some slow release carbohydrates and munched them without tasting them. Afterwards he couldn't recall what he'd eaten, but he had a full stomach and was ready to go.

He checked himself out in the mirror again. His clothes were rumpled from the nap, but that made them look like authentic work clothes, and not some he'd taken fully pressed from a storage chest.

He left the lug wrench and screwdriver, but the knife could still prove handy, so he wrapped it in a cloth and took it with him when he left the house. He went out the same way he entered, and was surprised to find that it was dawn, and mist was rising from the surrounding fields and swamps as the early-morning sunshine set to burning off the dew.

He crossed the yard past the outbuildings and approached the truck where he'd abandoned it in the lane. Checking inside, he found that some of his supplies were still there – not everything had been dumped during his assault on Neptune Island – and saw that his plan for taking Bradley Jorgenson was even more viable than before.

The truck started first try. Rather than trying to reverse it the length of the rutted trail, he drove into the rear courtyard of the farm, turned round, then headed out the way he'd come, making his way back through Aurora Village and seeking the highway.

As far as Bradley Jorgenson knew, yesterday's attacker was now sleeping with the fishes and no further threat. Under those circumstances, the man would want to return home to survey the damage caused and to murmur condolences to the families and friends of those killed. He'd also have to face the questions of the police investigators on the scene. Dantalion would be waiting for him.

He picked up the Dixie Highway, then the coast road and approached the island from the north. The roadblocks he anticipated weren't there. In all likelihood, they were busy looking for him at the crash scene. Cautious though, he watched for anyone following behind, anyone in front of him. He also looked for a silver sedan, skimming his eyes over vehicles parked on layovers along the way, watching for unmarked police cars. He didn't see anything. A black Audi A8 parked on a wide layover caught his eye, but it looked too immaculate to be a government-financed vehicle. Probably belonged to a businessman on the commute to Miami who'd stopped to enjoy a few minutes of peace and quiet before joining the Babel of the big city.

He continued south, driving adjacent to the wall that enclosed the estate. Parked opposite the main entrance was a group of assorted vehicles. They reminded him of newsreel footage he'd seen of hippy caravans that traversed the country in the late 1960s. Vans back then were decorated with flowers and 'peace' symbols and antiwar slogans. These vehicles were equally emblazoned, but the signs on these vans and cars declared affiliation to a greater movement than flower power. These were agents of the new media-hungry age, and the writing showed the names of their respective TV or radio stations.

Turning off the road, he wound his way through the assembled vehicles, parking up furthest away from the highway. Stepping out of the truck he settled his hat on his head, shadowing his face with a tilt of the brim. No one took much notice of him, and no one questioned why he hadn't arrived in an official vehicle.

A TV crew were passing the time of day in sarcastic banter while awaiting entry to the estate and he touched the brim of his hat in greeting. Eyes skimmed over him, but no one approached him for a comment. Leaving the throng behind, he approached the highway and started directing other arriving vehicles on to the layover, looking fully part of the scene in his Florida National Parks Warden's uniform. The cops guarding entry to the Jorgenson estate didn't give him as much as a sour look.

Within fifteen minutes he was just background, and went unnoticed as he walked away along the road, seeking a way into the grounds. When he'd checked out the area yesterday morning, he'd been concerned about CCTV cameras and motion detectors and pressure pads, but with the exception of the cameras all would now have been isolated. There were too many interlopers present

273

for the security devices to be viable. Also, no one would be expecting him to wander inside among dozens of police officers, so the cameras wouldn't be scrutinised as thoroughly as before. In fact, anyone watching the cameras would be concentrating on recordings from the previous evening.

A five-minute stroll found him a good distance along the wall. He found an empty oil drum partly concealed in the long grass on the untended no man's land between the wall and the highway. He dragged it upright, then rolled it end over end so that the accumulated sand and vegetation spilled out. Then he set the drum upright against the wall. Just a warden looking after the countryside. He waited for a break in the traffic. When it came, he hopped up on to the drum, then reached upwards and got a grip on the top of the wall. He was over it in seconds.

Striking out across the grounds, he headed for Bradley Jorgenson's house. He strolled like he was at home there and he went unchallenged.

He touched the book in his pocket.

Keen to rebalance the total.

CHAPTER 34

Pushing on down the coast road, I quickly discovered that the next layover was full to capacity with TV and radio crews. Space was at such a premium that a State Park warden had been drafted in to keep the traffic in order. Any vehicles that did not belong to the media were waved on by the curt man in the stupid hat.

Driving south, I looked for somewhere to park in solitude.

There were plenty of wide, sandy parking bays along the way, but each one had an abundance of tourists' vehicles already encamped on the parking lots, their occupants disgorged across the saw-grass above the beach, or walking on the sands themselves. A regatta of boats made its way through the Inter-Coastal Waterway and I understood why there was so much activity. The crowds had turned out to watch some sort of big boat race.

I finally found a spot to myself. I drove off the road and on to the grass itself. The Audi was equipped with a four-wheel-drive function, so I wasn't concerned about bogging down in the soft ground.

I tried Bradley's office number again but the phone was answered by the same brisk-voiced woman.

'Who is this?' she demanded when I kept my silence.

I hung up. It was time to call in a few favours.

Dialling a number that was committed to my memory, I waited while the call was shunted through various relays. It was some time before the call was picked up and I was asked to punch in a numeric sequence on my phone. I was asked to confirm the number, which I did, then was transferred to another telephone at the CIA headquarters, up the coast in Virginia.

Already a member of the British Special Forces, I had been drafted into a specialist counterterrorism team that pulled on the finest soldiers from across all the member countries of the United Nations. Rink belonged to the same unit. We were ultimately governed by our commanders at a base codenamed 'Arrowsake' after one of the locations where William Melville, head of the original British Secret Service Bureau, allegedly trained his new recruits in the fight against Nazi spies. However, because we were formed from the consolidation of a number of allies, we had facilitators in each country. My handler in the US was Walter Hayes Conrad IV, a Sub-Division Controller of the CIA.

When the face of modern terrorism changed post 9/11, so did the methods of fighting the war. Public relations campaigns and scrutinising bank accounts became more important than assaults on terrorist enclaves. In some eyes my unit were dinosaurs and belonged buried in history. Our fate was sealed, as the original dinosaurs' had been. I retired shortly before my unit was disbanded. Our handlers were absorbed back into their own security communities. Most of them still held great influence; as did Walter.

'I need a favour, Walter.'

'Why do you only ever call when you want something, Hunter?'

'Because I know you'll always come through.'

'Flattery, as you should know, will get you nowhere.'

'Better flattery than blackmail, huh?'

Walter owed me big time. For one, I had been instrumental in stopping the rogue Secret Service agent, Martin Maxwell, who had managed to stay one step ahead of those hunting him. More than that though, I'd kept the name of Tubal Cain – the Harvestman – secret, avoiding a massive embarrassment to both Walter and the US Government. Tubal Cain had gone to his grave as Robert Swan, and I'd made no one any the wiser.

'So what is it you want?'

'Cooperation from the local feds,' I told him.

My location must have been thrown up on some sort of Global Positioning Satellite screen on his computer monitor.

'Martin County, Florida,' he confirmed to himself. 'What are you doing there?'

'Up until now? Not a whole lot of good,' I said.

'Tell me.'

I gave him the brief version.

'I heard about the explosion on Baker Island. Homeland Security flagged it up. Thought at first that it was some kind of terrorist attack on the rich and deserving. When it came to light it was a good ol' gas explosion it was thrown back to Miami PD. Then bodies started turning up and the FBI jumped on board.' Walter ruminated a moment. 'Now you're saying that a contract killer's involved and it's all to do with the Jorgenson pharmaceutical contracts with *our* military?'

'That's as much as we've gathered,' I agreed.

'And you're up to your neck in it as usual.'

'You know me, Walt. Never can keep my nose out of other people's business.'

'Not when there's a damsel in distress, eh?'

'Doesn't matter who is in distress,' I corrected.

'You want me to put men on it?' Walter asked. 'Catch this killer before he gets at your mark again?'

'Suit yourself; I'm not interested in the killer. It isn't personal this time. All I want is a green light to speak with Bradley Jorgenson. The family estate is shut down as tight as a duck's ass. Can't think of a way to get in there without having to put some good people to sleep. I don't want to do that.'

'No, not a good idea, Hunter.' Walter tapped his

fingers. Thinking deeply. 'Can I ask you why you need to speak to the Jorgenson kid?'

'I want to get him out of there.'

'Why?'

'Because I promised his girlfriend that I would. He's not safe.'

'And you think you can protect him better than the police and FBI can?'

'Walt?'

'Yeah, I know. It was a stupid question.' He was tapping again, this time on a keyboard, and I guessed he was already on to someone in law enforcement. While he did that I told him what we'd patched together concerning Gabriel Wellborn and his network of contract killers named after the mythological fallen angels. I told him about Dantalion. Walter asked, 'But you don't know his true identity yet?'

'No. Only that he's decent at his job. I don't think he's military or police. He's, I don't know . . . different.'

'Self-taught?'

'Or privately taught. This guy looks weird. Very pale-skinned, white-haired, has some sort of condition with his skin?'

'Albino?'

'Perhaps, but I don't think so. Something else. But you might want to check historical medical records; it might throw up his identity.' I thought about the first time I'd seen Dantalion on Baker Island. 'He's also very good with disguises, Walter.

Maybe he has a background in theatre or the movie industry.'

'I'll pass all that on to the FBI,' Walter said. 'OK, all done. Go to the front gate; ask to speak with SAC Kaufman. He'll give you what you need.'

'Thanks, Walter.'

'Say nothing of it,' he said. To some that would be a throwaway remark. But I knew exactly what he meant. It was a reminder, and literal in its meaning. Say nothing of it. The Harvestman.

Pressing the end button, I pushed the phone in my jacket pocket. No sooner than I had done that than it vibrated and I pulled it out again. A text message from Harvey.

HOME AND DRY

Good, they'd made it back to the safe house. Time for me to get on with delivering Bradley there.

CHAPTER 35

There were obvious disadvantages to the disguise Dantalion had assumed on this occasion. For example, what was a State Park Warden's interest in the case? If anyone had thought to ask, or to scrutinise his uniform a little further, they'd have easily seen through the charade. He had no jurisdiction on the private estate, and would not be required to attend on official business or otherwise. On the other hand, his uniform was official, and therefore he was able to move among all the other officials without attracting undue questions. In fact, there were other advantages to his disguise. If, say, he had been wearing the uniform of a cop or medic, then maybe he would not have remained invisible for long. There were too many senior officers milling around throwing orders back and forth, demanding tasks from their people. But there were no other wardens in attendance. No one to question just who the hell he was, or what he was doing or to send him off on some errand that would divert him from his task.

By keeping his eyes averted and walking like

he had somewhere to be, he was able to go directly past officers from the local Sheriff's Department and towards Bradley Jorgenson's house. Commandos from the FBI Hostage Rescue Team had previously secured the area. With no viable threat evident, they had stood down. Dantalion saw a group of them standing around with their helmets off and their assault rifles slung from their shoulders. Talking and enjoying the sunshine. A couple of them smoked cigarettes round the side of the building, out of sight of their superiors. Most of the activity was carried out by ambulance crews and people from the Martin County Medical Examiner's Office. Apparently the thirteen-hours-old crime scene had been thoroughly picked through by the CSI technicians and had now been handed over to the men with the body bags.

Dantalion knew he'd be pushing his luck if he went inside the building, but his anonymity would be protected while in the grounds. As yet he wasn't even sure that Bradley had returned to the house. In fact, would it not be a better idea if Bradley went to another of the family houses where there hadn't been blood and mayhem? To one of the other family members who hadn't been in on the plot to have Bradley and Marianne murdered, for instance? That ruled out the houses of both Simon and Jack, but there were plenty of others to choose from. Was there a sympathetic aunt or uncle? Or would the officers in charge of the investigation have picked a house at random, commandeered it while they questioned Bradley and any other survivors about what had happened here?

He decided not to linger at either crime scene too long. The proliferation of law enforcement officers around both Bradley's and Petre Jorgenson's houses meant that the odds of blowing his cover were great. Though he'd remained invisible up until now, all it took was one eagle-eyed cop to challenge him, ask for identification, and that would be it. Contrary to all their faults as a collective beast, singly the officers were still trained professionals, and not to be underestimated.

Happy that there was no sign of the silver Lincoln sedan that Bradley and Seagram had made off in last night, he walked away. He headed northwards, towards the other half-dozen houses that lay strung out along the coast in that direction.

The next house belonged to Valentin's oldest sister, Hetti. Still a Jorgenson by birth, she now went by her deceased husband's name of Gorman. The family business meant little to her and she had made her own fortune in real estate. From the documentation supplied by Petre Jorgenson when he still remained Dantalion's client, he knew that Hetti kept herself aloof from the squabble between Valentin and her nephews. Aloof and unsympathetic; he doubted that Bradley would seek her out for comfort or support. Nevertheless he checked around her property for signs of the sedan, but it wasn't parked there either. He continued.

Christened Jan Jorgenson, but taking the Americanised form of John for the purpose of the business, Bradley's youngest cousin had always been referred to by the less formal name of Jack. His family home was next in line. He had no wife or children, and the house was somewhat excessive for the single man.

Simon, his brother, five years older at twenty-eight, did have a wife and a baby girl. However, the wife had taken the baby girl along with an out-of-court settlement of twenty million dollars when they'd divorced one year earlier. She'd moved with the child to her own place on Fisher's Island off Miami Beach. Like Jack, Simon lived alone, but there was a transient population of women coming and going at all times, something that had begun before the acrimonious divorce and had led to the breakdown of their marriage.

Dantalion bypassed both the brothers' houses.

He stuck to the coastline. The going was a little more difficult than if he'd walked along the road, but it was more in keeping with his disguise.

A full half-mile from Bradley's house, he found what he'd been looking for. Not the silver Lincoln, but a helicopter on the broad lawn of the next house. The helicopter was a Bell Jet Ranger, and it was decorated with the livery of the FBI. The only reason that Dantalion could think of for the presence of the helicopter was that it had some

284

pretty important passengers. The Special Agent in Charge from the local FBI office. He would be overall commander of the investigation, and there was only one reason why he'd be at this location. Bradley had come here for tea and sympathy from his elderly great-aunt, Eunice.

From where he was standing, Dantalion could see the pilot on board the helicopter. He was passing time by going through a series of checks, flicking buttons and reading dials. Dantalion quickly walked towards the house, striding purposefully. The pilot glanced his way, but didn't appear concerned and continued with his pre-flight checks. Dantalion kept going, rounding the house and approaching the walled yard at the back.

This house was not as impressive as those the cousins lived in, but was probably still worth a couple of million dollars. A two-storey wooden dwelling with porch and railings and a steepled roof and attic windows, it reminded Dantalion a little of a house in a movie he'd enjoyed: *The Amityville Horror*. One of the oldest houses on the island, it looked in need of renovation – not exactly dilapidated, but a lick of paint wouldn't go amiss. The elderly woman who lived here was in fact one of the first generation of Jorgensons to arrive here back in the 1950s. The house would have been grand in its day, but now it was as dated as the chintz curtains in the windows. It looked like the old woman was just sitting out her time. When she passed, the house would likely go to one of the younger generation, doubtless to be torn down and rebuilt.

He paused at the corner, studying the cars parked at the rear of the house. There was an older model Chrysler station wagon. Plus, there it was: the silver Lincoln sedan. He took a deep breath. Felt for the Taurus .38. Touched his book. Then quickly took a step backwards as he heard the rear door opening. The sound was followed by muted conversation. He couldn't quite make out what was said, but then he detected the crunch of tyres as a vehicle approached. Angling himself against the corner of the wall, he watched a car from the Martin County Sheriff's Department draw to a halt and a silver-haired man in a grey suit get in. The vehicle then did a quick U-turn and headed back along the road. What was that about? He waited until the car was shielded from sight by the swell in the land.

Yesterday's actions had been governed by fury. He'd acted recklessly and without thought of the repercussions. His thirst for vengeance had led him to slay his supporters. He'd left himself without back-up, the proverbial lone wolf. But, hadn't he always preferred it that way?

Gabe Wellborn had been useful, but he had also been a liability. His method of concealing his network of hired mercenaries had never been fool-proof. Sooner or later the FBI would chance upon his website, put two and two together and draw correlations between the fantasised murders and those they reflected in the real world. Dantalion had cautioned him. He did not want the names of his brethren used by the other killers for hire on Gabe's books. It cheapened his own identity when other men – nothing but thugs for hire in his estimation – plucked names from the Goetic pantheon with no thought for the true owners of those names. Dantalion had sought out each of those men in turn. He'd killed them all. He had planned to kill Gabe too. But not last night. That had been a reaction to the situation he'd found himself in.

This time things would be different.

He would be cool and rational. He wouldn't go in with all guns blazing: he would use subtlety and guile to take Bradley Jorgenson. Neither would he kill him instantly. He would give him a choice. Tell me where Marianne is and I won't cut off your hands. Tell me where Joe Hunter is and I won't cut off your feet. Ask kindly and maybe I won't chop off your balls and feed them to you.

Good plan, nothing psychopathic about it.

He scouted the building, looking for a sign that Bradley was inside. And found him almost immediately. He was sitting in the kitchen, his forearms resting on a table top. A man who Dantalion did not recognise sat opposite him. A digital voice recorder lay on the table between them. By the cut of the man's suit, his well-groomed hair, and the give-away clip-on badge on his breast pocket,

287

Dantalion saw that he was FBI. He appeared to be questioning Bradley – the digital recorder there to record the interview.

There were only two others in the room: one of them the bodyguard named Seagram, the one who had offered to help him get to Bradley. That, of course, had been before Dantalion had slaughtered Petre, who had obviously been bribing Seagram to switch allegiance. He doubted that Seagram would be so keen with his sponsor out of the picture. Now that Bradley had resumed the role of his main employer, it was in Seagram's best interest to keep him alive. The last person was a very elderly lady. She was sitting in a wooden chair and, despite the heat of the Floridian sun, she was dressed in thick wool and tweed and had a blanket over her knees. She looked like she hadn't a clue what was going on, and sat smiling and nodding as Bradley answered the FBI agent's questions.

There did not appear to be anyone else around. No bodyguards, no police, only the one agent and the helicopter pilot to give assistance to Bradley and Seagram.

This was about the best opportunity for taking Bradley that he was going to get.

He quickly walked away from the house, not wanting to leave himself open to an attack from behind. As he approached the helicopter he heard the engine whine as the pilot continued his pre-flight preparations. He slipped his hand into his jacket pocket and carefully folded it round a small cylinder.

He made it all the way up to the cockpit before the pilot noticed him. The man saw only the uniform and he lifted his chin in a nod of greeting.

'Hello,' Dantalion said. He smiled. Then flicked the brim of his hat. Sunlight flashed in his eyes. He adjusted the brim so his face was again in shadow. A natural enough action to explain why he kept his hand elevated.

'Hi,' said the pilot, 'Can I help you?' He leaned out of the open door to better see his visitor. He was reading the emblem embroidered on Dantalion's shirt. Behind the visor of his flight helmet, Dantalion saw the man's eyes narrow to slivers. He opened his mouth to speak.

That was when Dantalion swung his right hand as though he was holding a hammer. The bottom of his fist struck the man flush on the left side of his neck. The blow in itself could prove fatal if delivered with enough power and precision. Coupled with the hypodermic piercing his carotid artery and pumping in a lethal dose of ketamine, the man was guaranteed a rapid death.

The punch itself stunned him, the drug raced immediately to his heart, and he was dead within seconds. He didn't have the chance to shout or even to lift his hands in defence. Dantalion accepted his sinking weight, catching the man under each armpit, and dragged him bodily from the helicopter. Then he slid open the side door and bundled the man into the rear compartment. He followed him inside and closed the door behind him.

Minutes later Dantalion emerged a new man.

Wearing the pilot's jumpsuit and helmet, he crossed the lawn towards the house. As he got to the window of the kitchen he saw that the tableau had not changed in the couple of minutes he'd been gone. Boldly he rapped a knuckle on the window, even as he turned aside, gesturing to those within with a gloved hand. All they would see was the familiar figure of the chopper pilot. They wouldn't be alarmed, but one of them would come to the door to see what he wanted. He walked towards the door, watching in his peripheral vision as someone – Seagram from the shape of the brush cut – moved towards the door to intercept him.

He stood very close to the door. It was solid wood, so the person inside would have to open it fully before realising that there was something familiar about the bogus pilot's face. He readied himself. He preferred giving his victims a choice of how they would die, but he didn't have that luxury. This death had to be conducted in silence too.

'Yeah, what is it?' Seagram's voice.

'I need to give my colleague a message,' Dantalion said, purposely speaking a couple of octaves lower than normal.

'What is it? I'll tell him.'

'Can't do that, sir,' Dantalion said. 'Official FBI business, I'm afraid. You do not have clearance. I have to tell him myself.'

Seagram muttered a curse under his breath. He tugged open the door, which squealed on seldom-used hinges.

Seagram stood looking at him for the briefest of moments. Then it was there, the subtle movement of his jaw, the dilating of his pupils. He'd recognised the lie.

'Hello, Seagram,' Dantalion said as he stepped forward. The knife he'd brought from the dead warden's house went under Seagram's ribcage. All eight glistening inches of it. Dantalion's other hand covered. Seagram's gaping mouth. As the man's knees buckled under him, Dantalion supported him on the blade. He leaned close, placing his lips close to Seagram's ear. 'I've come to tell the FBI that the killer is here.'

Seagram knew he was dying, and that it was his greed that had brought him to this point. His eyes went large above Dantalion's cupped hand. He tried to shout, but the knife seemed to suck the words down into his throat as Dantalion pulled the blade out of his abdomen.

Dantalion placed Seagram on the floor just inside the vestibule, and swiped the blade across his trachea. His mouth still opened and closed like a fish on dry land, but no noises beyond the bubbling blood in his sliced trachea issued forth. Groping under Seagram's jacket, Dantalion pulled out a Glock 17. Not the model 19 he was used to, but still better than the five-shot Taurus.

He fitted his hands round both guns' stocks. The two-gunned assault had a decidedly intimidating quality to it that worked for him.

He strode along the hall.

The kitchen door was open and he could see the old lady sitting with her back to him. That would put the FBI agent on his right, Bradley on his left. The FBI agent was the most dangerous enemy in the room. By rights he should die first. Dantalion, however, had different ideas about rights and wrongs. He fired a single round through the old lady's back even before he was in the room. The Glock punched a 9 mm round directly through her and shattered something on the far wall. The woman toppled towards the table. As she did so her face twisted to one side, and Dantalion would have sworn that she was still smiling.

'Hello,' he called in his usual fashion. 'I'm Dantalion.'

Bradley and the FBI agent were too busy to take note of his words. They were half risen from their seats, Bradley turning away, the agent grabbing for the H&K inside his jacket.

Dantalion fired one shot from the Taurus, one shot from the Glock. Neither of them at Bradley. The .38 calibre bullet hit the agent above his right hip. A split second later the 9 mm struck him directly between the eyes. The opposing forces of the bullets made him jig in place like a disjointed puppet. Then he dropped straight to the floor, knocking over the chair he'd so recently been sitting upon.

Bradley was lurching around the far end of the table, seeking a way out. He had both arms over his head and was yelling something reminiscent of the defeated bellow of a bull as the matador serves the *coup de grâce*.

Aiming left-handedly, Dantalion fired the Taurus. The bullet struck the wall directly in front of Bradley who responded by dropping down and covering his head with his two hands. He shouted something but Dantalion's ears were ringing to the echo of his own guns.

'Surprised to see me, Bradley? Thought I was dead, eh? Must piss you off that the big bold Hunter failed to stop me? Stand up.'

Terror kept Bradley exactly where he was.

'I said "*stand up*",' Dantalion yelled. 'Or I will shoot you where you are. Cowering on the ground like a dog!'

Bradley came partly to his feet, but couldn't prevent his knees dipping again. Dantalion stalked over, kicking aside the dead FBI agent to get at him. He pushed the hot muzzle of the Taurus under Bradley's ear. 'Stand up. That's the only choice I'm giving you right now.'

Cringing like a wounded animal, Bradley came to his feet. He tried to protect himself with his arms but Dantalion struck at the meat of his forearms, forcing the hands away. Then he pushed Bradley back against the kitchen counter and forced him to bend backwards away from the pressure of the gun.

'Now, Bradley, it's choices time again. Do you die instantly, or would you rather I kept you alive as bait to bring Marianne to me?' Dantalion pushed the muzzle of the Glock under Bradley's chin. 'Come on, speak up. I'm giving you the opportunity of living a little longer.'

'Please,' Bradley croaked. His plea never came to a conclusion, and Dantalion was left wondering what decision Bradley had reached.

Dantalion heard a car pull up outside the front of the house.

So he made the choice himself.

He slipped the Glock in his pocket, pulled out a hypodermic syringe. Given in the same dosage, ketamine would kill Bradley as instantly as it had the pilot, but this syringe didn't contain ketamine. He'd brought this ampoule from the truck: sodium amatol left over from the hit on the Moore household. In small doses it caused the drugged person to become compliant. A higher dose caused unconsciousness. Too much and the person would die. Dantalion administered just enough to leave Bradley with no will of his own but with the use of his legs. He didn't want to have to carry him out of there.

CHAPTER 36

Special Agent in Charge Taylor Kaufman wasn't exactly pleased to see me. He extended his hand, but his shake was abrupt and his words dry. 'Walter Conrad says you're the best in the business.'

'Depends what business he's referring to,' I answered.

The silver-haired SAC studied me with eyes the colour of tarnished brass. He didn't appear impressed. Something about my accent seemed to irk him as well. I guessed it was because he'd already fought a jurisdiction war with the Miami PD and Martin County Sheriff's Department, which he'd indubitably won, only now to be faced with a Brit with carte blanche to take over his position of power. He straightened his grey suit. Nodded towards the squad car.

'You'd better get in. I'll take you to Jorgenson.'

'Go ahead,' I told him. 'I'll bring my own car.'

The Audi was no good to me a half-mile away.

'Prefer it if you came with us,' SAC Kaufman said slowly. 'I'll also have to ask you to hand over your sidearm.'

'Isn't going to happen.' I challenged him with my stare.

'I've got a man down there who has already survived two attempts on his life. Don't want to risk that again,' he said.

'I'm here to protect him, not harm him.'

'I don't know that.'

'Walter Conrad vouched for me,' I reminded him.

'Walter is CIA,' Kaufman said in reply, 'and we all know what *they* are famous for.'

'I'm not CIA,' I said.

'No. But that's the problem . . . I'm not sure what you are.' Then he turned his back on me and walked towards the sheriff's car.

'Kaufman.'

He turned.

'I'm not here to usurp you. We're on the same side.'

His mouth made a thin line, and he turned away again. I shook my head and then climbed into the Audi. The cop at the gate gave me room to bring the car in and I followed the police vehicle back on to the Jorgenson estate.

Approaching the village made up of estate staff lodgings, I was surprised when we took a left, skirted the village and approached a lone wooden house standing on the Atlantic shore. This house wasn't like the others; it was older, more homely. Less forbidding than the brick monstrosities that the younger Jorgensons had erected.

Why we were headed there instead of directly towards Bradley's house I didn't quite get, but then I saw the silver Lincoln parked adjacent to the back of the house and it made sense. Bradley had gone somewhere he felt safe.

SAC Kaufman climbed out of the police car. He leaned in and said something to the uniformed driver. The driver shook his head, then peeled away, heading back along the road towards Bradley's house. I parked the Audi next to the Lincoln Seagram had been driving the day before. Climbing from my car, I felt the phone vibrate in my pocket. I answered it and Rink said, 'I'm back from San Francisco. Harvey's got Mari tucked up safe and sound. I'm on my way back to you now.'

'Pleased to hear it, Rink,' I said. 'Your mom?'

'On the mend. She smacked me round the head for leaving you alone and told me to get my ass back here. How could I argue with that?'

'You know better than that.'

'You ain't kidding,' he laughed. Then his tone grew more serious. Back to business. 'The punk survived, huh?'

'Unfortunately, yes.'

'Where are you?'

'I'm back at the estate,' I told him. 'Had to pull a few strings via Walter Conrad, but I should be with Bradley in a minute or two.'

'Walter came through, huh?'

'He had no option, did he? He owes us big time.'

'No,' Rink rumbled. I imagined him touching

the scar on his chin. Like the knife wound in my chest, Rink's scar was courtesy of Tubal Cain.

'I'll wait here until you arrive, then we'll move Bradley between us.'

'Give me an hour or two, OK?'

'Should take that long to sort things out at this end,' I told him. 'I've got a fed here with a stick up his ass.'

'Nothing new there then,' Rink said.

I hung up.

'I heard that,' SAC Kaufman said.

'You were meant to, Kaufman,' I said. 'We started out on the wrong foot back there. Can we try this again? We're both here for the same reason, so let's agree to work together, huh? Truth is, I'm not going anywhere, so we may as well be civil to each other.'

Kaufman nodded. He swept the surroundings with one look. 'Would be a whole lot easier without *this* stick up my ass.'

We shook hands again, this time with meaning.

'Walter Conrad told me what you'd managed to piece together about the shooter. I've passed the information along to my people. Got someone on the skin-complaint angle, another on this demon stuff. Hopefully we'll have something useful before long.'

'He's unorthodox. I don't think he's been trained through the usual channels.'

Kaufman paused mid-step. 'That in itself could point us towards him. Maybe one of these private CQB courses or something?'

298

'Nah, close quarter battle's about protection. This guy comes from a different school. Maybe he has roots with one of those paramilitary Home Defence groups or something similar.'

Kaufman continued walking.

My step after him turned into a lunge.

I grabbed him by the shoulders, and powered my chest against him, taking us both down hard on the pavement.

Through the space we'd just vacated whistled two high-velocity rounds.

For all he was wearing an expensive suit, Kaufman was no slouch at crawling. He was off, scurrying for the cover of a low wall. He reached it within seconds and went over, landing on his back.

I had gone the other direction, rolling sideways. Another round chipped concrete from the paving stones, throwing splinters towards my face. Blinking to clear my vision, I continued rolling and got myself under a parked station wagon. Somewhere along the way, I'd drawn my SIG and was looking for targets.

My first reaction was to aim for the window where the shooter had fired from. It was the subtle shifting of his shadow, the pale face looming above it that had warned me of his presence. If my mind hadn't been tuned to recognise the danger of his ghoulish face, Dantalion would have got us cold.

The window had been smashed by his bullets, but I saw no movement there. He'd moved, possibly to get a clearer angle on me.

Just as I had that thought a round struck the front tyre next to my head and the hiss of air sounded like an angry snake. The car dipped slowly towards me, and I wormed further away from the collapsing corner of the chassis.

'FBI,' Kaufman shouted. He had one arm propped on the low wall, his service revolver aiming towards the empty window. 'Drop your weapon and come out.'

The FBI SAC wasn't a stranger to action. But it looked like it was some years since he'd engaged in a gun battle. His face was as pale as that of the man who was trying to kill us.

'Keep your head down, Kaufman,' I shouted across the intervening space. His gaze jumped to me, back to the house. I knew he was going to shout again even before his mouth opened.

'Come out with your hands in the air and you will not be harmed.'

Bullets smacked the wall beside him and I saw his gun arm drop. He cursed loudly and I wasn't sure if he'd been wounded or not.

My position was not the best for shooting back. I could only see a small portion of the house, and most of that was blank wall. On my belly, I used my feet to push me towards the station wagon's engine. That was a slightly better position, but most of my view remained obscured by the sunken front end of the car. It took me about a nanosecond to decide I wasn't staying there. All the shooter had to do was fire under the car and the ricochets would probably kill me. I scooted away, rolled out from under the car and came up on the far side.

In the movies, you will often see a cop hunkered behind an open car door. 9 mm Parabellums will pass through the shell of a car with no problem. Some more enlightened movie makers have their good guy place the engine block between themselves and the shooter, but again there are too many open spaces and fragile components to stop most bullets. The reality is, a car isn't safe to hide behind. Neither are trees or concrete walls. The only thing that will stop a high-calibre bullet is about six inches of solid brick or steel. Kaufman had the best hiding place. My own, other than offering enough cover so the shooter couldn't get a bead on me, was third rate.

As if he had read my mind, the man in the house fired again. He unloaded an entire clip from a semi-automatic. Not randomly either: he began at the front of the car, fired, moved his hand a fraction, fired, moved his hand a fraction and so on. Some of the rounds did flatten inside the engine, but for as many that were stopped, at least one got through. The hood buckled as rounds ricocheted under it. Holes appeared in the wing close by my body. I had no choice but run backwards, keeping my head down as bullets cut through the car and struck lumps from the ground beyond me.

Kaufman – jurisdiction battle or not – wasn't about to let me die. He bopped up, firing back at the house. He couldn't see his target, only hoped to offer covering fire while I raced for cover behind my Audi. I did so, sliding like I was headed for first base.

The retort of the shooter's gun changed. A lighter bore, but still enough to kill. I'd got myself all the way to the rear of the Audi and with its nose pointed towards the shooter it gave me much more cover than the other car had. Nonetheless, bullets punched through the galvanised steel body and lifted padding from the seats within. There was a loud pop – a tyre going. The semi-automatic was firing again and I had to drop as low as I could to the ground.

Then there was a lull. I quickly snapped a glance over the trunk. The door was opening and my first instinct was to shoot through it. Nevertheless I held my fire, waving over to Kaufman to do the same. Only someone with no sense would put themselves behind that door during a gun battle. Dantalion was as crazy as any other psycho out there, but he did appear to be knowledgeable about guns and their effects.

The door swung open, and there stood Bradley Jorgenson.

He swayed like he'd been out on a particularly heavy night's partying. His mouth hung open, a string of saliva knitting together his splayed teeth. His heavy-lidded eyes were unfocused. Drugged.

Bradley was a fair-sized guy. Maybe my height, but heavier. He was ample cover for the slim man crouching behind him. I could only catch a glimpse of white hair, an ear, one gloved hand that was under Bradley's arm and jammed into his armpit. Room under there for a .38 special. Over Bradley's shoulder the muzzle of a Glock.

'Anyone moves and I kill Bradley,' shouted the shooter.

'Put down the gun and move away slowly,' Kaufman shouted in return. He was again propped over the wall. No way could he take a shot, though.

The shooter twisted Bradley towards him. Fired once from the Glock. The bullet missed Kaufman but was enough motivation for him to drop down out of sight.

I watched, waiting for my opportunity.

'There are only two choices here,' the shooter yelled again. 'Drop your weapons or Bradley dies.'

There were actually three choices. I could shoot straight through Bradley and kill the fucker as well. Yesterday, before I knew the truth, I might have done. And, heaven forbid, if he did shoot Bradley, that was exactly what I was going to do.

'What's it going to be, FBI man? Do you want me to kill this innocent boy?'

Kaufman didn't reply. That put the ball back in my court.

'You aren't going to do that, Dantalion,' I said. I stood up. It meant putting myself at risk, but also gave me a clear shot through Bradley and into the shooter's central mass.

'So, you know my name?' Dantalion swung a fraction back my way. Still no clear shot though. 'Touché, Mr Hunter.'

'I know the pussy name you hide behind,' I told him. 'What is it with all you deadbeats, huh? Why the stupid name? All you sick-in-the-head mother-fuckers do that.'

Instead of riling him like I'd intended, Dantalion seemed pleased with my words. He chuckled to himself, even as he pressed Bradley to take a slow step forwards. I matched his step, moving away from the Audi.

'You're looking for an opportunity to shoot,' Dantalion pointed out. 'Go on. Shoot, then,' he dropped the barrel of his Glock so he could pull aside Bradley's jacket. Under it was a bullet-proof vest. Something Seagram had demanded his mark wear after it was too late. I wondered where the bodyguard had got to. Hell, probably. Dantalion went on. 'See the only problem now is you will have to shoot through Bradley's head. Are you prepared to do that?'

'Yes,' I said.

For effect I allowed my knees to bend slightly, exaggerating my shooter's stance. It was a gamble, a big one. But Dantalion didn't shove Bradley to one side and come out shooting as I'd hoped. If anything he took a tighter hold on the younger man. His face was barely visible beyond Bradley's lolling head.

'This is what's going to happen.' His Glock

was steady as it pointed my way, but I got the impression that he'd turned his head to one side. As he did, I took a step back towards the Audi. His gun was now pointing a yard to the right of my shoulder. He didn't note the subtle shift of my body, calling instead to Kaufman. 'FBI man, throw your gun over the wall. You have three seconds to comply or Bradley here will be as dead as your buddy inside.'

'Not giving up my gun,' Kaufman shouted in denial.

'Your choice. One. Two . . .'

Kaufman's service revolver clattered on the ground next to Dantalion's feet. I swore under my breath. We'd lost a major advantage and Dantalion knew it. But he didn't see me shift my weight to the side, putting an extra foot from the trajectory of his first shot.

'Same goes for you, Hunter.'

'No.'

'Three seconds.'

'When you reach three you will be dead.'

'One. Two . . .'

'Three!'

Neither of us fired.

'So how do things go now, asshole?' I asked him. 'You sound like you're a fair man. You like choices, don't you? How about you choose to put down your weapons? Let Bradley go, and maybe you'll get a comfortable prison cell instead of a hole in your head.'

'Don't care too much for prison,' Dantalion continued to edge forwards, Bradley a compliant partner in their slow dance.

'You look like you've spent a long time out of the sunlight already, but I guess that's because you've crawled out from under a rock.'

'You can goad me all you want, Hunter, but I'm not biting.'

'So you choose the bullet in the head?' I continued. 'Not that I blame you. Pretty white ass like yours would have them queuing up down at the State Penitentiary.'

Dantalion didn't reply; I'd come a little too close to the truth for his liking.

'Where'd you do your time? You've obviously done a stretch before? Don't care too much for prison,' I mimicked in an effeminate voice.

He didn't answer, just kept moving. What the hell was Kaufman up to? Where was his back-up weapon? We had Dantalion nicely triangulated now, and Kaufman could have put a bullet in his spine at any time. Only he wasn't making his play. He *had* been off the streets too long.

Dantalion was that much closer to Kaufman. He heard something that I didn't. 'The fucking cell phone, FBI. Throw it to me now!'

Kaufman's cell came sailing over the wall and Dantalion caught it under the sole of his foot and stamped it into fragments.

Dantalion was angry now. But it wasn't the senseless anger that I wanted to force him into.

His rage was controlled. More dangerous. He jammed the revolver hard into Bradley's armpit.

'I'm done playing games. Hunter, get your ass out of my way or – so help me, God! – I'm going to shoot this punk and then you.'

'I don't think God is on your side,' I didn't move an inch. 'You're forgetting that He chose to elevate man above His angels. Whose side do you think He's gonna pick today?'

'Think I believe all that stupidity?' Dantalion snapped.

'Yeah,' I said slowly. 'I think you do.'

'Think again!'

Dantalion fired at me.

I didn't have a shot, so I had to leap away.

His first shot missed by a mile, but he was turning, following me, vectoring in on my running form.

Now I fired. Not at him. Despite my threat, there was no way I could shoot Bradley through the head. I fired so that my bullet passed over their heads. But it was enough to make him flinch and his second shot missed its mark too.

Then I was back behind the station wagon and twisting round for a shot. Point. Shoot. That was what had been ingrained into my psyche during the hundreds of hours training at Arrowsake. My bullet went true, hit dead centre. Only it wasn't Dantalion I'd hit, but Bradley. The Kevlar vest absorbed the killing power, but it was still like he'd been kicked by a mule. His body collided with Dantalion's, knocking his third shot astray.

It was one of those do or die moments when everything can play out on the basis of a snap decision. He was off kilter now, and if I charged him he wouldn't waste time shooting Bradley, he'd turn all his attention on me. I would blast the fucker's face off the second he lifted it above Bradley's shoulder.

But before I could move, Seagram stumbled out of the house looking like the victim from a slasher movie. His shirt front was dark with blood; a mass of it had pooled round his waistband and was even now seeping into the front of his trousers. He had taken a serious wound to his abdomen. He had one hand cupped around his throat, and there was blood there too. Not as much as was coming from his guts, but I knew that this was going to prove fatal. In his other hand he held a Heckler & Koch semi-automatic pistol. His face was ashen and fixed into a mask-like rictus. There was no recognition when he looked first at Bradley and Dantalion, then at me.

He lifted the H&K.

Pointed at me.

He fired but I was already on the move. The problem was I had to dodge away, so could no longer rush at Dantalion.

Seagram didn't see me. Not as Joe Hunter. He was looking into a gulf into which he was about to fall on a one-way trip. The human body is miraculous. It can take horrendous wounds and survive and learn to function in new ways. Pity

308

our minds aren't as resilient. Seagram was gone from inside his own head, and whether it was terror or hatred or sheer instinct to come out shooting, that was all he was capable of. He pulled the trigger again and again.

I was loath to shoot the man, but I wasn't about to take a blind shot. I lifted my SIG and squared it on his forehead. I paused for a fraction of a second, then watched as a tiny rosebud blossomed in the centre of his face while the back of his head exploded in a welter of blood, skull and brain matter.

Dantalion had his arm extended over Bradley's shoulder, and there was smoke coming from the barrel of the Glock.

Then he was swinging it towards me, and I had no option but to look for cover. I got to the front of the station wagon and hoped that the engine block would be enough to save me.

In the few seconds I'd kept my head down, Dantalion had moved backwards and I saw then what he was aiming for. The silver Lincoln was the only car in a driveable condition. He opened the driver's door and shoved Bradley inside, encouraging him to move faster with slaps to the face. Bradley scooted over into the passenger seat and then Dantalion was starting the car. He must have taken the car keys from Seagram.

I rose up from my crouch.

I could fire, but I was afraid that I'd hit Bradley.

So I had no recourse but to watch the Lincoln screeching away up the road.

'Knowles? Knowles!' Kaufman came over the wall like an Olympic hurdler. He lunged forwards to pick up his service revolver and raced towards the house. I took a last look at the Lincoln powering towards the exit drive, then at my Audi and the station wagon. Both had deflated tyres. No way was I going to catch Dantalion now.

I followed Kaufman inside. The trail of blood led us into the kitchen and what I saw broke my heart. A man was on his back, eyes fixed in a cataract stare. The agent – Knowles – that Kaufman had been concerned about. Bad enough that this man had died, but he was a professional and death was sometimes a downside of the job. What made my heart shrivel was the elderly lady lying across her table. Her mouth was crooked in an eternal bow. She had been no threat to anyone. Dantalion had done it from a thirst for blood.

Earlier, I'd told Walter that it wasn't personal. Well, I was wrong. When Dantalion killed that old lady he'd ensured that I wouldn't give up until I tore the last breath from his throat.

Kaufman was gingerly probing through the dead agent's clothing. Looking for his cell phone to call for back-up, no doubt. I took out my own phone and called all the back-up I required.

'Rink.'

'I'm here, Hunter.'

'Change of plan, buddy.'

I told him what had gone down and he swore. I stood by the window, staring out across the lawn towards the bright sea. A dark silhouette hunkered on the lawn.

When I was done giving my instructions to Rink, I looked back at Kaufman. He was still yelling animatedly into Knowles's phone.

'Kaufman,' I said loudly.

It was as if he'd forgotten I was there.

My finger pointed out the window.

'Can you fly that thing?'

CHAPTER 37

Jean-Paul St Pierre – despite what everyone said – wasn't a sickly child. His vitiligo condition was purely external, and though it earned him cruel taunts from other children, even the occasional beating, it had never affected his physical boundaries. So long as he was careful under the Louisiana sun and took his medication at the dosage prescribed he could live a normal life. His mother loved him dearly, cherished him. Her little angel boy. She gave him all the kindness and support he needed. And he loved his mother in return.

He never knew his father. In a drunken stupor he'd been flattened under the wheels of an express train when his alcohol-addled brain told him he had right of way at a rail crossing. It wasn't much of a loss. He'd got on fine without him.

He blamed his father for his condition. It was his father's seed that had cursed him. But his father's curse was also responsible for making him the man that he would become.

He wasn't a sickly child. No.

He was strong and resilient and he looked after his mother as a good son should. When it came time to grant his mother her greatest wish he'd had the fortitude to do so, willingly and without an ounce of selfishness or self-pity. She had longed for it, asked for it, begged her uncaring god for it. So he couldn't understand why he'd been taken away and placed under guard at Juvenile Hall. They called him a monster. They did not understand him. He'd only been doing what his mother had begged for whenever he'd found her crying. His mother had been sad since the day of his father's death, and Jean-Paul had only wished to make her happy. He was even mindful to cause her as little pain as possible when he shot her in the back of her head with his grandpapa's old 'coon rifle.

Sociopathic, his doctors had called him. Psychopathic. Others called him worse names. More personal and hurtful. But he wasn't any of those things. He wasn't sick. Physically or mentally. Couldn't understand why they'd kept him locked away for eight years.

'*I know the pussy name you hide behind,*' Joe Hunter had said to him. '*What is it with all you deadbeats, huh? Why the stupid name? All you sick-in-the-head motherfuckers do that.*'

He had smiled at the inanity of it. He'd been hearing similar accusations all his life. They had been his bread and butter. They sustained him, nourished him, made him even more determined to show his doubters just how much further up the evolutionary ladder he was than they. They could not understand his singular take on reality, because they were blind. No one seemed to see it but him.

He had shown Hunter.

He was better than Hunter.

Primarily because he did not share Hunter's base weaknesses.

Where he would not have faltered in shooting through another person's head to kill his enemy, Hunter had paused. That was the difference between them, what made him better at killing than Hunter would ever be. Hunter was trained. His military masters had ingrained in him the technicalities of killing, but they had never fully eradicated that human foible: the reluctance to murder in cold blood another human being. Empathy and guilt are stronger than the finger that pulls the trigger.

That was why his doctors had proclaimed Jean-Paul a sociopath. No empathy. No guilt, they said. Just like his father, he supposed.

Hunter on the other hand did have empathy. He had it in bucket-loads.

Dantalion could use Hunter's weakness to bring all his targets to him. And he would kill them all. He would leave Hunter until last, so that his guilt was magnified tenfold. And, he thought, looking sideways at his hostage, he would start with Bradley Jorgenson.

His escape from the island was easier than he'd thought possible. When Hunter and the FBI agent

314

had turned up, things had looked like they were stacking against him. Only the fortuitous arrival of Seagram stumbling around like something from a zombie movie had allowed him to get away. The bullet he'd fired through Seagram's head had diverted Hunter long enough for him to make it to the Lincoln. Then the Lincoln had given him the speed and power to ram his way out of the metal gates. They were designed to keep intruders out, not in. The cop who'd tried to halt him by standing in the way and pointing his gun should actually have fired the thing, although his skull had starred the windscreen as his body was catapulted over the hood and on to the roof of the sedan.

Now he was ten miles north, travelling at high speed, slaloming in and out of traffic heading up the coast towards Jupiter. He was enjoying the freedom that the huge town car demanded from the other road users. A Dixie Highway turnpike was somewhere ahead, he recalled. He had to get off the coast on to the main route, then find a way across country. The FBI agent would set all available manpower on his trail. Roadblocks would be in place somewhere ahead of him, and a convoy of blue lights and sirens rushing in his wake. There was no sign of it yet, but the pursuit would definitely come.

Within half a minute he found the turnpike. Cars were backed up on the off ramp. He just went round them, forcing the car along the shoulder and leaving several vehicles minus their wing mirrors behind him. He swung into cross traffic and cars swerved and braked, and a refrigerated truck jackknifed into oncoming traffic, effectively closing the road behind him. Dantalion watched the carnage in his mirrors, wondering what tally he should add to his book from the pileup that ensued.

He sped up the highway, found a second exit on his left and blasted his way through the meridian across the path of more traffic at over sixty miles an hour. He almost lost control of the vehicle, but steered into the slide of the rear tyres, righted the sedan and took off at speed. The road went under another highway, swung north and then west, then he was rocketing along a single-lane blacktop, headed out into the swampy lands of the Floridian interior.

The road hadn't been designed for speed. It was ridged at its centre and there were more bumps and potholes than there were smooth patches. He could afford to slow down now that he'd lost any possible pursuers. He looked over at Bradley Jorgenson. The young man was oblivious of all that had occurred since Dantalion had jabbed him with the needle.

Dantalion backhanded him across the face.

'Wake up, Brad, you aren't going to be any help with your head in the clouds.'

Bradley's eyes opened but there was no recognition in their depths. He was mindless of the blood trickling from his nose and into the corner of his mouth.

Sodium amatol is sometimes inaccurately referred to as a truth serum. Movies show those who are drugged answering probing questions in a dull monotone, unable to deny their interrogators. Dantalion knew that was ridiculous. The drug did reduce a person's resistance to suggestion and had the effect of lowering their inhibitions, but it would never cause someone to give up their most closely guarded secrets. At a higher dosage it was no different than any other anaesthetic: it put you to sleep. Dantalion wanted answers, but he had other ways of forcing them from the man. He wanted Bradley awake and able to recognise the dilemma he was in.

He slapped him again.

Bradley muttered, turned his face away and promptly fell back to sleep.

Bradley would have to be woken by pain. Maybe the amputation of his extremities followed by a meal to remember.

On either side of the road scrubland was interspersed between the occasional irrigated fields. Tributaries of a swamp lying to the north were like the twisted fingers of an arthritic crone. Mangrove grew in dense clumps on hillocks standing above the streams. Birds broke from cover, startled by the passage of the Lincoln. Not the most densely populated area, but less wild than the swamps along the flooded banks of the Mississippi.

Bradley stirred beside him.

'Back with us?'

'Mmmmff!'

'Not yet, huh?'

Up ahead was a crossroads, giving him three choices. South, north, or continue heading west. Dantalion was all for choices, but occasionally you just had to throw the dice and go along with fate. He sped through the junction, the tyres kicking up gravel. The road ahead was as straight as an arrow's flight. Grass tall enough to conceal an elephant grew at both sides of the road, the upper reaches hanging over to create a natural tunnel.

The grass tunnel went on for the best part of a mile. Claustrophobia wormed at the base of his stomach, making him nauseous and out of breath. He was relieved when the Lincoln emerged into open space once more. A lake came into view on his right-hand side. Thousands of birds, myriad species he could not name, made the lake their home. Something splashed beneath the surface and moved away through the lake, leaving a wide wake on the surface.

There were trees ahead, then another one of those damn grass tunnels. Dantalion slowed the vehicle down and brought it to a halt. He'd seen something to his liking across the marshy field on his left. A collection of large red cubes surrounded by metal masts that glinted gold in the sunlight. Huge pylons made a forest of steel in the background. Power cables streaked away into the distant haze, and also towards him and over the Lincoln and across the lake. He could see another pylon on the far bank, standing tall above the slowly undulating marsh grass.

Dantalion nodded to himself, pushed the vehicle into drive and headed for the next grass tunnel. He had barely entered the green twilight when he nosed the Lincoln off the road and down the slight incline to the field of tall grasses. A flimsy wire fence was crushed under the tyres as he pushed the sedan into the grass's embrace. He didn't get far, feeling the car settling down almost immediately in the boggy earth. But he made it far enough into the tall grass so that the car wouldn't be immediately evident to anyone passing along the road. To make sure, he clambered out, wading through twisted stalks towards the road. His feet sank into the loam and were snagged by the tough grass, but he made it back to where he'd pushed over the fence. He righted the fence, even though it sagged from the nearby posts. Then he grabbed armfuls of grass and stood them upright against the wire. It wouldn't fool a determined tracker, but was good enough.

When he got back to the car, Bradley was gone.

CHAPTER 38

Back in the day, I'd frequently been a passenger on various helicopters: primarily Sea Kings and Chinooks, AH-6 Defenders and Huey Cobras. On those occasions I'd been on missions, usually in hot zones where I'd rappel from the guts of the choppers alongside Rink and the rest of my team on reconnaissance or seek and destroy. I'd never been in a Jet Ranger before, and this helicopter was the equivalent of a sleek limousine next to some of the cramped flying buses I'd experienced.

The FBI chopper was a five-seater, two up front and three in the back. When we'd clambered inside, with Kaufman reaching for the controls, we'd discovered the pilot dead across the back seats. His undressed state explained where Dantalion had got his disguise from. I couldn't find any obvious injury on the man's body, but located a small puncture wound in his neck.

Kaufman had once been familiar with helicopters, but – like his on-the-street days – it had been some time ago.

'Don't worry,' he told me. 'It's like riding a bicycle – you never forget.'

'Don't mind falling off a bike,' I replied as I settled into the passenger position next to him, 'only not from hundreds of feet in the air.'

Kaufman laughed.

Then he was flicking buttons and pulling levers and I heard a whine that grew rapidly to a shriek. Over our heads, the rotors began to turn lazily, scything the air as though cutting through molasses. Then the engine noise changed and the rotors became a blur before our eyes, then they were above us and we were lifting off the floor. I experienced a moment of weightlessness before I felt my stomach press down into my pelvis, and we were going straight up.

Kaufman banked to the right, and the world tilted on its axis. The sea was a blue wall over his shoulder, while the Florida sky stretched away into the hazy west over mine. Then we banked left and the view was reversed. Next moment we were past the house and the bird righted itself and we were streaking towards the highway about fifty feet up in the air.

'See, I told you. Piece of cake,' Kaufman crowed.

'I'll take your word for it.'

We flew past the village, then used the exit drive as a locator for the gate. Before we even got there I knew which way Dantalion had taken Bradley. The traffic was backed up on both sides of the highway, but I could see a broad smear of blood where some hapless cop had been hit by the fleeing car. People were crowding round the dead officer.

321

The TV crews encamped on the layover opposite the gate were charging across the road pointing their cameras at the victim. He'd been dragged about ten yards along the carriageway to our right.

'North,' I told Kaufman.

He was already turning the Jet Ranger in pursuit of the Lincoln. The nose of the chopper dipped, and then we were scooting along at top speed in pursuit of Dantalion. He had a good lead on us, but not for long.

When first we'd boarded the chopper, Kaufman had grabbed the co-pilot headphones. It left me without ear protection, and the sound was terrific. But I was fine; my head was ringing loudly with a jumble of chaotic thoughts anyway. Rather than recording Bradley's testimony on paper, the dead FBI agent, Leighton Knowles, had been conducting a taped interview with Bradley Jorgenson. When Dantalion had burst in on them, the recorder bore witness to the murders. Dantalion had neglected to turn off the recording device. Probably deliberately, as he'd spoken directly into it and said, 'The thunders of judgement and wrath are numbered. As are you, Bradley. Pretty Marianne Dean as well. All numbered. The same goes for your turncoat bodyguard. Hunter and Rink too. Do you hear me? Come to me, bring Marianne. Let's get this over with.'

When I'd first heard the recording I'd been taken aback. Dantalion had called me by name earlier, but I didn't at first understand how he could have known either my or Rink's name. It didn't take too long to draw conclusions. *Your turncoat bodyguard*, Dantalion had said. Seagram had obviously been involved with the plot to kill Bradley and Marianne. It explained why he had been at Petre's house when Dantalion had gone off on his initial killing spree. I'd known the man couldn't be trusted, that I should have had him cut loose the first time I saw him. It was apparent then that he was bitter about us usurping his status in the Jorgenson household. Worst, I'd missed taking Dantalion down because of his arrival, and maybe he hadn't been so blinded by impending death when he'd started shooting at me. The only thing I regretted now was that it was Dantalion and not me who'd put a bullet through the asshole's head.

Dantalion's words were a direct challenge. He was inviting me to try and take him down. He was confident. No bad thing.

He saw his escape with Bradley as a minor victory. He'd beaten me, yes. But minor victories never win the war. They breed self-confidence, which leads to complacency. And as any soldier will remind you, complacency will bring on your destruction.

Before boarding the chopper, I'd called Harvey. Now I used my mobile phone to call Rink. Shouting over the whine of the exhaust vents, I asked him if Harvey had done as I'd asked earlier.

'Yeah,' he told me. 'You know Harvey; he loves all that technical stuff.'

It was a ruse we'd employed once before to track the Harvestman. On that occasion, it had been doubtful if our idea would even work. But it had – until Tubal Cain discovered the mobile phone that we were tracking via satellite technology. Pretty soon after that I'd rammed a broken bone from his collection of skeletal parts through the monster's windpipe. Had Cain recognised the ploy earlier, maybe we would never have found him. Not until it was too late to save my brother John.

This time there was no concern about the killer spotting our makeshift tracking device. It was the phone in my hand that Harvey and Rink were vectoring in on. All I had to do was locate Dantalion, and if I failed to stop him at least Rink would get the opportunity to avenge me.

'You in some kind of aircraft?' Rink asked me. 'I'm watching my GPS and the land's scrolling along quicker than I can keep up with.'

'Chopper. Remember that FBI agent I was telling you about?'

'The one with the stick up his ass?'

'That's him. Well, maybe I was being a little judgemental. He's a good guy. Flew UH-60s on a couple tours of Somalia before becoming a fed.'

'UH-60s?' Rink said. 'You're talking Black Hawks?'

'Like I said, he's a good guy. Could even have been your pilot on a mission or two.'

The UH-60 Black Hawk is the helicopter of choice of the US Special Forces. Delta Force and

US Rangers, primarily. Before joining my team, Rink had belonged to the Rangers. Kaufman had just won kudos in both our eyes.

Beside me, Kaufman indicated the road ahead.

'Dantalion got away from us, Rink. He has Bradley with him as a hostage. I intend getting him back.' I saw a major pile-up of traffic on an intersection of the highway. Then more importantly, a silver Lincoln streaking west. Kaufman banked, following. He knew what I intended, so kept far enough back that we weren't obvious to the fleeing driver. To Rink, I added, 'Got him in sight now, buddy. Get to us as soon as you can.'

'Keep heading this way, and I'll be with you sooner than you think.'

I put the phone safely in my pocket. Took out my SIG and reloaded it.

Kaufman was busy calling up his own people. Nothing I could do about that. I only hoped that I could get to Dantalion before the FBI arrived in force and made a siege of wherever Dantalion intended holing up. Kaufman was an ex-Army aviator, used to working alongside the Special Forces. But now he was an FBI SAC and was governed by different rules. I had to give him his lead on this, as long as he gave me a few minutes' latitude before calling the shots direct from the FBI manual.

The Lincoln continued westward, passing through a couple of small towns, blew under the I-95 then continued going, out towards the wild lands that separated the coastal towns from Lake Okeechobee. The lake itself was a dark line on the horizon as we sped after the sedan.

Dantalion drove the Lincoln like a crazy man, careless of meeting any oncoming traffic on the single lane of tarmac. From our aerial perspective the land looked like it had undergone a barrage of meteors – a lush green version of the surface of the moon.

Fields of very tall grass spread out beneath us, and for a minute or so the Lincoln was hidden from view where the grass became a knitted roof over the road. But then the car was on to a clear stretch of road again and passing a lake. The Lincoln appeared to be slowing. I nudged Kaufman's shoulder and he banked away, taking the helicopter out of Dantalion's line of sight. We hovered where we could just make out a flash of silver.

'He's moving again,' Kaufman announced and he dipped the nose of the chopper and we moved forwards much slower than before. The Lincoln disappeared beneath a second field of long grass.

'You think he saw us?'

'Not likely. He maybe stopped to get his bearings.'

'Do you know where that road takes us?'

'All the way to Okeechobee. There he has only three choices. North, south or to the bottom of the lake.'

This latest field wasn't quite as large as the first. It should take Dantalion less than a minute to pass through it and come back in sight. We hung back, cautious, waiting for the Lincoln to reappear. I counted out sixty seconds in my head.

'He must have stopped again.'

'We can't be sure of that. He could simply be driving slower than he was before. Hold on, I'll get a little closer, see what's what.'

He put the chopper into a hover, then very slowly took us sideways. The helicopter began to rotate through a half-circle. It gave us a view of the entire field and where sunlight broke on the blacktop about three-quarters of a mile ahead.

'Don't see anything. I think you're right, Hunter. He's stopped somewhere along the way.'

'Can you put me down?' I asked. 'This end would be best. You can go to the far side and see if you can backtrack along the road.'

'He'll hear us coming. He could be waiting for us.'

'That's fine by me. There's no Seagram to fuck things up this time.'

'I know Walter Conrad said that you were one of the best that he'd ever worked with, but it'd be best to wait for back-up. I've a couple McDonnell Douglas 530s on their way here. We could round Dantalion up between us, no sweat.'

McDonnell Douglas 530s are commonly known as 'Little Birds'. They're the gunships employed by the FBI during aerial assaults; the type you see in movies with rocket launchers and men in black jumpsuits hanging out the side with sniper rifles. If Dantalion caught a glimpse of any of those, he'd kill Bradley there and then.

'Can't wait for back-up,' I said. 'He's stopped for a reason. Maybe he doesn't see Bradley as a hostage any more and wants to lighten the load. We need to stop him now, Kaufman.'

He knew that I was right, but I could tell he was considering all the different ramifications for his future career with the FBI. His decisions would be severely tested by his bosses up at Quantico and Washington DC, but in the end, I was my own man and not under his direct jurisdiction.

'Careful of those power lines,' I cautioned as we swung back to the open area next to the big lake.

'The ground is too boggy to land here. I'm going to have to look for somewhere firmer.'

'No time.' I took the Ka-Bar out of my boot and tucked it through a belt loop of my jeans. 'Just get us low enough so I can jump.'

He looked at me like I was insane. He probably had it in mind that I'd disappear up to my neck in a sink hole. But then maybe that would save him from the bureaucratic nightmare he'd have to face for allowing me to conduct my own vigilante action against Dantalion.

Suit yourself, Hunter, his expression said. Then he was going through the routine of bringing us down towards the ground. I pushed open the cockpit door and it slammed back against the side of the chopper. The downwash from the rotor blades flattened the deep grass beneath me. It lifted loose debris that swirled around us like we were in a cyclone.

'This is low enough.' I swung my legs out of the cockpit. I took out the mobile phone, held it tight in my left hand, and took my SIG Sauer in my right. Over the noise of the engine I shouted, 'My friend Rink is coming. Don't let any of your boys stand in his way. He's not as patient with people as I am.'

Kaufman gave me a tight-lipped smile. 'Just watch your ass, Hunter.'

I winked. Then dropped out of the chopper, hoping I didn't land in the gaping jaws of an alligator.

CHAPTER 39

Bradley Jorgenson could not have got far in the time it took Dantalion to conceal the Lincoln from the road. A couple of minutes, that was all. In his drugged and disoriented state, it was highly probable that he'd managed to get as far into the long grass as one determined rush would take him, before falling face down and going back to sleep. His trail was easy enough to see; there were bent and broken stems of the bamboo-like grass angling away from the front of the Lincoln into the green twilight.

Dantalion took out the Glock 17 he'd liberated from Seagram and checked the load. He fed spare rounds into the magazine as he started after Bradley. From somewhere ahead the sound of a body pushing through the long grass came to his ears. Then something else: the whup, whup, whup of rotor blades.

He craned round to see the helicopter, but he was surrounded by the tall grass, looking up at only a tiny patch of blue sky. The walls of this maze had the effect of distorting and redirecting the source of the noise and made it difficult to pinpoint where the rotor sound was coming from. He couldn't get a location, but he knew that this was the helicopter which had been on the lawn outside Eunice Jorgenson's ramshackle home. Hunter was proving to be one resourceful dude.

Bradley Jorgenson was still alive only because Dantalion planned to use him to bait a larger trap. He'd hoped to torture Marianne Dean's whereabouts from her lover, contact her, and then demand that she come to a prearranged location where he'd finish the two of them. Hunter and his friend Rink would be along for the ride, but Dantalion was capable of killing them all. He'd beaten Hunter every other time they'd met and felt sure he would do so again.

The sound of the chopper receded, and he assumed that Hunter would continue on towards Okeechobee, before backtracking this way. It would give him all the time he needed to catch up with Bradley Jorgenson.

Sure enough, he heard the drone of the chopper as it swung away to the west. Dantalion smiled to himself, then stepped into the tall grass.

Small biting insects called this grass home.

So did serpents and lizards and all manner of crawling things.

Not a place that Dantalion would choose to frequent. But he pushed through the grass happily, feeling that all was right in his world. The numerological equations in his book would soon be back in balance. He could write up the numbers of those he'd dispatched in the meantime, and he even made himself a silent bet that he was close to meeting the tally of the original Dantalion and his command of thirty-six legions of spirits.

The going was tough. The grass grew in great hummocks, but sent out feelers at ankle level that stretched taut across the clear areas, creating trip-wires as effective as any he'd ever laid. The grass itself was as strong and coarse as hemp rope. Sheaves on the stems made long prickly spines where they frayed and split from the main growth, and they scratched and plucked at his flesh and clothing with each step. His hands were protected from the spearing grass, but his face was bare now that he'd ditched the helmet.

He couldn't hear the helicopter now, but he could hear Bradley's stumbling progress. Everything else was still and silent, the indigenous creatures of this sea of grass fleeing before the presence of alien invaders. There was an overpowering stench of rotting vegetation. A breeze touched his face like the caress of the lover he'd never known. Instead of following Bradley, he swung to the left and pushed through the grass towards a wide-open field. Separating him from the cultivated land flowed a sluggish stream, cut out of the earth to help drain the swamp this field had once been. The stream, clogged with black mud and decaying foliage, was the source of the stench. Across the field he could see the buildings and pylons that he'd noticed from the road. Strange place to have a factory, he thought, maybe some sort of electrical substation.

Following the edge of the drainage channel, he could gain time and distance on the fleeing Bradley. He took off at a lope, peering back and over his shoulder as he did so. Giving up the cover of the long grass was great for manoeuvrability, but it made him visible to anyone chasing him. The helicopter would be back and he didn't want to find himself in the sights of an FBI sharp-shooter. Bradley's crashing flight through the grass was all he needed to tell he was still on his trail. He moved along parallel to the sounds, seeing every now and then a flash of clothing through the thinner stands of reeds.

Dantalion was aware that he carried injuries. Three bullet wounds were not to be trifled with. The one in his leg was the most troubling, and the most likely to become infected in this environment of clinging roots and decaying vegetable matter. A fall in the mud was only one stumble away.

He pressed on regardless, keeping pace with Bradley.

He was so close now that he could hear the rasp of Bradley's breath, and his sobs of sheer terror. Still under the influence of the sodium amatol, Bradley would be in a state of severe confusion. His last lucid memory would be when Dantalion shot the FBI man and jabbed a syringe into Bradley's skin. The rest would seem like a jumble of disjointed images interspersed with black gulfs of nothingness. He would slowly be coming awake in this world of green and brown prison bars, knowing he must escape, but not why or from whom he was running.

Maybe he should simply put a bullet through Bradley's head and have done, get out of this stinking marsh, and contemplate less muddy alternatives for luring Hunter, Rink and Marianne Dean to him. But he had come this far, so would see out his original plan. A gun was all he needed to ensure that the privileged scion of the Jorgenson Empire would do exactly as he commanded. A harsh word and a nasty promise and Bradley would give up his flight for freedom.

Dantalion swung round so that he was now facing the young man blindly thrashing his way through the long grass.

'OK, enough is enough, Bradley. Come on out now.' He lifted the semi-automatic handgun to add emphasis to the implied threat that there would be no second chances.

Bradley came to a halt. He held his breath, hunched over like a prey animal caught in the sights of an eagle. Dantalion's words would have carried like those God spoke to Moses from the burning bush – only a little wetter.

'You have three seconds to comply,' Dantalion added. 'One . . .'

Bradley turned and crashed back the way he'd come, yowling something unintelligible.

Dantalion charged after Bradley, then, as he overtook the fleeing man, he pushed his way through the bamboo-like stalks to intercept him. Bradley saw him coming, and there was recognition in his face that no amount of sodium amatol could conceal. Dantalion brought up the Glock, aiming it directly at Bradley's throat. Bradley skidded to a halt. But even the dark unwinking eye of a handgun couldn't compel him to stop and face his nemesis. He lurched sideways, dodging past Dantalion's left arm that groped in empty space as it tried to snag him. He was sinuous in his attempt at avoiding the clutching fingers with their long, discoloured nails and scaly flesh. And even in his irritation at not catching hold of his quarry, Dantalion felt a pang that people found his touch repulsive. The aversion that most people experienced when Dantalion laid hands upon them had often been a major weapon in his favour, but he'd always longed for that singular encounter when someone would reach out and take his hand, without squirming or averting their gaze. The last person to do so had been his mother. Moments before he'd pushed his grandfather's rifle against her medulla oblongata and sent her to the longed-for reunion with his father with a swift jerk of the trigger.

Bradley charged deeper into the grass before twisting to the side and racing for the open ground he'd spotted. Dantalion kept pace with him, so that Bradley was mere yards ahead when he burst through the last stand of grass and on to the embankment above the foul-smelling ditch. He lifted the Glock. His finger danced on the trigger, but he did not shoot. He wished to be facing Bradley when the boy died. He wanted to look into his eyes and watch the soul die behind them. He wanted to hear the final exhalation of breath, wanted to taste it on his lips.

'You are prolonging your death, Bradley. Is that really what you want? Why not take fate head on like an honourable man? Turn around, Bradley, and I will kill you cleanly and painlessly. Should you choose to continue running, there will be a worse alternative.'

Bradley couldn't possibly have understood the implications of the choices Dantalion offered. He didn't stop running and he didn't turn around.

Dantalion lifted the Glock so that he was running with his arm extended, legs pumping high to avoid stumbling on the uneven ground. 'OK, then, Bradley. Have it your way!'

The Glock's report was startlingly loud in this wilderness. Animals shocked by the sudden bang gave voice to their fear, and terrified birds broke from the cover of the long grass and launched themselves heavenward.

Bradley crumpled to the ground, landing so heavily that his upper body dug a trench in the soft earth. He gave a groan of agony as he half-rolled with his own momentum, then Dantalion was over him and the Glock was pointed directly at the back of Bradley's head. Bradley began to mewl like a cat, and his fingers stretched as the agony shrieking through his body sought outlet.

'Hurts like hell, doesn't it?' Dantalion shot a second bullet through the back of the same knee he'd just demolished. Bradley screamed. Dantalion kicked him over on to his back. He turtled up, hugging his damaged knee against his chest.

'You son of a bitch!'

'Don't,' Dantalion warned. 'Don't say anything about my mother.'

Then he shot Bradley again, this time through the bones of the foot of his right leg.

'Do feel free to tell me where Marianne is. Do that and I'll make the next shot count. The pain will end, Bradley.'

Bradley was in a place beyond comprehension. Dantalion's whispery voice wasn't registering; not when his entire being was screaming out in agony. Dantalion cocked his head, bird-like.

'I'm afraid you've outlived your usefulness,' he told the unheeding man. Then he aimed the Glock at the centre of Bradley's face. 'Your choice, Bradley. Tell me where Marianne is and I will kill you cleanly.' He lowered his aim so it was below the Kevlar vest. 'If not, I'll gut shoot you and leave you for the alligators.'

In a moment of clarity, Bradley stared up at him. The young man's face was contorted with pain, but it couldn't hide his revulsion. 'Go to hell,' he spat.

'No doubt about it,' Dantalion agreed. 'But you'll be there before me.'

Bradley sneered. 'Yeah? Well I'll say hello to your mother, shall I? Stands to reason that bitch will be there too.'

'I told you not to speak about my mother.'

'Tough shit, man!' Bradley yelled. 'If she's anything like you she's an evil, ugly, *diseased* old bitch.'

Dantalion's head swung from side to side.

'My mother was beautiful.'

'Yeah, right!' Bradley fought himself up to a sitting position. Beads of cold sweat broke along his hairline. 'So it must have been your father who was pig-ugly, then?'

Dantalion blinked his rheumy eyes.

'Ha! Thought so. You don't even know your father, do you? You're just another bastard born from a drugged-up whore!'

Dantalion felt a quiver of rage build in him. Bradley's words went beyond the insults he'd endured all his life. Aimed at himself, other people's insults had fuelled him, built him into the killer that he'd become, but he would not stand by while this pig of a boy cast aspersions on his mother. He loved his mother. He had proven the depths of his love when he'd sent her to be with his father rather than keep her all to himself. He could have been selfish, but, no. He had done

338

her a kindness, even though he wanted his mother to be his for all eternity.

He pulled the trigger and the Glock barked like an angry dog.

CHAPTER 40

The bang of a gun happened so close by I could have sworn that I felt the pressure of displaced air in my inner ear. It took less than a moment for it to register that the gun had been fired many yards to my left and it was an echo effect of the rippling grasses that made it sound so close.

Dantalion had made an effort at concealing the car, but I'd discovered the abandoned car within minutes of disembarking from the chopper. I checked it for Bradley's corpse, and – thankfully – found it empty. Two separate trails led away through the tall grass and at random I chose the nearest to follow. When I'd dropped from the helicopter I'd sunk almost to my knees into viscous mud. Water had splashed up my body and I had to take out the Ka-bar knife and wipe it clean on some scrub. It made sense to keep hold of it. My SIG was in my other hand. I moved through the green ocean in a crouch with both my weapons poised for killing.

The last time I'd stalked an enemy through grasses like these was on an island in the Indian

Ocean. Sinhala villagers had been butchered by a faction of terrorists and my team was sent in to punish those responsible. The terrorists were a particularly devout group of fanatics prepared to die for their beliefs. They were known to carry cyanide capsules, preferring suicide to capture. It was a good compromise. We caught the murdering pigs and made them chew on their own capsules, but still shot them in their final seconds. Sounds brutal, but the sight of headless women and children is enough to make you forget your humanity.

So does an old lady sprawled across her own table with a bullet through her heart.

Moving through the whispering grasses, I thought back to how Rink and I, and half-a-dozen of our comrades, had used the cover of the elephant grass to get so close to the men we hunted that we could've reached out and snatched them one by one. It was the same now. I'd moved to within a couple of yards of Dantalion and the white-faced freak wasn't even aware of my presence.

He was pointing his gun down at the floor, and it took me a moment to realise that Bradley was there, concealed from my view by a dip in the ground. Dantalion leaned over him, and for the briefest time I saw one of Bradley's arms waving him back. He was still alive then. Dantalion fired his gun again. Bradley began screaming. I lifted my own SIG, only for the damn thing to jam on me. Bradley was still shouting, even after Dantalion shot him a third time, and I guessed that the man was torturing Bradley by shooting his extremities. I had moments to save Bradley, the seconds ticking down. However, with my gun jammed I had no other weapon than the Ka-bar. I could throw the knife, but there was always the chance that I'd miss. Then it would be my bare hands against Dantalion's gun, and bullets would always be faster than my fists.

It was a risk, but I didn't think that Dantalion was ready to kill Bradley yet. I slipped backwards into the longer grass, giving me the cover I needed while I disengaged the slide on my gun. I'm a fan of my modified SIG-Sauer because it has no safety to snag on clothing, and the sights are removed for the same reason. Normally it serves me well. I could fire a thousand rounds in quick succession and it would never jam. It was pure bad luck that the gun had failed me this time at the very moment I needed it most. Typically, I found that it was the bullet and not the gun that had let me down. I quickly ejected the jammed round, then racked the slide a second time, ejecting a second. Happy that the gun was good to go, I moved back towards Dantalion.

Both their voices were raised. Bradley was more angered than terrified and he was goading Dantalion with insults about his heritage. Dantalion was rising to the bait. His face looked like molten wax as he stepped over the top of Bradley. It was now or never.

I fired.

So did Dantalion.

But I had fired first and my bullet hit him in the meat of his right shoulder. Blood puffed into the air. Dantalion was knocked sidelong and his finger tightened reflexively on the trigger, firing off round after round. He made a high-pitched howl and toppled out of sight. I heard a splash and saw a gout of dirty water erupt into the air. The stench of rotting vegetation filled my senses.

Immediately I came out of hiding. My bullet had hit the killer, but it wasn't a mortal wound. Only once I had put a wad of lead through his skull or his heart would I relax. I moved from the grass on to an embankment over a drainage ditch where I saw Bradley had survived. He was sorely wounded through his right leg, but he'd live.

'Did you get him?' he asked hopefully.

'Not as clean as I wanted to.'

I stepped towards the ditch.

The water was putrid, murky and full of weeds. Scum on the surface had been broken and an undulating circle showed where Dantalion had gone under. There was no sign of him. Part of me hoped that he'd been entangled in the weeds and drowned, his lungs filling with the rancid water, but then a greater part wanted to kill him outright. Things *had* become personal between us.

Three times I fired into the water. Maybe it was a waste of ammunition, but if he was down there I didn't want him coming back uninjured. I waited for blood to find its way to the surface, but I saw no sign of it. Dantalion had used the dirty water for cover. He'd have to come up soon, and close by, but it was awkward to cover two directions at once.

'Where is he?' Bradley hissed.

'Quiet,' I snapped. I took a step backwards so that I didn't offer a target from below the water, then stood poised with my SIG, waiting for the tell-tale eruption of water as Dantalion would make his play.

But then something intervened to take away all hope of hearing Dantalion resurface. The shriek of turbines and the whop, whop, whop of rotor blades were suddenly horrendously loud above me. My first thought was that Kaufman had returned to give support from the air. But that summation lasted only as long as it took for the pilot on a loud hailer to shout orders at me.

'This is the FBI. Lower your weapon or we will be forced to shoot.'

It was a sleek black craft. One of the McDonnell Douglas 530s that SAC Kaufman had brought in for back up. The 'Little Bird' hung in the air and an FBI sharpshooter sat in the doorway with his scope aimed directly at my chest.

'Drop your weapon!'

Bad luck was coming my way in spades that day. To the chopper crew I was the one standing over a severely wounded man and it must have looked like my gun that was responsible for shooting him. Fair enough under the circumstances, but no way was I about to give up my weapon; not when I knew that Dantalion was close by and would be seeking revenge.

It left me only one recourse. I rushed headlong into the long grass. The sharpshooter immediately fired and high velocity rounds peppered the earth behind me and cut fronds from the grass so that they sifted around me. I ran harder. The chopper had the advantage of a hawk's-eye view, not to mention a heat-seeking FLIR scope that would pick me out in seconds, but to stand still meant giving up my weapon and leaving me vulnerable to the killer under the water. I ran full sprint, slashing at the tough grass with my Ka-bar, trying to get out of the line of sight of the chopper pilot. It would take him the best part of thirty seconds to bring the chopper about, realise I was out of sight, then decide to switch to the heat-seeking camera on the nose of the cockpit. In that time I would be in a more opportune position to protect myself from the over-eager sharpshooter.

The loud hailer sounded again and the McDonnell Douglas swooped overhead, the downwash of the rotors knitting the grass over my head. As soon as it was beyond me I turned on my heel and sprinted back to Bradley.

Bradley had heaved himself up on to his elbows in the few seconds I'd been gone. I crashed out of the long grass and skidded to a halt at his side. His face was full of pain, and not a little bewilderment.

'What are they doing?'

'They think I'm the fuckin' bad guy,' I told him. And I was going to have to put them right. The problem being I still had a wounded man to protect from his would-be killer. 'Sorry, Bradley, but this might hurt.'

I grasped him under his armpits, pulled him bodily on top of me so that he was sitting in my lap like an overgrown child. Then I jammed the Ka-bar into the earth beside me, and held my right arm high, so that the sharpshooter could see I had my finger through the trigger guard, but that my SIG was suspended upside down and no immediate threat.

'Holy shit!' Bradley said, with the realisation that I was going to use him as a shield. 'What if they shoot me?'

'They won't do that,' I told him, confidently. 'And anyway, you're wearing a Kevlar vest.'

'They could hit my head!'

'Nah, they'll fire for centre mass. Only sure way of hitting the target.'

'What about the killer? He won't think twice about shooting me in the head.'

'Then you'll just have to count on me getting him first.'

'Goddamn . . .'

'Yeah,' I agreed. 'Not good odds, Bradley, but it's all we've got at the minute.'

Then I told him what I wanted him to do.

We sat like that until the gunship did a loop and

returned to its starting position. The chopper hovered over us and once again I was in the sights of the sniper scopes. My head was the only visible target, but my emphatic gesturing with the upside-down gun meant that I wasn't going to experience my last moments with the smell of Bradley's fear in my nostrils.

A second 'Little Bird' screamed into view. This one was about two hundred yards out, and it swept over the open field from the west. Passing over the top of the first chopper, it tilted and raced off over the long grass behind me. The combined roar of both choppers drowned out both Bradley's and my exhortations for them to back off.

Out of the side door of the nearest chopper, a black garbed Hostage Rescue Team trooper rappelled to the floor. He was armed with an assault rifle and he took up a crouched covering position while two more members of the team dropped from the guts of the chopper like large black spiders on fat webs. Once the two exchanged positions with him, the first agent came towards us, his gun braced to his shoulder. The 'Little Bird' swooped away and finally I could hear myself think.

The FBI agent's voice rang loud and clear.

'Drop the weapon, Hunter. Now!'

I wasn't surprised he recognised me. He was one of the men SAC Kaufman had been communicating with from the headset. Whatever Kaufman had told him, he wasn't taking any chances. Truth was, even with my gun in an awkward upside-down position, I could manipulate it faster than the human eye could follow and could've shot him.

'Lose the fucking weapon.' To emphasise the command he leaned into his rifle so that it drew a bead on my forehead.

'The killer is still out there,' I shouted back. 'I wounded him, but he's still dangerous. I'm not dropping my gun.'

'The perp's our problem now. I have orders from SAC Kaufman to make you stand down.'

'Bradley is *my* problem, and I don't stand down until I know he's no longer in danger.'

Switching tack, the anonymous agent said to Bradley, 'Mr Jorgenson, we are here to protect you. You need immediate medical assistance. We can't offer that while Hunter is armed. Tell him to stand down.'

'Look,' I said. 'We're on the same side here. Let's cut the crap and get Bradley the hell away from here. I'm going after Dantalion.'

'You aren't going after anyone.' He'd taken another step forward. The two back-up agents had also moved to flank me. I was the proverbial fish in the barrel. But out there in the water lurked a more dangerous creature in need of spearing.

Rising up from behind Bradley, I lifted the SIG so it was clear to all. 'I'm going to holster my weapon, but that's as far as it goes. You can load Bradley into one of those birds, but I'm staying.'

'Step away from Mr Jorgenson,' said the first

agent as though I hadn't spoken. 'The FBI will deal with this situation now. You do not have official sanction in this matter, Hunter. You are no longer on active duty and do not work with our government's agreement. If you refuse to step away you will be arrested for obstructing a federal agent.'

I stepped away.

I pushed the SIG into the waistband at the back of my jeans. One of the HRT agents came and laid a hand on Bradley's shoulder. He took a grip on the cloth of Bradley's shirt and pulled him round and away from me. As if I was the bad guy. The other two covered me with their rifles, but I was gratified to note that neither tried to disarm me. Not immediately.

I indicated the Ka-bar, hilt deep in the silt. 'I'm taking that as well.'

I stooped and picked up the knife. As I rose from my crouch I was already pivoting. The Ka-bar is a man-killer. To kill is its primary function, and all other applications of the fighting knife are side-products of its design. Not that I was about to kill an FBI agent in the correct execution of his duty. I used only the butt-end to thrust into the midriff of the man nearest me. He was wearing armour, but my blow was delivered with all the power of my upswinging arm and the force went directly through the vest and into his internal organs. Wind rushed out of his wide open mouth, even as I whipped the rifle out of his grasp and turned it on the first agent. I hurled the rifle at him, end over end. His reaction was to bat it away with the barrel of his own gun. And into the space he'd left me I stepped and launched a kick that caught him in the juncture of his thighs. He was wearing a box, but it didn't make a difference. Not when my shin lifted him a hand's width off the floor. I jumped in as he landed on his face, kicking away his gun with the side of my foot.

One and a half seconds isn't long in any violent confrontation. Viewed in afterthought it's amazing how rapidly a tableau can change. But there was a third armed agent to deal with.

'Now, Bradley,' I yelled.

Bradley immediately became less than the crippled weight he seemed. He threw his arms round the man supporting him, grappling the agent's rifle so that it was wedged between them. Bradley continued to drive into the man, and they went down on the ground, rolling in spongy earth. I charged over and grabbed the man's rifle away from him. Then I spun so that I was covering them all with the levelled rifle.

'OK, boys,' I yelled. 'The deal's the same. You get Bradley out of here, I go after Dantalion.'

The first agent was the first to recover from our attack. 'You have assaulted FBI agents in the execution of their duties. It is a federal crime, Hunter. You'll be arrested for this.'

'Get a fuckin' life,' I snapped. 'We all know how this is gonna go down. I'm leaving. You lot get the

350

fuck out of here. You tell Kaufman I escaped. I've gone after the demented killer we all want to see dead. Where's the fucking crime in that?'

I threw the gun aside, took out my SIG and raced away. None of them lifted a weapon, so it seemed they'd seen sense in my words.

I'd seen something too. Way ahead of me. A pale blur of a face turned my way. A dark-garbed figure loping across the field towards the huge buildings on the horizon.

CHAPTER 41

The bullet had clipped Dantalion's right shoulder when he was about to shoot Bradley Jorgenson in the face. It had cut away a large chunk of his hide, but had missed anything serious like an artery or bone. The wound was numb, likely very soon screaming in agony, but not totally debilitating. He could still hold his Glock, he could still shoot, and he could still finish his mission.

The force of the bullet had knocked him off balance, but that might prove a boon. It offered him another chance at killing Jorgenson. Next time it would take much, much longer and involve an infinite amount of pain.

The bullet had also thrown him headlong into the putrescent stream, providing salvation. If he'd fallen on the dry ground, Hunter would most definitely have killed him. The murky water had given him cover while he swam away. He was able to surface many yards west of where he'd fallen, concealed from the eyes of Hunter by over-hanging foliage. There he'd been able to catch his breath and check the two things most important to him. The Glock was wet, but serviceable. After his last plunge into the Inter-Coastal Waterway, he'd taken care to protect his book in cling film, so it was barely damp when he fished it from inside the jumpsuit. Everything was A-OK.

Then fortune smiled on him again. The FBI helicopters forced Hunter away from the stream, giving him the opportunity to make his own break for freedom. He heard the roar of the choppers, the hard snap of rifles, and knew that the FBI had confused Hunter with him. Maybe they'd kill the bastard and leave the door open for him to get at Bradley a second time. Or maybe not. He couldn't rely on Lady Luck. He had to make his own opportunities.

He scrambled along the stream bed, found a place to climb out and crawled up on to the far side. Lying on the embankment, he watched as a chopper set down three armed agents and witnessed Hunter dispatching all three in the space of seconds. Impressive. Hunter was proving a dangerous enemy. Time, he decided, to finish him off.

Glancing back over his shoulder, he scrutinised again the power station he'd intended taking Bradley to. The buildings had a decrepit look, as if they had not known service in some time. They were bordered by a chain-link fence, but here and there he could make out breaches in it as though vandals had broken into the compound many times over the years. One of the nearer buildings had metal sheets over its windows and doors, but he could also see a gaping doorway where the sheet had been prised loose.

Rising up, he cast a look backwards.

Hunter met his gaze, and he nodded in the direction of the buildings.

Come and get it, asshole.

Then he took off across the field, heedless of the two McDonnell Douglas choppers circling the nearby field. His leg pained him. His arm didn't yet, but it would only be a matter of time. He had to reach the buildings before Hunter could get close enough to shoot. Exposed as he crossed the open space, Hunter would be easy meat for Dantalion's bullets.

A chopper came over the top of the power station, rotors buzzing like an angry hornet. It wasn't one of the black gunships, but the liveried Bell Jet Ranger once piloted by the man whose clothes he now wore.

The sun was behind the chopper, but he could make out a single man on board. One of the agents from back at Eunice Jorgenson's home. Probably the asshole tasked with bringing him down.

Dantalion came to a standstill and lifted the Glock. He saw a widening of the eyes of the man piloting the chopper. Dantalion fired. Three rapid bursts that cut a zigzag pattern across the windshield. Behind the starred glass the cockpit changed colour, scarlet puffing in the air.

Then the chopper was dipping towards him and

Dantalion was forced to move as the whirling rotors cleaved air above him as if in a decapitating frenzy. He charged to the left and he felt the displacement of air as the chopper hurtled to the ground. Behind him it sounded as if the earth had exploded. Dirt and dust and grass showered around him. There was the screaming of an engine on overload, the *bang! bang! bang!* of rotors churning into the ground, followed by shrieks as chunks of hot metal were torn loose and thrown into the air.

He looked back.

The Bell Jet Ranger was reduced to scrap metal. Oily black smoke rose like a funeral pyre from the burnt-out engine components. The rotors had been reduced to gnarly stumps. Still, the dying helicopter was groaning, but only until sparks jumped from the overheated engine into the spilled fuel and it gave out one final roar as the entire craft exploded.

The concussion sent Dantalion sprawling to the ground. Searing heat washed over him and for the briefest of moments he felt as though all life was being sucked from his body. An image flashed through his mind of the petrified victims found in the ashes of Pompeii after the eruption of Mount Vesuvius, charred and desiccated corpses twisted into foetal balls. He thought that was how he must look. Except now the heat had gone, the in-gust taking the flames back towards the wreckage of the chopper, and he realised that –

apart from singed hair and a throat that felt like it burned – he was unharmed.

He was face down on the ground with his arms over his head. He had no recollection of striking the pose. He quickly snapped to attention, wondering how much time his killing of the chopper pilot had taken, and how much of his advantage had been torn away in doing so.

Rolling to his feet, he looked for Hunter. He was two hundred yards nearer and gaining. Then smoke from the doomed chopper rolled across the intervening space and Hunter's charging form was lost from view. Dantalion broke into an ungainly lope, hand fumbling for his book. The book was there, but it took him a second to register that the hand he'd used should have been holding a Glock. He ground to a halt, turned round, searching for where the explosion had thrown the gun to.

He couldn't see it. Smoking debris lay everywhere. Chunks of hot metal and divots of earth obscured the ground all around where he'd fallen.

'Son of a bitch!'

Hunter burst through the smoke bank, his seething eyes picking out Dantalion like lasers.

He wasn't at an advantage any longer and the nearby building offered only a place to hide.

If he could even get there before Hunter was close enough to use his handgun.

This time his flight was fuelled by adrenalin and all his hurts were forgotten.

CHAPTER 42

It seemed my CIA friend, Walter Hayes Conrad, wields only a limited amount of power. He'd pulled enough strings to ensure Kaufman offered me a level amount of leeway that I was allowed along for the ride. But SAC Kaufman had said that I'd only be given free rein until his own men arrived. It had obviously been his plan to take me out of the picture as soon as he had back-up at the scene. I'd been wrong about Kaufman. He was as much a bureaucratic asshole as most others in his position. He was still *the* Special Agent in Charge, and he wasn't about to allow me – a loose cannon – the glory of bringing down the professional hit man who'd killed his colleague.

It was bad form taking down Kaufman's men the way I did. I probably hadn't endeared myself to anyone. My only saving grace was that I hadn't left any of them severely injured. I could foresee that Walter was going to have to kiss a few butts before this was over with. Maybe I would have to as well. But I didn't let that concern me. I had Dantalion in my sights.

The white-faced killer had a good lead on me. I jumped the irrigation channel, raced after him. I could have taken him out with a rifle, but something had made me throw down the FBI agent's gun in favour of my trusty SIG. Things had grown very personal between us and I'd only be happy if I was looking into the bastard's face when I killed him. Using my SIG meant I'd be able to see the whites of his eyes.

It wasn't hard to see where he was heading – a complex of buildings surrounded by a chain-link fence. My best guess was he wanted to find cover and then pick me off while I was in the open and exposed. So I ran harder, taking that option away from him.

Then a chopper rose into view from behind the buildings.

Recognising it as the Bell Jet Ranger I'd hitched a ride here in, I realised that SAC Kaufman was on an ass-covering expedition of his own. There was the roll of automatic gunfire and I staggered against the blast as the chopper went supernova.

SAC Kaufman didn't need to worry about answering awkward questions any longer.

The air was full with the stench of aviation fuel, as viscous as warm treacle on my skin. Smoke billowed, but I caught a snatch of movement as Dantalion came to his feet. He set off running, and it was more than my approach that lent wings to his heels. The fucker was unarmed. And he was running scared.

The thunders of judgement and wrath are numbered, you freak!

I charged after him. Lifted my SIG and fired a quick volley.

Contrary to popular belief, even a trained gunman like me can't hit targets at a run. Handguns are notoriously poor for killing people unless you are very close to a static target. But that was OK. My only wish was to keep him running and keep him frightened. My bullets kept him moving, and his face when he glanced back at me was a mask of horror.

Dantalion reached the fence and he launched himself at a rent in the wires. His clothes snagged and he tore at the wire to free himself. All the while I was gaining on him and I fired again. Sparks marked where my bullets cut through the wires.

Fifty yards or so separated us. But that distance was shortened with each step. So, I told myself, was Dantalion's time left on this earth.

The phone in my pocket vibrated.

Without halting my charge I plucked the phone out of my pocket.

There was only one person it could be.

'Rink?'

'Just lost your signal, buddy. Thought I'd check you were still alive.'

Above my head was a tangle of high-voltage cables. The buildings appeared derelict but I could hear the faint buzz from the wires, felt the hair stirring at the nape of my neck. There was still power surging through the network, so we were lucky to be able to speak at all.

'Still alive, Rink,' I huffed as I ran. 'Where you at?'

'Can't be far off. I can see vultures circling in the sky, and if I'm not mistaken they're looking for pickings from some big old barbecue.'

Snatching a glance over my shoulder, I saw Rink's vultures. The two 'Little Birds' circling the devastation of the Bell Jet Ranger. The barbecue was SAC Kaufman's funeral pyre.

'Follow the portents,' I told Rink. 'You ain't too far off. The FBI are playing at assholes now. Can you keep them off my back so I can finish Dantalion?'

'I'll do my best.'

'Would have liked you with me, Rink, but things are about to come to a head here.'

'Just kill the frog-giggin' asshole so's I can go back to my mom.'

The phone cut out.

I jammed it back in my pocket, then vaulted through the hole in the fence that Dantalion had used. A metal door in the large building directly in front of me had been pulled askew. Dantalion must have rushed through the door and into the darkness inside.

I was pretty sure that Dantalion had lost his gun. But I would have been an idiot if I'd blundered inside and been cold-cocked if he was waiting just inside the door. I slowed down. Peripherally I was aware of one of the sleek gunships racing my way. Perhaps they blamed me for the death of their leader. Maybe they were coming to shoot me. But I didn't think so. I waved to the pilot, directing him over the building to cover the exits at that side. The chopper had to swing around the high-voltage cables strung above the compound, but it looked like they were complying with my directions. The other chopper headed away, taking Bradley to safety.

Marianne Dean was safe. So now was Bradley Jorgenson. There was only one thing I wanted: to ensure that Dantalion couldn't threaten either of them again.

Pressing myself against the wall to the side of the open door, I drew my Ka-bar. Dantalion could be hiding anywhere, and the knife would be a better weapon than my gun if I stumbled into him in the dark. I shoved the SIG into the waistband at the small of my back, then quickly slipped inside the building.

My first act was to move away from the light seeping in through the door. Randomly choosing to go left, I moved silently through the shadows. Then I came to a standstill. I held my breath, closed my eyes against the darkness. Even in a pitch-black place the eyes can play tricks on the mind. You see movement in the darkness that isn't there, you jump at images conjured by the mind as the brain attempts to make sense of the sudden blindness. Far better is to trust your other senses and shut off the one suffering deprivation. We naturally close our eyes, so the brain does not rebel against the act; rather it heightens your hearing, your senses of smell and taste and touch. I'm also a firm believer in a sixth sense, that extrasensory perception that warns of impending danger. Maybe it is simply all the senses working in complete unison, maybe it's something paranormal, but it's there. I attuned myself to the dark, listening, smelling, tasting the air. A cool but steady draft wafted from deep inside the building. It caressed my face, but there was no flutter in the breeze, nothing to indicate that a human body moved nearby, disturbing the flow.

Confident that Dantalion did not lurk close by, I moved further inside. Ten paces on, I paused again. The breeze remained constant. But something plucked at my olfactory senses, and I realised I could smell blood. The coppery tang was faint. But it was there. I moved again, and the smell grew stronger.

I'm no bloodhound, so it wasn't as if I could sniff the killer out, but I was pretty sure that I was heading in the correct direction. A change in the draught told me that something ahead had affected the dynamics of the atmosphere. Dantalion had silently opened another door and was seeking refuge in an antechamber.

The smell was now of rusting machinery coupled with a hint of ozone. Somewhere nearby I could detect a static buzz. I tried to tune all these things out, but it was no good. I opened my eyes, and my night vision had adapted so that I could now make out the bulk of machines on either side of me. They squatted like amorphous creatures, silently watching my progress through the building. Ahead of me I could detect a darker shadow. I edged towards it, the Ka-bar held tight to my body so that Dantalion couldn't knock it from my hand. My boot touched a raised plat-form and I found I could step easily on to the first of a number of concrete stairs. Grit crunched underfoot. I halted. Listened for a response to my movement.

Nothing came back at me, so I continued.

The stairway took me to the door I assumed Dantalion had used to leave the room. Probing for the door with my free hand, I readied the Ka-bar with the other, wedging my fingers into the narrow gap between the door and the frame and exerting the slightest presure. The door swung silently away, and I stepped into the space beyond.

I was in a narrow passage, some sort of vestibule that led deeper into the guts of the building. I listened for any hint that Dantalion waited for me. But there was nothing.

The air was close, like it had been sealed within this corridor for too long. Dust sifted on to my lips, so delicate, but apparent to my heightened senses. Someone had moved through here very recently, kicked up the motes of dust that were only now beginning to settle. I pressed on.

Twenty yards further I came to a second door, this one wooden. I touched it with my fingertips and they came away sticky. Dantalion's blood. He had obviously brushed his injured arm against the door. I smiled to myself. Then I turned quickly on my heels, bringing up the Ka-bar.

It was an old trick. One I was infinitely familiar with. A false trail misled the hunter while the pursued person backtracked, waited until the hunter passed by and then launched an attack at his exposed back.

Dantalion wasn't as clever as he thought he was.

As he burst from a doorway to my right I was ready for him.

He came at me, throwing a punch aimed at what he thought was the nape of my neck. Instead I was facing him and he ran full tilt on to my Ka-bar. Six inches of razor-sharp steel rammed to the hilt into his gut.

I twisted the blade, even as he slapped at me with both hands. His blows were ineffectual, but I felt a scratch from one of his ragged fingernails. He slumped on the blade and I grabbed hold of his windpipe, closing my hand into a tight fist to halt his sour breath exploding over my face.

'Die, you freak.'

He couldn't answer. Not with his windpipe crushed in my fist, but I could have sworn that his shudder was one of humour. What was so damn funny?

I felt a weird rushing in my head.

And I knew.

That was no fingernail. It was a needle. A fucking hypodermic syringe!

Then it was my turn to slump.

CHAPTER 43

He waited in darkness.

Coming here, stumbling twice as he'd sought concealment within the shadows, he'd put down his ungainliness to the human shell that his spirit inhabited. It was Jean-Paul St Pierre who'd stumbled, not the great Dantalion.

It occurred to him that the racing of his heart, and the endorphins flooding through his system, had negated most of his pain, and after this he would be laid up for days, unable to function while his body healed itself. Feeling the ache in his many wounds, he knew he would continue to suffer the agonies of *ordinary* men until his book was put right. He didn't consider this long; he didn't believe that he would exist in this weak shell of mortality much longer. His mind had been working on a subconscious level, calculating formulae, figuring the numerology of all those that he'd killed, and it had come to a conclusion. The agent he'd recently killed had raised his tally exponentially. He needed only kill Hunter and he would equal the original Dantalion. All his worldly troubles would be behind him.

Dantalion did not fear Hunter now. He was confident in his abilities. He was a professional killer. He was an angel, and even one who'd proven as adept as Hunter was no match for a divine being. He would destroy him.

Hunter had a gun but that did not faze him. There were more ways to kill a man than with bullets. Guile and trickery could defeat even the most powerful enemy.

I'm better than Hunter is, he thought. I've beaten him every other time. Hunter has shot me a number of times and his bullets haven't killed me yet. Why should things be any different this time?

With the syringe with which he'd controlled Bradley Jorgenson and the sodium amatol it held, it would be enough to put Hunter to sleep. It would be a simple task to take his gun from him, then use it to ventilate his head in a number of places.

The thought brought a smile to his lips. He liked shooting people in the head. There was an undeniable finality to it.

It was why he killed his mother that way.

She wanted to join his father. So he'd answered her wish. The single bullet had instantly severed her spine at the point where it met her brain. She died instantly.

He didn't need to keep on shooting her until he had no bullets left, but he knew now that he'd done that out of inexperience. And love. He didn't want to shoot the woman only to find that he'd failed and that she would be a cripple for the rest of her days. So he made sure. No walking away, he told himself. Like he wouldn't walk away from Hunter until he was sure he was dead.

'Now,' he told himself. 'Do it now.'

He attacked. Jabbing with the needle.

He felt the solid thud of Hunter's hand connect with his gut, but it did not deter him.

'Die, you freak.'

Dantalion was not sure who had spoken those words. Hunter, or maybe it was even himself; he could not tell.

Hunter's hand twisted against his abdomen. Dantalion felt a corresponding twisting of his gut. Then red searing pain flared and he realised only then that the man had not simply punched him: he had jammed a knife into his body.

So it was Hunter who'd spoken?

Let him have his little moment, he thought. Let him think he's won.

Dantalion smiled. He felt the man slump and knew that his drug had done its work. And his book had been his salvation. Hunter's blade had pierced his book. It had pushed through the cover and the pages within, exited out the back of it, but with barely an inch of the blade embedded in his flesh, nowhere near his internal organs. It wasn't he who was going to die.

The fingers round his windpipe loosened and Dantalion sucked in air. Hunter was lying against his shoulder, as though seeking support. Dantalion stepped away and the man went to his knees. His fingers were still on the hilt of the knife, but he had no strength to use the weapon. Dantalion reached down and teased away each finger individually.

Hunter grunted.

Dantalion snorted and kicked the man over backwards. Hunter slammed against the door marked with Dantalion's blood, throwing it open to reveal a room much brighter than the dark places they'd already traversed. A raised platform made up the nearest end of the room, then dropped away to ground level. The light was coming from below.

Dantalion looked down at the knife standing out from his body. It hung suspended, held by the wound and the weight of the book caught up in his clothing. Dantalion tugged on the hilt, wincing as he felt the knife pull from his flesh. Warm blood trickled down his abdomen and pooled around his groin. He wasn't overconcerned. Once he finished off Hunter his flesh would mend as he transformed into the higher being he'd always been destined to become.

He pulled out his book and wrenched free the blade.

Military issue Ka-bar, he noted. Man-killer by definition. Useless against angels.

Hunter had rolled on to his side in an effort to get up. Dantalion saw the confused expression on his face and was only sorry that Hunter wasn't fully coherent. He wanted him fully aware when he was killed by his own weapon.

Hunter made it to his hands and knees.

Dantalion stood to his side, lifted the Ka-bar.

Then he saw the gun thrust into the waistband of Hunter's jeans.

The thunders of judgement and wrath are numbered.

It was always about the numbers.

He could offer a choice.

'One: knife?' he asked. Then he plucked out the SIG Sauer. 'Two: gun? Which is it going to be, Hunter? How shall I kill you?'

CHAPTER 44

O ne of the more obscure facets of my training had been how to endure torture. I've ran the gamut of methods employed by those who find it necessary to prise information from an enemy soldier. Sleep deprivation, mind games, physical beatings: I had to suffer and defeat them all when a member of the Special Forces. When I was drafted into the team headed by the shadowy men who became known as Arrowsake, I was introduced to further methods. The Geneva Convention forbids torture. But those I fought did not give a fuck for conventions. So it was necessary for me to be exposed to the other methods that some governments and terrorist groups used with impunity.

As soon as the needle went in, and I felt the rushing in my skull, I knew what drug was coursing through my system. I'd felt its effects before. Sodium amatol. Truth serum as it's sometimes referred to. It's an inhibitor. It lowers resistance. It makes you feel drunk. But at the low dosage Dantalion had squirted into me, it wasn't going to kill me. It wasn't even going to send me to sleep.

What it would do was disorient me, take away my strength and make it difficult to fight back. But I knew I could shake off the effects. Given time.

Dantalion kicked me over.

He didn't know, but the pain acted in my favour. It shook off some of the debilitating fog in my brain. I rolled on to my side, looking for him.

My eyes rolled in my skull and I could see his silhouette in triplicate as my vision swam.

Aim for the one in the middle, I told myself. The thought struck me as funny, even as I knew that he was moving to kill me.

I rolled on to my hands and knees. A tide rushed through me, and I was almost sick. My heart felt like a massive bellows in my chest, blood pumped supercharged through my veins. Blackness clouded at the edge of my consciousness. I shook my head. Clear the cobwebs. Clear the cobwebs, I chanted to myself. Fight the drug, push it aside.

'One: knife?' I heard.

Couldn't quite comprehend his meaning.

'Two: gun?'

Fingers tugged at my back and I realised my mistake. I'd shown him my SIG. I didn't have the strength to stop him taking it. I barely had the strength to hold myself upright on my locked forearms.

'What's it going to be, Hunter?'

I sucked in air, holding it, making pressure in my skull to push back the fluttering shadows from my mind.

'How shall I kill you?'

'With boredom,' I told him.

Then I kicked out, pistoning from the knee so that my heel crunched into his nearest shin.

Dantalion howled with pain, and the sound did more to clear my mind than all my previous attempts.

Pushing upwards, I came to my feet. My head swam, and it felt like I was on the deck of a ship in the storm of the century. But I didn't stop. I slammed the heel of my palm into Dantalion's groin, took hold of anything I could find and squeezed with all my might.

Now his pain was given high-pitched voice. Ah-ah-ah-ah-ah, sounding like he was going to sneeze. To give him something else to think about, I smacked my forehead into his face.

Not the best idea. The effect of bone on bone set off a tsunami inside my own head, and we reeled apart, equally stunned.

I grabbed for my gun: it wasn't there.

Dantalion was holding both my weapons.

Have to change that scenario.

But even as I lunged at him, he brought up my SIG and fired.

Luck rather than skill had caused me to dodge at the same time and the bullet punched through the space beneath my left armpit. I threw a looping right hook and drove my fist into his ribs. Dantalion was flung round by the force of the blow, but his left arm swept up and the Ka-bar slashed a line through my jacket. Dantalion stumbled away from me and I followed, chopping at his gun hand with the stiffened edge of my hand. My blow caught him on the mound of his forearm, shocking the radial nerve, and his hand opened in reflex spasm. The SIG clattered to the floor. It was out of reach for both of us and if I lunged for it I'd be inviting a knife in my back. So I threw a punch at his face instead.

Still under the influence of the drug, my punch was neither powerful, nor precise. I didn't knock him out, but I did flatten his nose against his face. Blood splattered, a torrent ran down his upper lip and into his mouth. He exhaled harshly, making droplets of his blood fleck my clothes.

He stabbed out at me and I grappled his arm. Holding his wrist with both my hands, I hauled him round even as I turned side on. His ankles bumped against my outstretched leg. It wasn't an expert judo throw, but it was enough to over-balance him and he went down to the floor. I fell on top of him, and loosening one hand from his wrist I drove my clawed fingers into his eyes.

Dantalion pushed me off him and I didn't have the strength to resist. We rolled away from each other. Then it was a fight to be first to our feet. Dantalion won and came at me, launching a kick into my ribs. I felt something crack and white hot pain flared through my body. He kicked again, but this time I hooked an arm round his heel and swept his leg high into the air. He toppled backwards and his fall took him almost to the edge of the platform. Then he rolled back towards me and I saw my own Ka-Bar glinting in his hand.

I had only one option. My SIG lay on the platform not half a dozen feet from Dantalion. We exchanged stares for less than a heartbeat, and then we were both rushing for the gun. Dantalion got to it first. He snatched at the SIG, even as he scythed the air in front of my throat with the knife.

But I'd never been going for the gun, I simply wanted him in a position where I could finish the bastard off. I leaped feet first at him. He fired, but he hadn't brought the gun round far enough and the bullet missed by a mile. Both my boots drove into his chest. I slapped down on the edge of the platform, my hip and right shoulder taking the brunt of the fall. It knocked the wind out of me, but nowhere near as much as my drop kick had done to Dantalion. He was thrown backwards, legs and arms windmilling as he disappeared over the edge of the platform. I heard the dull thud of him hitting the ground, but then there was silence. Painfully, I crawled to the edge of the platform. He was lying in a pool of light ten feet below me, squirming as though his spine had shattered during the fall.

I took stock of my surroundings.

I was in a large room that had once been a loading dock of some kind. A large roll-down shutter dominated one wall. It was partly open, letting in the harsh Florida sunlight. Glancing to my left, I saw a flight of metal steps leading down from the raised dais I was kneeling on. A guard rail would support me going down.

Down was where I wished to be.

Dantalion was injured, but he wasn't dead yet.

Pushing up to my feet, I again had to fight the disorienting effects of the drug in my body. The steps were a challenge, but I went down them hanging on to the rail, my feet clanging on the metal stairs. At the bottom I faced Dantalion.

Apparently his back wasn't broken.

He was on his hands and knees. His head swung up and he met my stare with a grim smile.

'I cannot die.'

'Want a bet?' I demanded as I moved towards him.

'Yes,' he said. Raising my SIG.

Suddenly all was sound and movement. The light went even harsher as the roller shutter was forced up and black-garbed men swarmed in. Laser scopes stabbed red beams through the room. Men shouted orders and commands.

I kept walking towards Dantalion and he rose up to meet me.

The gun was aimed at my face, but I just kept going.

Dantalion waited. Fisting both hands round my gun, he swayed where he stood, his legs braced wide. There was a book trailing on the floor behind him, attached to him by some kind of chain.

'Do not move!' someone shouted.

Neither of us was of a mind to listen.

Dantalion swung towards the FBI commandos swarming into the room and fired. The bullet passed above their heads, but it had them dropping for cover. Then he swung back towards me and a smile played across his lips.

One FBI man lifted his rifle and a red dot blossomed on Dantalion's chest.

'Drop your weapon or I will shoot,' yelled the commando.

'No you won't, asshole,' said a familiar voice. I heard the racking of a pump-action shotgun. The laser dipped away from Dantalion.

I didn't have to look to know that Rink was there.

Dantalion knew he was there as well. 'I owe you for ramming me off that bridge, Rink,' he said. 'Stick around and I'll kill you too.'

Rink laughed.

'He's all yours, Hunter,' my friend called.

I ran at Dantalion.

Dantalion jerked the trigger.

There was only the empty click of a firing pin in an equally empty chamber.

In my mind's eye I saw an innocent old lady lying dead on her table. I thought of Bradley brutally wounded. And, thinking of Marianne Dean – of what this beast intended doing to her – I barrelled into him with my shoulder, hooking my arms behind his knees, lifting and throwing him backwards at the same time. He slammed down on his back with me on top. The SIG went flying from his hand. I struck him in the chest with an elbow, holding him there even as I crawled up and sat astride him. His arms were free and he gouged at my face with his horrible fingernails, but it was futile. I drove my fist into his face, once, twice, three times.

His face was flecked with blood, and his pale eyes rolled up at me from swelling eyelids. His mouth opened in a grin and I saw tusk-like teeth. 'You're wasting your time, Hunter. I can't die. But you can.'

Peripherally, I caught the blur of movement. Men shouted and over the top of them all, I heard Rink's warning. My brain wasn't so clouded by drugs that it hindered my natural response.

I caught Dantalion's right wrist in my left hand. He continued to push, and he was surprisingly strong. The blade pressed against the flesh below my ribs. I felt the prickle of steel, but that only served my determination. Squeezing with all my might, I felt his bones grating together. The pale-faced bastard must have had something wrong with his bones, because I heard them snapping like green twigs.

Dantalion screamed. The knife fell from his nerveless hand.

'You can't die, huh? Let's see about that.'

I snatched at the book trailing like an abnormal appendage between his legs. It was attached to him by a silver chain and I wrenched it from him.

378

He was stunned by the pain of his broken arm, but when he saw me holding his book, strength flared. He bucked upwards, grabbing at the book with both hands.

'Give it back!'

Hooking my heels under his kidneys, I rode him like a rodeo bronco. Then I slammed the book against the side of his head and jammed his face against the floor. He squirmed beneath me, spittle shooting from his mouth as he cursed me. His hands clawed towards my face again, so I grabbed his broken wrist and gave it an extra squeeze. He shrieked in agony. Both hands dropped on to the book and touched it spasmodically. I wrenched it from him.

'What's so fucking important about this damn thing?' I demanded. I flicked it open and saw nothing but row upon row of numbers written in a scratchy style.

The numbers meant nothing to me.

Evidently they meant everything to the killer.

'You want it back, do you? Well, here you are! Have it!'

I tore pages from the book, crumpled them in my fist, then as he shouted in alarm I jammed the wad of paper into his open mouth. He gagged, but I forced the wad further in. Then I held his mouth shut and placed my other hand over his sealed lips and nostrils. Adding to the pressure, I threw my weight on top of him and stared into his eyes. We were inches apart and I saw his pupils dilate in realisation that he was wrong. He could die.

There were shouts of consternation from behind me. A rush of bodies. Hands clawing at me. But I trusted Rink to keep the FBI off me long enough for it to be finished. Dantalion thrashed under me in one final attempt to break free but there was nothing he could do to stop me now.

It didn't take long.

I wasn't sure he was dead until I felt a hand on my shoulder.

'He's dead, Hunter,' Rink said. 'You can relax.'

I looked down at the man beneath me. Marianne and Bradley would be safe now. The old lady was avenged.

His eyes were bugged wide, pale and milky in death.

The flesh round his mouth was blackened, lips blue. Blood vessels had erupted all along his jawline.

'That put a little colour in his cheeks.'

CHAPTER 45

Rink and I made an unscheduled visit to the local FBI field office. We were in cuffs and treated like we were the ones responsible for slaughtering upward of two dozen people. But then Walter Hayes Conrad IV arrived and a few asses were metaphorically kicked. When we walked out of the FBI building it was with handshakes all round and congratulations on a job well done, even if the plaudits weren't reflected in the faces of the men doing the congratulating. Maybe the way in which I'd killed Dantalion had something to do with it.

Not that anyone lamented Jean-Paul St Pierre's passing. He was a psychopath with delusions of grandeur. He was responsible for murder from a very young age. He'd murdered his mother, an uncle and a school friend when he was only thirteen years old and had spent the next eight years incarcerated in a high-security hospital. At age twenty-one, he'd been released into an unsuspecting world. He had enrolled in a school for performing arts where he'd learned all about theatrical make-up and the assuming of other

381

personas. Later he'd trained to be a stuntman and studied driving, guns and unarmed combat. He should have stuck to the fantasy world of movies. His training was all make-believe. All fake skills when it came to the very real, very serious world of a contract killer. He thought he was a professional, but he wasn't. He was simply crazy. But that was what had made him so dangerous.

Walter didn't hang around.

He stayed only long enough to remind me that his debt to me was cleared.

'Nothing like this can happen ever again. I can't keep on advocating murder, Hunter.'

'Won't ever come to that again,' I promised him. But we both knew our words were hollow.

Violence follows me around like stink on a mangy dog.

Anyway, my treatment of Dantalion wasn't murder. The fact I'd stopped a maniac who'd murdered dozens outweighed my 'drug-clouded' actions and I wouldn't be facing any charges.

Rink took a flight out of Miami International, headed across the country chasing the setting sun. I promised him that I'd follow in a day or so, as soon as I'd finished up here. I told him to give his mom a kiss for me.

'Kiss her yourself when you get there,' Rink told me. 'She isn't going anywhere. She's getting stronger all the time.'

I called Richard Dean.

We met at a diner a whole lot nicer than

Shuggie's Shack. The food must have been good judging by the clatter of cutlery on plates. People talked and laughed with each other. Patsy Cline was playing on the jukebox.

It wasn't the kind of atmosphere I wanted, so I led him round the back into a service alley. The smell of garbage rotting in a dumpster was more conducive to setting the scene. It kind of fitted my mood.

I felt like smashing him in the face there and then. But I didn't. For all that Marianne had been an inconsequential pawn in his scheme, his daughter still loved him. I wasn't going to hurt her by hurting her father.

Plus, he was a pathetic man when all was said and done. Beating him wouldn't have proved anything.

'When we first met I told you I wasn't the man you were looking for,' I said to him. 'I told you I wasn't a hit man. But that's what you wanted.'

'I only wanted my daughter back,' he said, but his eyes told the lie.

'No, Dean. You wanted your son back. But you knew that couldn't happen. So you wanted the person you blamed for his death to die also. Sending me after your daughter was just an excuse. It was a way to get at Bradley Jorgenson.'

'Bradley Jorgenson killed my boy.'

'You're wrong.'

I explained to him how Bradley opposed the military contracts, how he was working hard to make amends for the mistakes made by his predecessors. I explained how Marianne had brought all this about. How ultimately Stephen's death had brought about the change. How he should be proud of all that his children had done. But my words fell on deaf ears.

He remained a bitter, twisted man who refused to see the truth.

'You lied to me, Dean.' I pulled out the photographs he'd falsely used to build his case against Bradley. Then I jammed them into his jacket. All but the one lifted from the police file. I pushed that under his nose. 'I don't know how you managed to get a hold of this – it doesn't really matter – but I want you to take a good look at it. This girl loves you, Dean. *And you did that to her.*'

His eyes clouded as he looked at the photograph. I thought he'd accepted that his anger had been misguided. Of all the people in the world, Marianne should have been the last one he should strike out at.

'She won't be coming home,' I told him. 'But it was never really about getting Marianne back. You didn't care what happened to her. All you cared about was that Bradley got hurt along the way.'

'How do you expect me to feel? She was in bed with the man who killed my son,' Dean said. 'Marianne betrayed Stephen's memory. She betrayed me.'

'No, Dean, you betrayed her. I sympathise with

the loss of your son. You blamed the Jorgensons for that, but losing your daughter I don't sympathise with. That is all down to you.'

Dean blinked up at me, and I could see that his tears weren't of shame; they were too bitter for that.

'I paid you,' he said. 'You have to bring her back.'

Pulling an envelope from my pocket, I slapped it against his chest.

'It's all there. Every stinking cent of it.' When he didn't reach for it, I allowed the twenty thousand dollars to fall at his feet. 'Take that as notice of my resignation,' I said. 'Effective immediately.'

'You can't back out. You gave your word.' He set his jaw angrily. 'You have to finish what you started.'

'I just quit, Dean.'

'Suit yourself,' Dean hissed. He stooped quickly, grabbed the envelope and waved it in front of me. 'I'll send someone else . . .'

Grasping him by his jacket, I pushed him up against the alley wall.

I stared into his eyes. 'A short time ago I killed a man who was trying to hurt Marianne. An old friend of mine told me he couldn't advocate murder. I promised him it wouldn't happen again. But, do you know something, Dean? I'm not sure I can keep that promise.'

Releasing him, I smoothed out his jacket. I fixed his tie. 'Let it go, Dean. Let it all go.'

Then I left him to consider what would happen

if he raised a finger to Marianne again. Or to Bradley.

I was twenty grand down, but it didn't hurt too badly. While I'd been smoothing down Richard Dean's jacket I took payment in another kind.

CHAPTER 46

I found Marianne at Bradley Jorgenson's hospital bedside. Bradley was sedated, his leg in splints and raised on some sort of pulley contraption. Marianne leaned close and kissed him on the forehead before she came to me.

We stepped out of Bradley's private room and I looked down at her uptilted face. She was beautiful. But there was still a shadow of fear behind her eyes.

'It's over.'

'How can you be so sure?'

'Trust me.'

'I do.'

I told her that the FBI was going to launch an investigation into the attempts on their lives. It was apparent that Petre Jorgenson had been the force behind the plot to have them murdered. He had also ordered the death of Caitlin Moore just because she had been instrumental in influencing Marianne, who had in turn influenced Bradley to cancel his involvement in military contracts. Petre Jorgenson couldn't stand to lose his share of the billions of dollars those contracts meant. He'd preferred to lose family members instead. What no one was sure of was to what depths the plot had gone, and who else among the Jorgenson family had been involved. Jack and Simon were currently answering serious questions.

'Any sniff of trouble, you let me know, OK?'

'I will,' she promised. 'But what about . . . ?'

'Your father? He knows you won't be coming home.'

'He was happy with that?'

'He sends his love,' I lied. 'He also sent you this.'

She held out her hand and I slipped her mother's crucifix into her palm. It was looped on a silver chain.

Marianne studied the chain.

'This isn't mine.'

'Souvenir for you,' I said.

It was elegant and expensive. An antique piece of jewellery. It had once held the weight of a book containing thirty-six legions of spirits. The weight of the cross would easily balance that out.

Marianne looped it round her neck and lifted the cross between her fingers. She kissed it, and I saw the fear recede. Then she stood on tiptoes and pressed her lips to my cheek.

'Thanks, Joe.'

All the gratitude I required. She turned away and re-entered Bradley's room. I leaned against the wall next to the door. I could hear her humming something under her breath, the same song she'd been humming in the garden on Baker Island. Only this time it didn't sound so sad.

ACKNOWLEDGEMENT
AND THANKS

There are so many people I am grateful to this time that I'm sure to miss some of them out, but you know who you are, so thank you.

Special thanks go to Jim H, Richard G, Col B, Mark T, Stu H, all of whom have kept my creative juices bubbling in different ways.

As ever, huge thanks to Luigi and Alison Bonomi and all the team at LBA, without whom Joe Hunter wouldn't be the same. Also to George Lucas at Inkwell Management, and to everyone at ILA, who champion my books throughout the world.

To Sue Fletcher, Swati and Eleni at Hodder and Stoughton, and to David Highfill, Gabe and Sharyn at William Morrow and Company, thank you for all your invaluable editorial advice and support.

Thanks also to Jacky and Val Hilton.

Matt Hilton

LS	12/09